An Ohnita Harbor Mystery

The Secrets of the Old Post Cemetery

From the New York Times Bestselling Author

PATRICIA CRISAFULLI

The **Secrets** of the Old Post Cemetery

PATRICIA CRISAFULLI

Woodhall Press | Norwalk, CT

Woodhall Press, Norwalk, CT 06855

WoodhallPress.com

Copyright © 2025 Patricia Crisafulli

Cover design: LJ Mucci
Layout artist: LJ Mucci

Library of Congress Cataloging-in-Publication Data available

ISBN 978-1-960456-39-7   (paper: alk paper)
ISBN 978-1-960456-40-3   (electronic)

First Edition
Distributed by Independent Publishers Group
(800) 888-4741

Printed in the United States of America

This is a work of fiction. Names, characters, business, events and incidents are the products of the author's imagination. Any resemblance to actual persons, living or dead, or actual events is purely coincidental.

For Jeannie—
devoted sister and lover of history

It is not down in any map; true places never are.
—Herman Melville

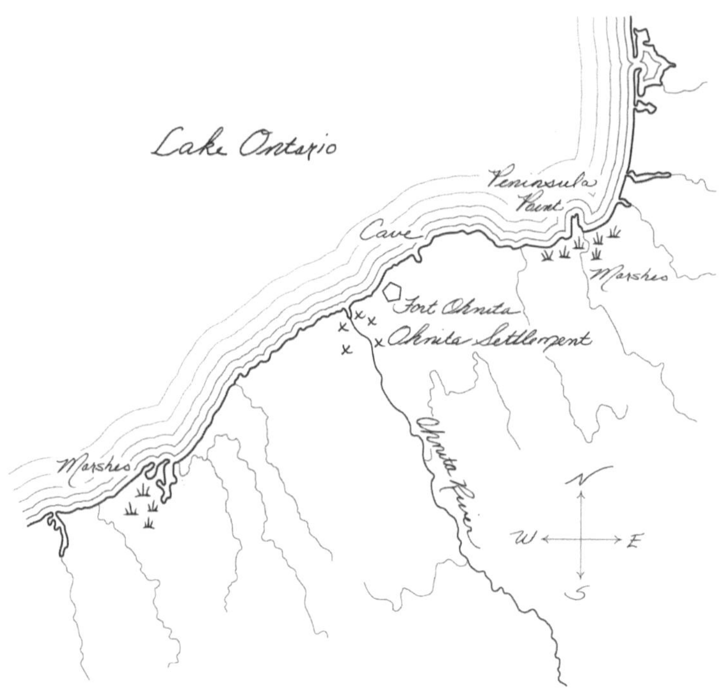

"The Traitor's Map"
Credit: Dave Imus of Imus Geographics

Prologue

Peninsula Point
17 miles due east of Ohnita Settlement
June 2, 1777

Heart thumping, lungs tightening, Henry gulped air as he ran through the woods. Tripping over a tree root hidden in darkness and old leaves, he scrambled to find purchase on the muddy ground and flung out his arms for balance. He paid for it with a crack of his wrist against a tree trunk. Pain registered, but he neither stopped nor slowed his pace, knowing they would not wait for him.

Henry cursed himself for lingering after dinner so as not to disappear from the household too soon. For two hours, he'd had to endure his brother, Jacob, holding court with his circle of sycophants and cronies; but if any of those men were to be questioned about his whereabouts on this night, they would have to admit he'd been right there with them. Even Jacob couldn't deny it. That thought pulled the corner of Henry's mouth into a half smile.

The soggy ground underfoot told him he'd finally reached the edge of the swamp. Glancing up at a three-quarter moon and a few visible stars, Henry changed direction and pushed on. Wind off the water carried the sound of waves, rhythmic and soothing, and he took a little comfort. At the lapping edge of Lake Ontario, he splashed in, hoping they would hear him—and praying no one else could.

A lantern blazed for only seconds, then extinguished. Henry swam in the direction of that brief glimpse of light and a boat he could not yet see. His exhausted muscles seized up in the cold, and panic gripped him until strong hands grasped his arms and hauled him over the side of a dinghy. He collapsed at the feet of the oarsman.

The hard toe of a boot nudged his ribs. "You have it?" a voice asked.

Dragging himself up on his elbows, Henry reached inside his shirt and extracted a long, thin leather pouch he'd stitched himself. Lanolin and duck fat waterproofed the exterior, keeping the contents dry. He fondled the soft, damp leather a moment, then handed it over.

The lantern glowed again, glinting on a knife blade that slit the seam and exposed the interior of the pouch. The light went out, and the oarsman began rowing.

As the boat moved, Henry let his thoughts drift to her—how she would hate him if she knew what he was doing. And why shouldn't she? He hated himself.

The ale he'd drunk that evening returned to his throat, burning its way upward. Leaning over the side of the dinghy, Henry retched until his stomach emptied. Cupping water from the lake, he splashed his face, a baptism that could never expunge an unforgiveable sin. He was a traitor to cause and country.

Chapter One

Ohnita Harbor, New York
Present Day

Pulling up the collar of her long black coat, Gabriela scrunched her shoulders up to her ears to block a bitter wind off Lake Ontario. It was the first day of spring, but here in Ohnita Harbor, winter's icy grip did not let go easily. Despite the damp chill, she lingered at the edge of the bluffs overlooking the shore, feeling a deep connection to this place where land, water, and sky intersected.

She turned her gaze inland toward a gray stone structure some fifty yards behind her—Fort Ohnita, which overlooked the harbor in the center of the town that had grown up around it. Like every Ohnitan, Gabriela had learned its history back in elementary school—stories of hunters and fur traders, explorers and settlers, conquerors and defenders. They had come here in vessels of every size and purpose, from canoes to ships. Between 1755 and 1814, battles from three wars had been waged right here, on the land and on the lake. Today she hoped to bring that history alive for her own students.

Glancing at her phone, Gabriela acknowledged that she had arrived a little too early for this field trip that would take two hours out of her schedule. Mentally, she ran down the list of all the unfinished tasks and unwritten emails she'd left behind at the Ohnita Harbor Public Library, where she was the executive director. *It will wait*, Gabriela told herself.

Taking in a deep breath, she reminded herself of the joy she'd discovered since becoming an adjunct professor at the community college two months ago. It surprised her just how much she looked forward to every Wednesday and Friday, from eleven to twelve thirty, when she taught one course—History 201, Artifacts and Authentication. It was her specialization from her days at the New York Public Library, where she'd worked in Archives and Documents, and the few surprising opportunities she'd had to identify the origins and histories of artifacts right here in Ohnita Harbor.

With a glance at the parking lot—still empty—she hoped today's class would be intriguing for a bunch of mostly nineteen- and twenty-year-olds. For two of them it would be, she knew, and thought of Emilie Hernandez and Ricky Seymour, her best students.

At 10:55 two cars pulled into the parking lot, followed by two more. A minute later another car arrived, followed by a young man on a bicycle. Gabriela raised her gloved hand to attract their attention, then headed to the far corner of the fort grounds and a wrought-iron fence that marked the perimeter of the Old Post Cemetery.

The students approached a few at a time, most with wide grins, though a few wore pinched expressions from being underdressed for the cold weather. Gabriela led the group into the oldest part of the cemetery, where headstones leaned at odd angles. She drew them closer for warmth and launched into the story: "Imagine that it's August 1756. France and Britain are at war—the Seven Years' War, as it will be known in Europe, and the French and Indian War in the colonies. At stake was nothing less than domination of North America."

Pointing toward the fort, Gabriela asked them to picture the fortress not as they saw it now, with its impenetrable-looking stone walls, but as a frontier stronghold constructed out of rough-hewn timber. Back then, British soldiers from His Majesty's Fourth Battalion—the Royal Americans—hunkered down in the fort along with a band of colonial fighters and some civilians. For days they had prepared for an attack by the French out of Canada to the north. But as night fell, they had no idea the enemy was already on the move.

Under the cover of darkness, the French maneuvered their flat-bottomed bateaux along the shoreline, hugging its cliffs. At dawn the next morning, the French and their Iroquois allies attacked, quickly overwhelming the British and colonial forces. More than one hundred soldiers at the fort were killed and five hundred soldiers and civilians were captured.

Gabriela scanned the students' faces for comprehension or confusion. "You with me so far?" she asked, and heads nodded.

"As the fort fell, a teenaged boy was sent by a British officer as a runner to warn the people of Ohnita Settlement. His name was Jacob Thorsen. That's a name you'll want to remember."

Then, stepping closer to a double row of short markers with rounded tops, Gabriela drew the students' attention to the inscription on each one: *Unknown Soldier, 1756–1757.* "Whoever they were—colonists or soldiers in the king's regiment—everyone buried in this corner shared an important commonality. In 1756 they considered themselves British subjects, loyal to the Crown." She pointed to the Union Jack and the Stars and Stripes snapping side by side on twin poles flanking the cemetery entrance. "That's why both flags fly here today."

Gabriela beckoned the students to follow her across the small cemetery to a twin phalanx of a dozen markers also inscribed with

Unknown Soldier, but this time with the dates of the American Revolution: 1776–1783. A few other stones bore specific names and dates—two officers of the Continental Army, an officer's wife, three soldiers, and a blacksmith who, as his inscription stated, was "a man of strength & courage who manned the mighty cannons."

"The people buried here were Americans, fighting for the cause of independence. But it wasn't that way for everyone. The Declaration of Independence didn't make for a clean break—allegiance switching from the Crown to a newly formed republic."

Gabriela paused and scanned the students' expressions a second time. Most eyes looked back at her, though a few focused on the graves, the lake, or the fort behind them.

"Early on, when the Continental Army lost battle after battle against the British, independence seemed like a lost cause," she continued. "New York was a hotbed of Loyalist sentiment, particularly New York City and Long Island—"

"What'd you expect from a bunch of Mets fans," one of the students interrupted.

"Take them over the Yankees any day," another replied, and a short round of good-natured sports trash-talking ensued.

"Ah, yes. Rivalries run deep," Gabriela added with a chuckle. "Keep that in mind for the next part of the story."

In the back corner of the cemetery rose a five-foot obelisk atop a broad base some four feet wide and three feet high. It bore a small brass plaque indicating the monument had been donated by the Daughters of the American Revolution, replacing the original stone. The inscription read:

Colonel Jacob Elijah Thorsen

Survivor of the Attack on Fort Ohnita, 1756

Gravely Wounded Defending Fort Ohnita, 1781

Hero of the Battle of Ohnita Harbor, 1812

Born Aug. 10, 1740—Died Dec. 11, 1818

Emilie Hernandez, a tall young woman with straight dark hair topped by a heather gray knitted hat, raised her hand. "Jacob Thorsen—that's the kid who got sent out of the fort, right?"

Gabriela nodded, glad that at least one of the students had been paying attention.

Emilie ran her finger down the long inscription. "So, wait. He's badly wounded during the Revolution. Then he's a hero in 1812 at the age of—what? Seventy-two. And he lives to be seventy-eight. Who was this guy—superman?" She landed hard on the word *guy* with her strong downstate accent.

"Colonel Thorsen does seem to have been larger than life," Gabriela replied. "But during the Revolution, several generals were commissioned when they were in their sixties. So Jacob Thorsen's age was not entirely out of the ordinary."

Gabriela extracted a book from her tote bag. "But here's something very unusual about Colonel Thorsen, and it's a big part of your assignment. He helped capture three spies during the Revolution—and one of them was also named Thorsen."

She turned to a marked page and began reading:

Execution was set for the precise moment of dawn, June 8, 1777. But when the prisoners were led from the stockade, Henry Thorsen, the younger brother of Colonel Jacob Thorsen, was missing and presumed escaped. Enraged, Colonel Thorsen ordered the two other prisoners flogged to make them reveal what had happened to Henry, but both men pleaded ignorance. Colonel Thorsen then aimed his flintlock pistol, condemned the two men to the devil, and executed them himself. Henry Thorsen was never found.

"Well, that's a dysfunctional family!" quipped Ricky Seymour, a slightly built student huddled inside a parka that looked like he'd borrowed it from someone two sizes bigger. The other students laughed.

A flap of olive-green fabric from a tear down the sleeve of Ricky's parka caught the wind like a tiny flag. Noticing it, Gabriela remembered what the young man had told her about working odd jobs to scrape together tuition. His father, he said, didn't believe in banks and loans.

"I'm betting on bad blood between those two brothers long before this spying business," Emilie added.

"To understand more about this rivalry, we have to go one more place," Gabriela said, leading the way out of the cemetery. "It's only five minutes away—and fortunately, it's heated."

Tall, with a shock of stylishly coifed short white hair, Charmaine Odele greeted them at the front door of the Ohnita Harbor Maritime

Museum. She wore leggings and high boots, a turtleneck, and a thigh-length poncho in deep purple and blue.

At only five-foot-two, with her shoulder-length dark curls severely windblown, Gabriela tried not to feel diminished in Charmaine's dramatic presence. Patting her hair with both hands, Gabriela tried to tame the mess, then gave up. She pointed to the students browsing among the museum's displays of nautical artifacts, navigation charts, and the hull of an old dinghy. "I think I hooked them on the story of the Thorsen brothers."

"Of course you did." Charmaine leaned down, and Gabriela stood eye-to-eye with the woman who not only chaired the community college history department but also headed the library's board of trustees—her boss, twice over. "You know, you could add another course next semester. It's inspiring to see students this engaged."

Gabriela warned herself not to get roped in by flattery. Dropping her chin and widening her eyes, she gave Charmaine her best *you've got to be kidding me* expression. "I don't have enough time to teach this one course, let alone add another one."

Charmaine held up both hands, fingers splayed, and smiled broadly. "Just saying. It's a possibility."

A lanky student in jeans and a flannel shirt approached them and cleared his throat. "Professor?"

Gabriela paused. As an adjunct, she didn't have the professor title and encouraged the students to call her Ms. Domenici or Gabriela. Then she noticed his eyes were on Charmaine, who indeed was a professor, Dr. Odele.

"This is all really interesting, but I have to get to my job at one o'clock."

Gabriela rounded everyone up and led them into a dimly lit alcove where a framed map hung on the wall. "You're among the first to see this on display," she said. "It was donated to the museum just a few weeks ago. When I heard about it..." She smiled over at

Charmaine, who stood behind the students. "...I knew this would make the perfect final project."

She turned to the map, which had been drawn in ink on parchment the color of autumn leaves. A heavy line showed the shoreline, with indentations for coves and inlets, and a few spits of land that jutted out into the water. One of them on the far right of the map was labeled "Peninsula Point." In the center, a curvy line was labeled Ohnita River, and crosshatches on both sides indicated Ohnita Settlement, the town's original name from three centuries ago.

As Gabriela scanned the map, her chest swelled with excitement and longing, a feeling she associated with the most compelling artifacts and documents she'd handled throughout her career.

Charmaine moved through the knot of students, handing each of them an eight-by-ten photograph of the map. Holding up her copy, Gabriela relaxed into what she loved best—telling the stories of artifacts, giving historic objects a voice in the present. "This map is believed to have been drawn by Henry Thorsen, who handed it over to the British," she told the students. "It sealed his conviction as a spy. That's why it's known as the Traitor's Map."

Murmurs rippled through the students, and Gabriela's smile widened. She pointed to several features on the map and explained that the coves and marshes likely had been used by the Continental Army to stash their boats and keep watch for movements along the shoreline. "But here's the odd thing," she said. "This map is inaccurate. Ohnita Settlement is clearly marked, and you can see the Ohnita River. But many of the other markings don't make sense. About a third of them are either in the wrong place or don't exist at all. There seems to be a huge cave here." She pointed to a clearly marked indentation. "But it simply isn't there."

"Could the shoreline have changed since then?" Ricky Seymour asked.

"Most definitely it has, because of erosion and improvements to modernize the harbor. But this cave appears too large to have changed over 250 years—a mere blink in geological time," Gabriela said. "This brings us to your final assignment. And remember, it counts for half your grade. I want you to describe in detail how you would go about authenticating the Traitor's Map."

The students' expressions ranged from bewilderment to excitement. But when Gabriela told them they could work in pairs, most of them seemed relieved. As the students chose their partners, Gabriela wasn't surprised when Emilie pointed to Ricky. They couldn't be more different—the young woman from downstate whose parents were both in tech and could work remotely from anywhere and the local young man from a hardscrabble background.

"I don't expect you to actually prove whether the map is real or fake. This project is about describing your authentication process. Use your research skills. Think about where you would go for more information. Use your imagination. Think about who you'd interview if you could go anywhere and what questions you'd ask."

"How about a time machine? I'd like to talk to Jacob Thorsen," one of the students joked. Several others laughed; a few rolled their eyes.

"There are other ways of hearing the voices of the past—journals, diaries, and correspondence," Gabriela said. "Primary research, remember?"

Ricky stepped closer to the original map, even as he held a photographic copy. "Forget time travel. I want a boat."

"If you tried to navigate using this map, you'd soon find out just how inaccurate it is," Gabriela said. "But we know that already. The big question is authentication. We just don't know that much about the Traitor's Map."

She saw several of her students thumbing on their phones. "If you're googling it, you won't find anything. It's been in a private collection until just recently."

"So why doesn't the collector know more about it?" Ricky asked.

Gabriela looked at Charmaine, who shrugged, then turned to Ricky. "You'd be surprised what can sit in someone's attic without anyone knowing what it is," Gabriela said.

"What if we really can authenticate it?" Emilie said. "You know, prove what it is."

"That would be amazing, not to mention ambitious," Gabriela told her. "Authentication takes time—a lot longer than the six weeks until the project is due."

Emilie's chin rose an inch, as if she'd just taken on a challenge. Gabriela understood completely. Ever since her first look at the Traitor's Map two weeks ago, she'd wanted to dive into authenticating it herself. Perhaps this summer when her schedule wouldn't be quite so busy, Gabriela mused. *As if,* she added to herself.

Her cell phone buzzed in her pocket, but she ignored what was undoubtedly a call from someone at the library. "Who knows what any of you might find! Luck certainly does play a part in authentication." Her phone buzzed a second time. "I'll see you in class on Friday."

Still wearing her coat, Gabriela bustled into the executive office suite on the second floor of the Ohnita Harbor Public Library. Delmina Duro, the executive assistant and bookkeeper, handed her several messages written on pink *While you were out* notepaper. No matter how many times Gabriela protested that they had voicemail, Delmina insisted that during business hours callers should talk to a person, not a recording.

Gabriela also suspected that intercepting every call was Delmina's primary method of intelligence gathering. Not that she'd call Delmina a spy, Gabriela thought as she rifled through the short stack of names and phone numbers, but she couldn't deny Delmina's extraordinary connections at City Hall, across Ohnita County, and even state government in Albany.

Two of the messages were from the mayor with "call immediately" underlined twice. Gabriela dialed Mayor Duncan Phillips and cradled the receiver under her chin as she hung her coat on a hook on the back of her office door.

"We got it!" the mayor crowed.

Duncan's excitement could only mean approval of a $1.2 million New York State Beautification Grant, with 10 percent of the funds going to the library. Gabriela squealed, then apologized with a laugh for piercing his eardrum.

"Can you make a two o'clock meeting tomorrow?" the mayor asked.

Gabriela thought of the $120,000 infusion into the library's anemic budget. At last they could start some restoration at the library. As long as they could justify the work as beautification, the grant would pay for it. Top of the list was restoring the original plaster ceiling hidden behind ugly acoustic tiles on the main floor.

Lost in her musings, Gabriela's brain finally registered that Duncan had said something about a citizens' committee, and she quickly voiced her agreement.

"Awesome!" Duncan replied. "I thought twice about asking you to chair it, knowing how busy you are at the library, but you're the best on community relations."

Chair the committee? She'd missed that part but couldn't back out now. "Okay, see you tomorrow at two."

Gabriela disconnected the call. "The grant came through," she trumpeted, waving the phone in the air.

Delmina's placid smile deflated her bubble of enthusiasm. Of course Delmina had already heard the news, Gabriela realized. She might even have known before the mayor himself.

Chapter Two

Thursday afternoon's meeting at City Hall was half victory lap, half planning session. Gabriela confirmed her willingness to put together a citizens' committee and to chair it, even as her anxiety rose over being stretched too thin. To make this work, she really needed a great committee who would commit both time and effort.

She thought of Daniel and all his qualifications: local business owner, experience in roofing and construction, great connections with all the contractors in the area. He didn't have any more free time than she did, but working together would be fun. She'd ask him this weekend—her birthday weekend, she reminded herself, and wondered what Daniel might be planning.

On Friday morning, Gabriela got to class at the community college one minute before the starting time. All her students were there, and several of them, from the sounds of it, were discussing old maps.

An hour and a half later, as the clock ticked toward the end of class, Gabriela tried to impress upon her students the importance of the process. "These aren't just old documents. Artifacts are more than curiosities that may or may not be worth something. They all contain stories waiting to unfold. That's what we're after—the stories."

Back at the library, Gabriela ate lunch at her desk and worked straight through the afternoon. She triaged what needed to be done in the half hour before her son arrived after school. At 4:15 a text buzzed on her silenced cell phone: *Ben at your house with me. XO D.*

Gabriela reread the text as if she had missed something the first time. What was Ben doing at home with Daniel?

Everything okay? she thumbed.

Daniel's next message appeared a few seconds later. *All good.*

Those two words gave her the assurance that she shouldn't worry. Daniel had become a steady presence in Ben's life and, increasingly, a partner in hers.

This have anything to do with my b-day? she texted back.

B-day???????????? A kissing emoji followed.

Whatever these two might be scheming, she'd go along with it. Being surprised—or at least pretending to be—was half the fun.

⁂

On Saturday morning, Gabriela brewed a pot of strong coffee, started the first load of laundry, and logged into her library email account from her home computer. Ben got up late, gobbled breakfast, begrudgingly picked up his room, and, an hour later, came back to her office to announce he was off to the park and then to his friend Ryan's house.

She took off her low-powered reading glasses and rubbed her eyes. *Welcome to forty-one*, she thought. "Okay but call me before you go anywhere else. I need to know where you are."

Gabriela got up from her chair and walked to the kitchen, where Ben was pulling on a sweatshirt before heading out. Reaching over, she tugged at the hood that bunched around his neck then gave him a goodbye hug that made him squirm. From the doorway, she watched him pedal his bike down the driveway. In the past two years, from age ten to almost twelve, he had become so much more independent, she mused—with so much more change to come.

Two hours later, sunlight shone through the side window with western exposure, streaking glare across her computer screen. Gabriela got up to adjust the blinds, surprised to see that it was almost three o'clock. She hadn't eaten lunch.

In the kitchen, Gabriela peeled a banana and ate it with slow bites. Maybe she should go for a run before Ben came home and Daniel showed up with her birthday surprise. She hadn't yet figured out what it might be.

Fifteen minutes later, she was out the door. Her muscles loosened as her body warmed. Lengthening her stride, Gabriela pushed on toward the center of town.

Somewhere up ahead, a siren blared. Reflexively, she looked around, trying to pinpoint the origin of the sound. Back when she lived and worked in New York City, police cars, ambulances, and the occasional fire truck had composed the cacophonous soundtrack of everyday life. But here, even one shrill alarm reverberated across the quiet city of twelve thousand people. Hearing a second siren, she knew something had to be wrong and hoped it wasn't too serious.

Approaching the intersection before the bridge over the Ohnita River, Gabriela looked down the cross street. Red and blue emergency lights flashed in the distance, near the turnoff to Fort Ohnita. Curious, she veered off her jogging route and went to investigate. Three blocks later she joined a small crowd gathered where two police cars idled grill-to-grill, blocking the street.

A young police officer admonished them all to go home, but nobody budged. A second officer appeared, and Gabriela recognized Thelma Tulowski. *Inspector Tulowski*, she corrected herself, recalling Thelma's promotion a month ago. She waved, but Thelma frowned.

Gabriela approached her anyway. "I was out running when I heard the sirens."

"And you just had to see what's going on." Thelma's blue eyes narrowed under her hat's visor. "Body washed up on the shore. Some college girl found him. She's pretty shaken up. Seems she knew him."

Thelma's words sent a chill through Gabriela that had nothing to do with the cold breeze off the lake. "Who are they, Thelma? I've got a really bad feeling. I brought my class to the Old Post Cemetery on Wednesday. One of my students talked about getting a boat."

Gabriela waited for a reaction. She and Thelma were friendly, though not exactly friends, having become acquainted through previous police investigations. "What if I say two names and you tell me if they're somehow involved?" she added.

Speaking the names aloud felt as reckless as opening Pandora's Box, unleashing pain and anxiety that could never be contained again. But she had to know. "Ricky Seymour and Emilie Hernandez."

Thelma opened the driver's side door of one of the parked cruisers and motioned for Gabriela to get in the passenger side. As Thelma drove the half mile down the road to Fort Ohnita, Gabriela fumbled on her cell phone to call Daniel.

His voice sounded playful when he answered. "What's up, birthday girl?"

"There's been an accident," Gabriela blurted out.

"Oh my God. Are you hurt?"

"No, not me. Someone drowned. I think my students are involved."

"Where are you? I'll come get you."

Yes, Gabriela begged silently. She didn't want to go through this alone. "No, it's okay. Can you wait there for Ben? He went to the park, but he's probably at Ryan's by now."

"I can leave the back door open for him. Let me get you."

"No, I'm fine. I'm with Thelma Tulowski—at the fort. I'll be home soon."

"Please be careful. Call me if you need me."

The worry in his voice tore at her heart, and not knowing what had happened at the lakefront intensified the agony. Gabriela asked Thelma again for details.

"I'll tell you this much since you're about to see her. The girl who found the body is Emilie Hernandez," Thelma said.

Gabriela clamped a hand over her mouth and spoke through her fingers. "Oh, God."

"Emilie says she was meeting another student who had a boat—*access to a boat* is the way she put it. But he never showed up. So that's when she decided to climb down the bluffs to the beach. She found her friend in the water."

Gabriela swallowed hard. "Ricky Seymour?"

"Can't say until we notify the next of kin," Thelma said.

"Dark hair, small stature. Probably wearing a parka that's too big for him." Tears strangled Gabriela's voice. "Is it Ricky? Just say yes or no."

In the fort parking lot, Thelma pulled into a space beside another cruiser. "Yeah."

A sob escaped, and Gabriela crumpled forward, leaning her head against the dashboard. This was her fault. If she hadn't taken the class on that field trip, if she hadn't assigned them the Traitor's Map project, Ricky wouldn't have gotten the idea of going back to the lake. Her mind spun faster, trying to imagine what had happened. The boat could have capsized. Or Ricky might have been walking along the edge of the bluffs on the other side of the fence when what looked like solid ground gave way—especially given all the snow and rain in the past few weeks.

Getting out of the car on shaky legs, Gabriela followed Thelma to the other cruiser and saw Emilie in the back as if she were a suspect. She shot Thelma a sharp look.

"She was cold, so we let her sit inside. That's all," Thelma said, opening the door.

Emilie rushed out, swamping Gabriela in a hug. "Ricky said he'd meet me at two o'clock. I kept calling and texting. And now, he's...he's dead."

Stroking Emilie's hair, Gabriela tried to make soothing noises but had no words of comfort to offer.

Pulling back, Emilie wiped her eyes and nose with her gloved hands. "I don't get it. Ricky said we'd meet here and get the boat. So why was he on the beach—with no boat? The police won't tell me anything."

"They're trying to figure out what happened. We'll know more soon." Gabriela looked over at Thelma, who conferred with another Ohnita Harbor police officer, then back at Emilie. "Are your parents coming?"

"My mom is. Dad's out of town on business."

A few minutes later, an SUV pulled into the lot, and a woman with short dark hair and a face creased with worry rushed over to Emilie. She introduced herself as Marcia Hernandez and thanked Gabriela for being there with her daughter.

"I just happened to be out jogging," Gabriela said.

Emilie began to cry again and embraced her mother. As Gabriela stepped away to give them privacy, Thelma came up beside her and spoke in a low voice. "Take a little walk with me."

Arms bolted across her chest, Gabriela tried to still the chills that rattled her body as she and Thelma made their way across the fort grounds.

"She say anything?" Thelma asked.

Gabriela looked straight ahead to the steely gray of Lake Ontario, somber and foreboding. "The same thing you told me. Emilie thought they were going out on a boat—but there's no boat, is there?"

Thelma said nothing.

"So that means Ricky fell and drowned. Did he hit his head?"

Thelma cricked her neck to the right as if dodging both the question and a direct answer. "There's a head injury. Let's leave it at that."

Gabriela stayed on the scene far longer than she'd needed to but would not leave Emilie and Marcia. Once Thelma told her the college authorities had been notified, Gabriela called Charmaine from her cell phone and related her version of the events.

"Which student?" Charmaine asked.

"They're not releasing the name until his father has been notified," Gabriela said. "Besides, I don't think you know him."

"I need to know," Charmaine added, her voice softening.

"Do you remember the small kid with dark hair, the one in the parka that looked like a tent on him?" Gabriela asked.

"Big tear down the sleeve," Charmaine said. "I noticed that."

"That's the student." Gabriela's eyes flooded and her voice cracked. "He wanted to go to a four-year college, maybe get a degree in history or archaeology. I told him there would be scholarships for him."

Charmaine mumbled an expletive. "Listen, I have to ask this. Did you tell the students to investigate the lakeshore?"

"What? No!" Gabriela spoke more loudly than she intended and saw Thelma turn her way. "I took them to the Old Post Cemetery to see Jacob Thorsen's grave, then we went to the museum. Why do you ask?"

"Because right after the college administration expresses its condolences, they are going to be looking to mitigate any liability," Charmaine said.

"Ricky..." She paused, remembering the name was being withheld. "The students came here by themselves without telling me." It was the truth, Gabriela knew, but that didn't lessen the guilt she felt for taking them to the cemetery.

It was after five o'clock when Gabriela left. Before starting her jog home, she called her house phone but only reached her own voicemail. She sent Daniel a text: *Heading back. Pls stay with Ben.*

Cold cramped her muscles as she shuffled along Main Street. Block after block, she pushed on. After about a mile, Gabriela recognized Daniel's pickup truck, the doors emblazoned with the DRD Roofing logo—his company name and his initials, for Daniel Red Deer. With a wave of relief, she bent over and planted her hands on her thighs. A moment later, strong arms enveloped her, pulling her gently upright.

"Let's get you home," Daniel said.

Gabriela looked in the truck cab for Ben and released a grateful sigh that he wasn't there.

"Ben's keeping an eye on dinner, which basically means watching television," Daniel said. "And Agnese is with him."

"My mother?" Gabriela couldn't imagine walking into the house with her entire family there.

"I had to pick her up. She had something...for our dinner tonight." Daniel looked over sympathetically. "I asked her to stay with Ben."

Clicking her seat belt, Gabriela wished she and Daniel had more than a three-minute drive; there was so much to say. She blurted it all out.

Daniel pulled over to the curb about two blocks from the house and turned toward her. "How did you know this had happened?"

"I didn't. I saw the police cars at the turnoff to the fort. When Thelma told me someone had died and a college girl had found his body, I had the worst feeling." Fisting her hand against her mouth, Gabriela turned away. "I feel responsible," she said against her knuckles.

Daniel reached for her free hand. "You know you're not. It's just a terrible accident."

"Ricky was a good kid. He told me once it was just him and his father. Money was really tight. I don't think his father worked. Why does a kid like that have to die—at nineteen?"

"I don't know. Bad things happen to good people all the time." Daniel squeezed her fingers.

"Emilie is never going to be the same. We both know that." Gabriela thought back to what had happened last September when she and Daniel went hiking at Still Waters Chasm and found two people—one dead, one dying. On sleepless nights she still saw those bodies in her mind, and she hadn't known the two victims. How much worse would it be for Emilie, who had been friends with Ricky?

Releasing her hand, Daniel put the truck in gear. A moment later, when they pulled into the driveway, Gabriela saw Ben standing at the front window and waved, but he disappeared. Then the front door swung open.

Daniel touched Gabriela's leg, stopping her from getting out of the truck cab. "Listen, Ben is really excited about your birthday, but I can tell him that we need to postpone. I also need to take Agnese home. She wants this night to be for the three of us since we're seeing her tomorrow."

"She'll stay," Gabriela told him. "Mama's too curious to go home."

As Gabriela got out of the truck, her facial muscles tightened, her lips pulling back in a parody of a smile. Reaching her son, she wrapped her arms around him, and he did not pull away.

"Where'd you go?" Ben demanded.

"A couple of my students needed help." Gabriela settled her arm around Ben's shoulders and led him into the kitchen. "What do I smell?"

"You!" Ben wrinkled his nose. "You stink."

She couldn't do this—just pretend that nothing had happened. But seeing her son's face, Gabriela knew she had to.

Looking through the archway into the kitchen, Gabriela glimpsed her mother slicing a tomato. "Hello, Mama."

Agnese turned toward her, hands jammed onto her hips, her tiny figure sharpening into angles. "This is no good. What trouble you get into?"

Her mother's Italian accent thickened, a sure sign she was upset. "It's okay, Mama."

"Okay, okay. *Va bene, va bene.* I don't believe you."

Turning her attention to Daniel, Gabriela asked, "Do I have time for a shower before dinner?"

"Take as long as you like."

⸺⸺•⸺⸺

Gabriela soaped herself twice, washed her hair, and finger-combed conditioner through the wet strands. The water turned from scalding hot to warm to tepid before she finally turned off the tap. Wanting to look presentable for her birthday dinner, she dressed in tights and a thigh-length sweater, then applied foundation, a neutral eyeshadow, and a little mascara.

Four plates marked their places at the table in the tiny dining room. Gabriela took a seat and asked Ben about his adventures at the park that afternoon as she ate her salad despite a clenched gut. Daniel brought a large bowl to the table heaped with pasta tossed in tomato sauce and dotted with meatballs, which she knew her mother had made.

In the other room, her cell phone rang. "Probably a telemarketer," Gabriela said, even though she suspected it might be Emilie or the college administration or even Thelma Tulowski.

"You need to get that?" Daniel asked.

"It can wait." Gabriela took a forkful of pasta, chewing slowly, her appetite gone.

When the house phone rang, Daniel started to get up from his chair, but Gabriela held up her hand. "Let it go to voicemail."

She reached for her wineglass and took a sip. "That was delicious. Thank you." Her plate was nearly full.

"Why you don't eat?" Agnese asked.

Gabriela smiled at her mother but received a frown in return. "I took a big portion. I'll save it for lunch tomorrow."

Ben scrambled to his feet and rushed into the kitchen. Daniel set his fork down and got up slowly. "I guess the next course is ready to be served."

Gabriela heard drawers opening and closing, Ben's loud whispers about wanting to light the match, and Daniel saying he'd better do it. A chorus of two voices—one low, the other still high pitched—sang "Happy Birthday." Her eyes moistened at the sight of Ben carrying a cake ringed with flaming candles and Daniel walking behind, his hands on the boy's shoulders.

Her cell phone rang again.

"...birthday to you—*oo*!" Ben squeaked the last note.

Gabriela got up from the table. "Maybe I better answer it."

"Stay. Your son, Daniel—" Agnese scolded.

"Make a wish!" Ben demanded.

"I'll get it for you." Daniel left the dining room to retrieve the phone.

Gabriela stared at the tiny flames around a cake frosted white with pink rosettes, her name in a gooey green that always reminded her of toothpaste.

"She's here," Daniel said, coming back to the table with her cell phone. "It's Thelma Tulowski."

"Sorry to disturb you." Thelma sounded very much like she was deep into police investigation mode.

Gabriela watched wax drip onto the sugary frosting, puddling at the base of the candles.

"Just heard from the medical examiner. As we suspected, Ricky didn't drown. He was shot."

Gabriela felt the phone slip in her sweaty palm. She gripped it tighter.

"One bullet, behind the ear," Thelma said. "Happened last night, probably around midnight. Body was in the water about twelve hours."

The information ricocheted inside her brain. Her stomach lurched, and Gabriela panted through her open mouth. She headed toward the living room, not wanting Ben to overhear any of this conversation.

"Emilie is coming back to the station now with her mother," Thelma said.

Gabriela bit her lip to keep from blurting out just how unnecessary that seemed. "What more can she tell you? She and Ricky just wanted to look at the shoreline. I'll give you a copy of the map they were following."

Thelma's sigh hissed in her ear. "This isn't a field trip report. It's a murder investigation. Somebody shot Ricky, execution-style. And believe me, it has nothing to do with some old map."

"I'll be there," Gabriela said.

"You don't need to be. I'm just telling you as a courtesy."

Pacing across the room, Gabriela rested her forehead against the living room wall, feeling the coolness of the surface. "Ricky and

Emilie wouldn't have gone to the lakeshore if it weren't for me. I have to come."

"Suit yourself." Thelma hung up.

Chapter Three

When Gabriela returned to the dining room, her birthday candles had been extinguished. She looked from her mother's disapproving face to Daniel's sympathetic expression. Ben seemed to switch from excitement to worry.

She gripped the back of her chair. "There's been a, uh, development. Emilie, one of my students, has to go back to the police station. So I'm going there too."

"What's going on?" Daniel asked.

"The police need to ask some questions." She hitched one side of her mouth into a half smile. "Save me a piece of cake?"

Ben jumped up. "But there's presents, and you didn't make a wish!"

"Don't worry. I'll do all that when I get back."

"No! You should wish now. For something good." Ben rounded the corner of the table and stood in front of her. "Like the two of you getting married."

The room got very bright. Gabriela pulled out her chair and sat down. She and Daniel had made only the briefest references to what their future might look like, as a prelude to a bigger discussion they might have one of these days. Just not right now.

Ben's face reddened the way it did when he got upset and tried not to cry. She reached toward her son, but he stepped back.

"It's okay," Agnese said and started to clear the table. "We do the dishes. Then you come back, and we have cake."

Her cell phone rang again. Gabriela wanted to ignore it, but Daniel answered it for her. He mouthed "Emilie" and handed her the phone.

Before she could say hello, Gabriela heard Emilie's disjointed tumble of rapid words. "They think somebody murdered Ricky. That's stupid—who would do that? I don't understand why they want to talk to me."

A woman spoke in the background, and Gabriela recognized the voice as Emilie's mother. "We moved here to live in a quiet town and now this," Marcia Hernandez said.

"I'll be at the station," Gabriela told Emilie. "Soon as I can. I promise—I'll be there."

Ending the call, she looked over at Daniel. "Walk me out to the garage?"

Closing the back door behind them, Gabriela told Daniel about Ricky being shot. "Execution-style, Thelma said. I just can't...I just don't believe it."

When they reached the car, Daniel wrapped both arms around her. "Let me go with you. Agnese will stay with Ben."

Gabriela shook her head. "We have to tell Ben what's going on; Mama too. They're going to find out."

"I'll give them a minimum of details," Daniel said. "One of your students died and another student is pretty upset about it. That should satisfy Ben. Your mother is another story."

He grinned at her, but Gabriela noticed his smile didn't reach his worried eyes. Gripping his hand, she held it close to her heart. "Thank you. I'm so sorry. This is—"

"Unavoidable," Daniel added. "Go now and come home as soon as you can."

Sitting in the waiting area outside the office marked "T. Tulowski, Inspector," Gabriela heard only muffled voices. After about twenty minutes, the door opened and Emilie emerged, clinging to her mother. Gabriela stood but did not approach until Marcia Hernandez stretched out one arm to draw her into the embrace. The three women hugged.

"My husband is coming home tonight," Marcia said. "He'll be here in a few hours."

"If there is anything I can do," Gabriela said.

Marcia put her hand on Gabriela's shoulder. "You've done a lot just being here. Thank you."

Thelma stepped into the hallway and motioned toward Gabriela. "Got a second?"

Gabriela gave one last hug to Emilie, then entered the office and shut the door. She took in the off-white walls, scratched wooden desk, black laptop computer. Without a single photograph or scrap of anything personal, it had all the charm of a holding cell. She sat on a folding chair and crossed then uncrossed her legs, trying to get comfortable.

Thelma leaned against the corner of her desk. "So, you didn't tell these kids to go out and look at the lakefront?"

"No!" Gabriela said with more force than she intended. "It's a research assignment into authentication."

"Well, Ricky had other ideas. He told Emilie he could get a boat for them to use. He went to see someone Friday night to arrange everything. That little tidbit of timing—which Emilie just told me—explains why the coroner thought the body had been in the water twelve to fourteen hours."

Fishing was popular in and around Ohnita Harbor, Gabriela thought. Every angler in the county probably had a boat or access to one. "Could the boat belong to Ricky's father?"

Thelma rolled her eyes. "That would take effort. Walt Seymour has gotta be the laziest human on this planet. We're still looking for him, but he'll turn up eventually."

Gabriela winced at the thought of a parent coming home and learning their child was dead. *Murdered*, she corrected herself.

"So, just between us," Thelma went on. "Why do you think somebody might want to shoot this kid?"

"It makes no sense to me. I only knew him from class, but he was a good kid. Always prepared. He really wanted to make something of himself."

A memory flashed of a conversation they'd had a month or so ago, when Ricky had asked Gabriela where she'd gone to college. When she'd told him Syracuse University for undergraduate and New York University for her graduate degree, Ricky had gotten a wistful look in his eyes and asked if he could ever do something like that. She had told him yes and promised to help.

"I know you liked him," Thelma went on. "And clearly Emilie did too. But nobody gets shot in the back of the head if they're not involved in something."

"What—drugs?" Gabriela slapped her hands against her thighs. "Ricky never seemed like the type. Comes to class early. Does extra work on an assignment. Hangs around with Emilie, who is a very nice young woman."

"But he was desperate. No money. No help from anybody. My guess is he wanted to impress the girl. He got himself into something." Thelma leaned over and picked up a folder from her desk.

Gabriela straightened her spine, expecting Thelma to show her the contents. The folder stayed shut.

"So, what do you think happened?" Gabriela asked. "He had some rendezvous, and somebody shot him? The fort's right in the middle of town. Somebody would have seen them or at least heard something."

"No, I don't think that at all," Thelma replied. "My guess is whoever Ricky went to see on Friday night took him out on the boat, shot him, and pushed him overboard. That would explain why no one heard gunfire anywhere near the lakefront. The body just happened to wash up by the fort."

Standing, Thelma took a ring of keys out of her pocket. She selected one, unlocked her desk, put the folder in a drawer, and turned the lock again. "Go home, Gabriela. You've done all you could possibly do. And happy birthday."

Every light in the house was on, both upstairs and down. Standing in the darkness of her backyard, Gabriela took in the illumination. The three people she loved best in this world waited inside for her, yet she lingered in the shadows that gave her one more moment to grieve before stepping inside. She would need to mask those feelings for Ben's sake.

The back door opened, and Daniel stepped out onto the small deck. "You gonna stay out here?"

Gabriela made her way toward the house. "Just thinking."

"About?" Daniel descended the steps of the deck and met her halfway.

She paused a beat. "How good it feels to be home."

Daniel gathered her into an embrace. "You've had such a tough day. We're going to make it up to you tomorrow. Ben and I have been planning it for a few weeks now."

"Really, where're we going? Paris?" The false brightness in her voice felt like a lie.

"It's a surprise." Daniel led her in the door. "Just don't expect anything fancy."

In the living room, Ben slouched on the sofa, eyes on the television. He sat upright when Gabriela entered. "Hi, sweetie," she said on her way to the closet where she hung up her coat. Shutting the closet door, she rested her palm against the smooth wood.

"Why did that student die?" Ben asked.

"We don't know yet. He was a nice young man, and I'm very sad that he died." Gabriela crossed the room in four strides and gathered her son in a hug. A tear trickled down the side of her nose and disappeared into his hair.

Her throat felt scraped raw as she feigned a light tone. "Any more of that cake left? Or did you and Nonna eat it all?"

"I didn't have any," Ben said.

"I have to make one phone call, then we'll light up the candles."

Passing the dining room, Gabriela saw her mother sitting at the table, her hands folded. She gave her mother a hug.

"It's no good," Agnese whispered. "All the time, you get involved."

"They're my students," Gabriela said. "I have to be there for them."

Agnese pulled out of the embrace. "You should be with your family first."

Gabriela opened her mouth but knew trying to explain to her mother would amount to futile effort. "I'm here now. We'll have cake in a moment."

Stepping into her home office, Gabriela shut the door and called Charmaine again to update her about Ricky's death being ruled a homicide.

Charmaine gasped. "Someone *shot* him?"

A headache throbbed behind Gabriela's eyes as she repeated what she'd learned from Thelma. "So, what do I do about Wednesday's class? Should I cancel?"

"That's a tough one," Charmaine said. "But I do think the students need to be together. They'll want to talk about their classmate. Just don't expect to do anything other than talk."

Gabriela knew the students would want to hear from her too. "What if the students want to have a vigil or a memorial for him?"

"Then that's exactly what we'll do," Charmaine told her. "The circumstances don't change the fact that one of our students has died."

When the call ended, Gabriela returned to the kitchen, washed her hands, put the candles back in the cake, and relit them. With each little flame, she said a prayer for Ricky and for Emilie.

Carrying the cake into the dining room, she sang her own happy birthday song, with Ben, Daniel, and Agnese joining in. This time Gabriela really did make a wish and closed her eyes before blowing out the tiny sparks of light.

After Agnese went home and Ben fell asleep upstairs, Gabriela and Daniel cuddled on the sofa together, both drifting off in front of the television. It was late, and she didn't want him to leave. Getting up, she tugged at his hand. "Stay. I need you here."

"Okay," he agreed. "But I'll be gone before Ben wakes up."

———◦———

When Gabriela awakened a little before seven o'clock the next morning, she felt the emptiness of the other half of the bed, the sheets already cold. Downstairs on the kitchen counter a note rested against the coffeepot. "Went to my place to shower and change. Be back for breakfast around eight or so." At the bottom of the page,

Daniel had sketched an elaborate heart wreathed by flowers, like an old-fashioned valentine.

Using her phone, Gabriela scrolled through the local news on the *Ohnita Times-Herald* website, reading about the unidentified male whose body was found at the lakeshore. There was no mention of the gunshot wound, though surely that detail would be reported in the next update once the police released the coroner's report—along with Ricky's name and, perhaps, Emilie's as well.

She clicked off the screen and made her regular morning call to her mother. Agnese was full of questions about their plans for the day and whether they were going to church that morning.

"I'm not sure, and no," Gabriela answered in order.

Her mother's sigh turned to a low growl of impatience. "I leave in a few minutes for eight o'clock Mass. You should take Ben to ten thirty. Daniel too."

"First of all, Ben hates going to church, which makes it feel like punishment—not spiritually meaningful. And Daniel comes from completely different traditions."

"*Bah!* Everybody go to church. It's good for them."

Gabriela needed to change the subject. "So, you want to have dinner with us again tonight?"

"I tell Daniel you come here."

Gabriela couldn't remember the last time her mother had cooked a big meal in her own home. "Won't it be too much for you?"

"*Va bene.* I see you at six o'clock." Agnese hung up without saying goodbye

A short while later, Daniel arrived, carrying a pastry box. As they sat at the kitchen table with their mugs of coffee, Gabriela lifted the lid and selected a carrot cake muffin. Daniel took a plain doughnut, dipped it into his coffee, and took a bite.

"Oh," Gabriela said. She'd never seen him do that before, a small discovery that spoke of the newness of their relationship.

"Sorry, is that gross?" Daniel asked.

"No, just the opposite. My dad always dunked a doughnut in his coffee. Seeing you do that reminds me of him."

"At least I have one thing in common with your dad."

Vincent Domenici had been a hardworking man with three loves: his wife, his daughter, and fishing. "I think you have more than one commonality," Gabriela replied. "A lot more."

By the time they refilled their coffee mugs, Ben joined them at the table, still in his pajamas. He picked up a frosted confection with sprinkles and asked for a hot chocolate.

Daniel slid his chair back before Gabriela could get up. "I got this, birthday girl."

"Did you tell her?" Ben asked Daniel.

"Why don't you?" Daniel tore open a packet of cocoa mix and dumped it into a mug.

"We're going to a place with lots of spies and smugglers," Ben said to Gabriela.

Her eyebrows shot up. "Oh?"

"Not exactly. It's called Peninsula Point. A small state park along the lake—about a half hour or so from here," said Daniel. "Is that okay, you know, after yesterday?"

"Of course. Sounds fascinating." Living in Ohnita Harbor, it wasn't like they could avoid Lake Ontario for long, and staying home would not change anything that had happened. Gabriela knew from her own past traumas that life had to go on. Emotional and physical survival depended on it.

Getting up from the table, Gabriela went into her office and returned with a copy of the Traitor's Map. Spreading it out on the table, she ran her finger along the shoreline from Ohnita Settlement in the center to the far right where a thin protrusion of land jutted into the lake. A faint script labeled it as Peninsula Point. "That's it, right?"

Daniel nodded. "That's it. About twenty miles from here."

Gabriela felt her pulse quicken as she studied the map. Amid all the inaccuracies and omissions that made the Traitor's Map so frustrating, Peninsula Point was one of the few places that appeared to be precisely marked. That fact alone made her want to visit it.

Chapter Four

After packing a lunch of sandwiches, fruit, and trail mix, they piled into Daniel's SUV he drove for personal use. Gabriela did a quick search on her phone and read aloud from a local history blog about how Peninsula Point had been used over the past 250 years by spies and smugglers.

"Told you!" Ben announced, stretching the length of his seat belt to look over her shoulder at the screen.

Her son's excitement churned up a wave of guilt over enjoying this day when Ricky's body lay on some slab at the morgue and Emilie mourned her friend. Perhaps more than a friend, Gabriela considered, remembering how the two of them always sat near each other in class and had partnered on the final project. Emilie and Ricky had seemed like a study in contrasts, but perhaps that had been part of the attraction. The thought of young love made Ricky's death even more tragic, if that were possible.

When they arrived at Peninsula Point, a chain blocked the entrance. Beyond it, snow mounds dotted the dirt-and-gravel access road. From the look of it, no one had been there since the previous fall.

"I was afraid of this." Daniel maneuvered the SUV back onto the pavement. "Boat launch won't open until May. But that's why we brought boots."

They parked at a gas station about a quarter mile away, where Daniel topped off the tank and spoke to the manager about leaving their vehicle for a couple of hours. For once, Ben didn't protest over having to wear boots; he even pulled on a hat and gloves when Daniel put on his. Bundled up against the cold, they walked back to the park entrance and skirted the chain, which seemed to delight Ben, who kept talking about "breaking into the place."

Mud and puddles from melting snow turned the road into an obstacle course. Ben ran ahead, splashing through standing water while Gabriela yelled after him not to get soaked. As she and Daniel walked together, Ben increased his distance from them.

"Wait up," Gabriela called out.

"It's okay. He can't get lost." Daniel explained that Peninsula Point was about a mile long, jutting straight into Lake Ontario and forming coves on both sides where cattails and thick, towering grass grew. Marsh Creek emptied into the larger of the two coves, and the state had built a boat launch there several years ago.

Ben came running toward them bareheaded, his hat protruding from his pocket and face flushed red from exertion. "The road is flooded."

"Maybe we should turn around," Gabriela said.

Daniel gave her a wink. "I think we can make our way through."

Ben fell into step beside them, talking a mile a minute about the water being knee-deep and needing to climb through the trees to reach the other side. A boy's hyperbole, Gabriela smiled to herself, relishing how Ben could turn an ordinary road into an adventure.

How many more years before he'd become too self-conscious for such flights of fancy?

The path snaked through the trees, and several times Gabriela had to duck out of the way of branches that snagged her hair and jacket. Although it wasn't quite the Amazonian jungle Ben had described, deep puddles forced them into the bushes and brambles growing along both sides of the road. As they pushed their way through the wooded detour, Daniel explained that state crews would be out later in the spring to cut the brush. Gabriela had to admit she liked the overgrowth. It helped her imagine what it had once been like: a stretch of undeveloped shoreline crisscrossed by rivers and streams and footpaths made by the Iroquois people.

When they rejoined the road and continued their walk, Daniel told the story that had made Peninsula Point famous. During the Revolution, two Continental Army soldiers on night patrol had come upon a British battalion secretly encamped on a small island in the middle of one of the peninsula's marshes. Hiding in the vegetation, the soldiers overheard a British brigadier general and his lieutenants plotting an attack on Fort Ohnita. "Those two soldiers made it back to their commander, reported everything, and became heroes," Daniel said. "The defeat of the British at Fort Ohnita was an important victory in the American Revolution."

Gabriela wondered if that was the battle in which Colonel Jacob Thorsen had been wounded. She tucked the details away to look into later.

"The spies weren't the only ones," Daniel went on. During Prohibition, smugglers had outrun the Coast Guard and risked storms on Lake Ontario to bring boatloads of liquor out of Canada. Larger vessels anchored off Peninsula Point, and smaller boats ferried shipments to land. From there, cases of alcohol were loaded onto horse-drawn wagons and hauled to the main road to be transferred to trucks. The contraband went off to Syracuse, Buffalo, or New York City disguised as milk and produce going to market.

He nudged Gabriela's arm. "Can you tell I did my homework?"

"Very impressive." Gabriela looked around for Ben, who had gotten ahead of them again. She called out his name but heard nothing except the wind rustling the marsh grass.

"Where are you, buddy?" Daniel shouted.

"Over here."

They followed the sound to a marshy area where Ben sat in a small boat with an old outboard motor. "Look what I found."

"Ahoy—permission to come aboard." Wearing Wellingtons that went almost to his knees, Daniel splashed in the water.

Pulling out her phone, Gabriela took several pictures of Ben in the boat and Daniel posing beside him.

Daniel stretched out his hand toward Ben. "Come on. Let's get you back on dry land."

"But they just left it here. Can't we use it?"

Gabriela folded her arms across her chest. "You know better than that. It belongs to whoever left it here."

"We're not stealing, just borrowing it," he protested.

Ben stood and the boat tipped. Daniel clasped Ben's hands to steady him, then swung the boy over the side and onto the ground next to Gabriela.

"A friend of mine has a boat. I'll ask him to take us out on the lake to do some fishing this summer," Daniel promised.

A friend's boat. Gabriela's thoughts turned back again to Ricky, who had been on her mind all day. She pictured him, the local kid, wanting to show off a little for Emilie, the downstate girl. It had cost Ricky his life.

"There's a small bridge up ahead," Daniel said, and Gabriela roused from her musings. "When we cross, you'll see where the British camped."

The arched bridge spanning Marsh Creek led to a small island rimmed by a rocky shoreline. Ben climbed onto a driftwood log, and Daniel sorted through stones on the beach to find flat ones for skipping. He let a stone fly, and it kissed the water twice. When Ben tried, he hit the water with a plunk. After a little more coaching, Ben managed one skip and let out a victory whoop.

"Try it, Mom," Ben coaxed, but Gabriela didn't want to take her gloved hands out of her pockets.

Walking along the shore to keep her feet from going completely numb, she thought about the boat in the marsh. There had been no truck or trailer tracks along the road, which meant someone must have motored down the shoreline and left the boat in the marsh. But why would they do that? Maybe it had gotten loose from someone's dock and floated there.

She gave her curious mind a rest and drew herself back into the moment. Using a piece of driftwood as a makeshift table, Gabriela set out their lunch and called Ben and Daniel over to eat. Taking a bite of a cold sandwich, she wished she'd brought a thermos of soup too. But Ben didn't seem to mind as he ate his sandwich, leaving only a corner of crust before going back to skipping stones.

Sitting on the log, Daniel slid closer to Gabriela and took her hand in both of his. "Not exactly a trip to Paris."

Gabriela looked up at him. "No. It's a hundred times better."

Out of the corner of her eye, she saw that Ben had just managed to skip a stone with three hops. "Way to go," she called out.

"What Ben said last night about us—you know. Well, it got me thinking," Daniel continued.

"I hope you don't think I ever said anything to him about us getting married," Gabriela interjected. "I don't know where Ben got that idea."

"Kids get ideas. But would that be such a bad birthday wish?"

Before she could answer, Daniel reached into his pocket. In the palm of his hand, he held a silver ring set with three turquoise stones the color of a robin's egg. With his free hand, he tugged off her glove. Top heavy and with a band that was too large, the ring would only fit her right index finger with room to spare.

"My grandfather made that for my grandmother," Daniel said. "She wore it all the time."

Holding it up for a closer look, Gabriela saw how the silver had been worked into a scroll design around the stones. "It's beautiful."

"Consider this a placeholder. We'll get you a real engagement ring. That is, if you agree."

Gabriela felt the unfamiliar weight of the ring.

Say yes, say yes, say yes, the voice in her head screamed over the practical thoughts about how they would all adjust to daily life together, the inevitable challenges when Ben became a teenager, and the reality that her aging mother would need to live with them one day. Her house was too small for all of them, and Daniel's was impractical.

"Okay," she said.

"Okay?" Daniel repeated, bringing his forehead down to touch hers. "Think you can find a more enthusiastic response?"

Her arms slipped around his neck. "Yes."

Although Ben's back was turned to them, their kiss was brief. "I love you," he whispered. "You and Ben and Agnese—you are my family now."

Gabriela leaned into Daniel, smelling damp woods and the clean scent of the soap he used. "My home and my family," she repeated.

The wind picked up, frothing the incoming waves and pushing them higher onto the shoreline. Skipping stones became harder, which helped Gabriela persuade Ben that it was time to leave. Back over the arched bridge and down the path that bisected Peninsula

Point, Gabriela and Daniel strolled hand in hand while Ben ran ahead. Inside Gabriela's glove, the ring pressed against her index finger, a sensation that would take getting used to. All of it would, she knew.

At the gas station, Gabriela used the restroom and bought a cup of coffee out of a push-button cappuccino maker, not caring about the taste as long as it came out hot. As she approached the counter to pay for her coffee and a snack for Ben, she overheard Daniel talking to the man who worked there about a nearby plot of land on which custom homes, a nine-hole golf course, and a marina were planned.

"Where's this place?" she asked.

"About a half mile down the road. They've got seventy-eight acres," said the man behind the counter. "They think all them people downstate are gonna move up here."

Daniel nodded. "Yeah, I believe it. And I'd love a piece of that. Not just roofing, but some of the construction."

"You work too hard as it is." Gabriela glanced at the clock on the wall—nearly three o'clock. "I want to hear more but tell me in the car. We've got dinner at Mama's tonight, remember?"

They rounded up Ben and left the convenience store. Daniel started up the SUV and headed out of the parking lot toward Ohnita Harbor. Then he turned the steering wheel in the other direction. "Might as well take a look. It's right down the road."

An eight-foot placard just off the shoulder advertised custom-built homes on half-acre lots. "Golf course and full amenities," the sign promised. It was the name, though, that captured Gabriela's attention: Thorsen Manor. "Who's developing this?" she asked.

Daniel squinted through the windshield at the sign. "EBR Properties. Why? You interested in buying?" He smirked at her.

"Hardly," Gabriela replied. "But I'll bet Thorsen Manor refers to Colonel Thorsen—the brother of the Traitor's Map guy."

"Let's find out," Daniel said.

Across the pavement, a bright red arrow pointed down a dirt access road. Daniel drove slowly as the SUV pitched and rolled over the ruts. Great swaths of woods and fields had been cleared and staked off. Fluttering tails of neon-orange streamers marked the boundaries of oversized lots, but no other signs of any real progress could be discerned.

The access road ended at a parking area that looked to Gabriela like it could hold at least twenty cars. In the rear stood a farmhouse with a sagging porch and a swayback roof. Three chimneys sprouted from the top, a sure sign of its age.

Daniel switched off the engine and got out of the SUV. "The guy at the gas station says this house is over two hundred years old."

Gabriela quickened her pace to keep up with Daniel, calling for Ben to stay close and not wander around the construction site on his own.

Shading his eyes with both hands, Daniel looked up at the roofline. "Complete tear off. Plus, the upstairs would need to be reconstructed."

Gabriela slipped her arm around Daniel's waist. "Then go find out who this EBR Properties is and go for it. And when you do, let me know what the connection is to Colonel Thorsen."

Looking around for Ben, she spotted him heading toward the back of the house. She followed her son into an overgrown backyard where a hulking lilac bush had gone feral and Virginia creeper vines snaked over an old garden shed. Just beyond the small building, a low iron fence topped with decorative scrollwork ringed a grassy area. The gate hung off its top hinge and stood permanently ajar. Inside the perimeter, a tall slab rose above overgrown grass.

Gabriela approached the stone and squatted down. Touching the grave marker, she shivered. A cool breeze off the lake whipped her hair across her forehead, and she pulled the collar of her jacket up to her jaw for warmth. Moving her hand over an inscription nearly erased by time, wind, and weather, she felt a sensation. Not a shiver, she registered, but something else. Goosebumps, she thought, and recalled another word—*frisson.*

Then her eyes made sense of the faint indentations carved into the stone:

Penelope Stanton Thorsen

Devoted Wife & Mother

Mistress of This Manor

Born April 11, 1748 ~ Died October 15, 1832

"Daniel!" Gabriela cried and began pulling at the grass with both hands, uprooting clumps from the muddy earth.

"What's up?" Daniel asked. Ben stood beside him.

"This has got to be Colonel Thorsen's wife." Gabriela kept yanking at the grass, uncovering a smaller marker to the right that bore one word: *Infant.* Daniel helped her, and soon another stone on the far right emerged, though it had crumbled beyond recognition.

"You know we're trespassing, right?" Daniel said. "Although I doubt anyone would fault us for pulling some weeds."

Gabriela got to her feet, scanned the overgrowth that engulfed much of the property, and tried to picture what it might have looked like when Colonel Thorsen and Penelope first settled here. Great stands of oak, beech, and hemlock, hundreds of years old, would have made this place a sea of bark and leaves all the way to the lakefront. Back then, the journey to Ohnita Settlement would have taken half a day, maybe longer. But this virgin land, with its proximity to the lakeshore, also would have been accessible by boat, making it all the more prized.

Getting her bearings, Gabriela headed in the direction of the lake. Daniel called for her to wait, but she kept moving, drawn by the distant sound of waves. She pushed back the brush with both hands and found a footpath leading through a tangle of vegetation. She imagined Penelope Thorsen walking there, a basket over her arm, gathering berries or wildflowers.

Daniel and Ben caught up with her, and the three of them made their way through the woods to the shoreline. Wind, water, rock—elemental and primal. Instead of recalling the brutality of Ricky's death near the fort grounds, some twenty miles away, Gabriela felt shielded from that tragedy in the timeless bubble of her imagination.

The guttural putt-putt of a motor broke into her thoughts, and Gabriela saw a boat pushing across the waves, calling to mind the skiff Ben had found in the marsh. It traveled parallel to the shoreline, in a northerly direction—away from Peninsula Point and Thorsen Manor.

As Gabriela watched, a man in the boat turned toward her. She waved instinctively, but he did not return the greeting.

The motor whined more loudly, and the boat picked up speed as it made a ninety-degree turn and headed out toward deeper water. A fisherman, Gabriela surmised; as spring took hold, every cove and cranny of this lakeshore would be filled with them.

Chapter Five

With the heat blasting in the SUV and her feet pressed against its floor vents, Gabriela began to regain the circulation in her extremities. They were headed back to Ohnita Harbor and would arrive in a half hour or so. Her eyes heavy, her head bobbed a few times. Daniel said something, and she murmured about needing to rest for a moment. The next thing she knew, the car had stopped. Opening her eyes, Gabriela recognized her own garage. In the back seat, Ben leaned his forehead against the window, still asleep.

Rousing her son, Gabriela guided him into the house, where the boy kicked off his muddy boots inside the kitchen. She didn't insist he bring them into the basement as usual but instead sent him upstairs to take a shower and put on clean clothes. A minute later, she heard the water running.

Daniel filled the coffee maker with water and spooned grounds into the filter. As the machine gurgled on the counter, Gabriela stepped into Daniel's embrace, resting her face against his chest. "I liked going to Peninsula Point," she said, "even though my feet got wet."

He kissed the top of her head. "We need to get you some Wellies. Big green ones."

"Uh-uh. Red's my signature color."

The phone rang, and Gabriela knew who had to be calling. "Hello, Mama."

"What time you come?" Agnese asked.

"Five thirty?" Gabriela suggested.

"*Bah*, the braciole won't wait. Overcooked for sure."

"Mama, your braciole is always perfect. We just need to clean up and rest a little. We'll be there as soon as we can. I promise."

Gabriela quickly drank her coffee and headed upstairs to shower. Wearing her bathrobe, she looked through Ben's partly opened door and saw him dressed in clean clothes, asleep atop the quilt on his bed.

Across the landing, she found Daniel fully dressed and sprawled out. She crawled in her bed beside him. Sleep dragged her under like water over her head. The sensation triggered a short dream of being in a boat and wanting to get to shore before the retreating tide pulled her into the depths. Although the boat had no motor and no oars, it moved with steady speed. Gabriela gripped the gunwale and shouted for it to stop.

Her eyes snapped open.

Daniel curled on his side, looking at her through lowered lids. "You yelled."

Gabriela sat up. "Really? What did I say?"

Daniel rolled over on his back and stretched. "Stop, or something like that."

She covered her eyes with both hands. "Just a stupid dream." Twisting her body toward the nightstand she read the clock: 5:15. They should get going, but the warmth of Daniel's body, the rise and fall of his chest, made her wish they could stay like this forever. *She belonged*—not to, but with. The difference was important.

Raising her hand above the covers, she admired the old silver and turquoise ring and silenced the nagging voice that wondered whether Daniel's late wife, Vicki, had ever worn it.

Daniel stroked her hair. "I'm glad you like it. We'll get you a real engagement ring soon."

Cautionary thoughts elbowed their way into her consciousness—the reality of daily life with Ben and her mother, and the issue that weighed most heavily on her mind. *Where would they live?* Gabriela pictured the dramatic interior of the farmhouse Daniel had rehabbed himself: interior walls eliminated to open the space to display his artwork, the upstairs converted into a sleeping loft.

Daniel brushed a strand of hair off her forehead. "When you start working something over in your mind, you scrunch your face up really tight." He pressed his fingertip between her eyebrows.

"Are you saying I need Botox?" She laughed lightly.

"Uh-uh. I'm saying you should tell me what's going on in there."

Gabriela heaved a sigh. "We're going to outgrow this house, especially when Mama can't live on her own anymore. And we can't all live in your house. There's only one sleeping loft. But that's your dream house."

"It was my dream once, but that time has passed. I'm going to convert it back to something more conventional so I can sell it."

"But what about all your memories there—with Vicki?"

Sitting up, Daniel bent his long legs and rested his arms on his knees. "I loved Vicki. We were happy together and still would be if she hadn't died."

Gabriela balled a corner of the sheet in her hand. What he said was true, but that didn't make it less painful to hear.

"It's the same if you and Jim had found a way to reconcile," he went on. "But that's not how life turned out. You and I are together now. You're forty-one, and I'll be forty-nine in August. What are we waiting for?"

"I know. I just—I suspect I'm very different from Vicki. You might not like daily life with me."

"Oh, you're different all right," Daniel said. "I can't imagine Vicki ever getting caught up in murder investigations. You can't seem to stay away from them."

Despite the freshness of Ricky's death, Gabriela had to smile.

"You share other important qualities, though," he said. "You're both loving, loyal, and very intelligent. But without any disrespect to you or to her, I say with all honesty that I don't want another Vicki. I'm with you now, with all the mess and drama that make up life with you."

Gabriela studied his sharp nose, deep-set eyes fanned by lines, his long straight gray hair loosened from the ponytail he wore at the nape of his neck. The artist-turned-roofer who could create or repair anything, including her wounded heart. "Okay," she said.

Daniel brought his face close to hers. "I thought you already said yes."

Gabriela closed her eyes and exhaled. "I'm saying it again. But I don't want to rush it. We need to figure out the logistics."

"I won't push you into anything. I promise," Daniel said. "But I can't speak for your mother."

Groaning, Gabriela pulled the covers over her face. Once her mother knew they were planning to get married, Agnese would pester her about a church wedding. She had skipped that the first time around with Jim and had no intention of pursuing it now. Simple and uncomplicated suited them, but neither of those words applied to her mother.

Agnese's kitchen filled with an aroma that had Gabriela already tasting the braciole—beef pounded thin and wrapped around a filling of breadcrumbs, grated cheese, and herbs. She had tried to describe it to Daniel but told him he could only understand once he'd had a bite.

Daniel kissed Agnese on both cheeks and repeated the words she spoke in Italian to him. "*Buona sera.*"

Gabriela took her jacket into the living room to hang it up in the narrow front closet. She passed Ben, stretched out on the floor in front of the television. Extracting his zip-up hoodie from him, she made space in the closet next to a man's brown tweed jacket. Recognition caught her breath. Taking the old wool blazer from its hanger, she held the fabric to her nose and closed her eyes. Her father had been dead for almost five years, but Gabriela thought she detected a faint scent of wood and lime from his aftershave. Tears welled in her eyes. "I miss you, Daddy," she whispered into the thin padding of the shoulders, then returned the jacket to the back of the closet.

In the kitchen, Gabriela offered to transfer the meat to a serving platter, then stood back as her mother cut the first slice of the braciole, revealing the pinwheel pattern of beef and filling. "Perfect, Mama," she said.

Agnese shrugged. "We see, maybe not too overcooked."

Daniel poured wine into three stemmed goblets and set a glass of milk at Ben's place.

With a clap of her hands, Agnese summoned them all to the table. "You say grace." She nodded in Daniel's direction.

"How about I toast the cook instead?" Daniel held up his glass of wine. "Here's to Agnese. Thank you for making this amazing dinner. And to Gabriela as she turns forty-one."

"Soon," Gabriela giggled. "I still have about two hours of being forty."

Daniel turned to the boy sitting at his left. "And to Ben for being so adventurous today. And to all of us for this time together."

"Cheers." Gabriela clinked her glass against Daniel's.

"Amen." Agnese crossed herself with her right hand and sipped wine from the glass in her left. "What you wear?"

Gabriela set her wineglass down on the table. "My sweater?" Dark blue with a metallic thread, it shimmered a little in the light. She hadn't put it on since Christmas but felt festive tonight for her birthday.

"On your hand." Agnese reached toward her.

"This belonged to Daniel's grandmother. His grandfather made it for her." The ring slipped off easily and she deposited it in Agnese's outstretched palm.

Agnese studied the ring, her mouth turned down in concentration. "Why you wear it?"

Under her mother's scrutiny, heat rose in Gabriela's cheeks. "Daniel gave it to me. I think it's lovely." Taking the ring back, she put it on.

"It's a placeholder," Daniel said. "We'll be going ring shopping soon."

Agnese leaned toward him. "You get married?"

Ben looked up from pushing his salad around with his fork. "*What?*"

"We're talking about it," Gabriela added quickly.

Daniel cocked his head at her. "A little more than that."

"It's yes or no. You wear a ring, it's yes." Agnese pursed her lips.

"When?" Ben asked.

Gabriela reached her hand across the table to Ben, but he didn't take hers. "Not for a while. We've got a lot to figure out."

"Not that much," Daniel interjected.

"Where we're going to live for one," Gabriela added.

"We have to move?" Ben took an enormous bite of bread.

"No," she told Ben. "Well, maybe another house, but not now."

"Why you wait?" Agnese said. "You are not getting younger."

When Gabriela looked over at Daniel, he gave her a smile that she couldn't help returning.

Throughout their dinner, every time Agnese pressed for details, Gabriela steered the conversation to the tenderness of the braciole, the fun they had that afternoon, Ben finding what she called the mystery boat.

"Who comes for the wedding? Your family?" Agnese asked Daniel.

"I don't really have anyone." He explained that he'd never known his mother's family. His paternal grandmother out West had raised him and his sister after their parents died. But his grandmother had passed away many years ago.

Agnese put another slice of braciole on Daniel's plate despite his protest that he'd already eaten two. "Where is she now—your sister?"

"Albuquerque," he replied. "Or that's where she was the last time I knew. I don't hear from her very often. It's been years since I saw her."

"You call her." Agnese pushed back her own plate and folded her arms on the edge of the table. "Bad blood no good in families."

Daniel set down his knife and fork. "It just happened. We drifted apart over the years. Not quite sure why."

"She married? Have children?" Agnese asked.

"No. Divorced, the last I knew."

"She has nobody. You call her."

Gabriela widened her eyes to make her mother stop. "Sometimes it happens in families. You and Aunt Cecelia left Italy. You never saw your mother again."

Agnese hit the table with the flat of her hand and raised her voice. "That was different. No money, no future. Cecelia, she had to leave, and I go with her."

"I understand, Mama," Gabriela said, trying to smooth things over. "I just meant that when people move, sometimes it's hard to stay in touch."

Agnese got up from the table. "Cecelia came to see me today. She brings me cannoli from the bakery in Syracuse. She says happy birthday."

Gabriela raised her glass. "Well, thank you, Aunt Cecelia. I'll call her tomorrow."

Her glass still suspended, Gabriela watched Agnese head back into the kitchen, her mouth a firm line. Since childhood, she'd heard her mother describe daily life in Italy—the olive groves on the hillsides, the basil growing in the kitchen garden, ripe tomatoes that clustered like oversized grapes on the vine, and a hundred other scents and sensations. And she reminisced about early days in the States, especially meeting Vincent Domenici. But her mother never said much about why she and Cecila had left Italy as young women—alone and unaccompanied—no matter how many times Gabriela asked. She'd always assumed it was too sad or painful to discuss.

Seeing her mother's angry expression now, Gabriela wondered if there was more to it than that. *I bring that into the coffin with me*—it was Agnese's version of taking secrets to the grave. When it came to her departure from Italy nearly sixty years ago, Gabriela realized, her mother meant it literally.

Chapter Six

An angry voice split the quiet of the library on Monday morning. From her office on the second floor, Gabriela heard the commotion and raced down the stairs. When she reached the circulation desk just inside the main entrance, her eyes locked on a short, stocky man in a gray plaid shirt unbuttoned to show a dingy thermal undershirt and jeans that rode low under a rounded belly.

"I want to see the professor," the man thundered.

Pearl Dunham, a circulation clerk who had worked at the library longer than anyone else on the staff, held up her hands, palms out. "Back up the truck, buddy." Her gravelly voice took on a twang. "Why don't you start by telling me who you are?"

"Seymour," he said. "Walt Seymour. My boy got killed."

Gabriela drew in a sharp breath. It was hard to see any resemblance between this raging man and the jovial student in her class. She stepped forward and extended her hand. The man did not take it. "Mr. Seymour? I'm Gabriela Domenici, the executive director here. Your son was in my class at the community college. I am so sorry for your loss."

Bloodshot eyes bore into her, and a thick finger aimed in her direction. "Because of you he's dead."

Gabriela turned toward Pearl and murmured, "Call Thelma." The police station was a block away, which meant Thelma or another police officer could be there in a minute or two.

She addressed him again. "Mr. Seymour, please know that we are all deeply saddened by what happened to Ricky. He is missed by all his classmates."

"It's your fault. All he could talk about was you and that map."

His fury tore at Gabriela. She couldn't imagine the depth of this father's grief; if anything ever happened to Ben, she would be inconsolable. "We all want to pay our respects to Ricky. I'm sure the college will hold a memorial—"

Walt's face crumpled. "What good is that gonna do? My boy's dead."

Behind him, the front door opened. Gabriela made eye contact with Thelma Tulowski and the young patrolman accompanying her. "What's going on here, Walt?" Thelma asked.

He rubbed a beefy hand over his face. "Ricky would be alive if he hadn't gone to the lake that night. How come it was him who died?"

Gabriela felt lightheaded and wanted to sit down but stayed where she was. In her peripheral vision, she saw a few patrons peering around shelves toward the circulation desk. A couple of women ducked down behind the magazine rack.

"You know the circumstances," Thelma said. "We talked about this. Ricky went out Friday night to ask somebody about using a boat on Saturday. And we think that *somebody* shot him. Gabriela had nothing to do with that." Thelma stepped closer to Walt. "But I've got a feeling you might have some ideas who owned that boat."

"I don't know nothing about a boat 'cept what *you* told me. Maybe you know who killed him and you're hiding it," Walt said.

"Why don't you come with us to the station, and we'll talk some more about it?" Thelma said. "But you're not going to bother these good people in a public place."

Walt's shoulders sagged and a deep keening came out of the man. He stumbled, and Thelma grabbed one of Walt's arms and the young patrolman steadied him on the other side. Together they escorted Walt out of the library.

Gabriela stepped toward the circulation desk and gripped it tightly. From behind her, Mike Driskie, the library custodian, came forward. "You need some water?" he asked.

"I'll be okay. I think I forgot to breathe for a minute."

Pearl rounded the corner of the circulation desk. "Man, if anybody thinks working at a library is boring, they oughta spend a day or two with us." She held out her hand to Gabriela. "Come on. Let's go down to the breakroom and get you some coffee."

Gabriela wanted to retreat to her office and out of the spotlight of attention from staff and patrons but accepted the invitation. As they walked across the main floor, Gabriela doled out reassuring smiles to people who glanced and quickly looked away and to a few who stared as she passed.

"You know you have a knack for getting yourself mixed up in stuff, right?" Pearl said as they descended the stairs to the lower level jokingly called the dungeon, both for its gloominess and the fact the old library had been built 160 years ago to look like a castle.

"Yes, I do realize that," Gabriela said, accepting the ribbing that Pearl was known for.

On the counter of the breakroom, a pot of coffee made sometime that morning rested on a burner. "Maybe we dump that out, brew a fresh pot," Gabriela suggested.

"Nah. Just add a little more sugar." Pearl filled two mugs and handed one to Gabriela.

Gabriela's first sip almost made her gag. She poured in another packet of sugar and spooned in more nondairy creamer.

Pearl raised her cup. "To courage."

An hour later, Gabriela still had the taste of that bitter coffee in her mouth and decided to walk down to A Better Bean for a latte. Passing through the coffeeshop she overheard scraps of gossip—"an execution-style murder" and "all those college kids on drugs." When one man started up about "this kid being involved in a meth ring," Gabriela gave him an icy stare. He looked back, his expression blank.

Don't engage, Gabriela chided herself. In time, Ricky's murder would be forgotten and these busybodies would move on to the next thing. But it angered her to hear Ricky maligned by people who hadn't known him.

On her way back to the library, Gabriela stopped at the police station for an update on Walt.

"You bring a coffee for me too?" Thelma asked when Gabriela entered her small office.

"Sorry, wish I'd thought of that." Gabriela took a seat in one of the folding chairs against the wall.

"Just kidding," Thelma sat down at her desk. "I don't think Walt is going to bother you. I told him if he shows up again at the library, we'll arrest him for harassment."

"No, you don't need to do that. He's in pain—any parent would be." Gabriela took a sip of her coffee. "So, I just left A Better Bean."

"Little City Hall," Thelma interjected. "That's what we call it around here. Everybody sits around and discusses what they think they know."

"Well, the gossips are accusing Ricky of being in a meth ring."

Thelma shook her head. "People with nothing better to do are going to speculate. You see the Syracuse paper today?"

Gabriela shook her head. "Just the *Times-Herald*. The reporting seemed pretty accurate."

"Yeah, our local guy got it right. Syracuse paper got a little carried away—said it was a mob-style hit because of the bullet in the back of the head." Thelma cocked her forefinger and thumb, aiming them behind her right ear. "Ricky's death has got some imaginations running wild."

Gabriela gripped her coffee cup. "So, any idea what did happen?"

Thelma gave her a sideways glance. "Really? You're going to ask me that?"

"I withdraw the question." Gabriela got up. "But when you do know something, you'll let me know?"

Thelma let out a little laugh. "I'll ask you for the same favor, since you're always poking your nose where it doesn't belong."

Two days later Gabriela arrived at the community college a half hour early for her Wednesday class. It was the first time they'd come together since Ricky's death, and Gabriela had no idea how many students would show up, but she wanted to be there when they walked in the room. Charmaine Odele came by and offered to speak to the students before class. Gabriela gratefully accepted the support.

Shortly before eleven o'clock the first students arrived. Gabriela tried to read their expressions—most of them sullen, a few of them neutral. Glancing toward the door every few minutes, Gabriela waited for Emilie. At two minutes after the hour, she entered the room.

Charmaine stood at the front of the classroom and reminded students that counseling services were always available at the health center. "Don't struggle in silence about Ricky's death or anything else," she told them. "You can get help."

Watching the students as Charmaine spoke, Gabriela noticed Emilie touching her eyes with her fingertips. Another student leaned over and whispered something to her.

When Charmaine headed toward a seat in the back of the room, Gabriela took her place in front. Looking out at the students, she felt a tug of protectiveness. "I thought we might talk about Ricky today. The college is going to arrange a memorial for him, but for now let's remember our classmate."

No one spoke up. The room radiated with tension.

"I asked Ricky once why he signed up for this class," Gabriela began. "He told me it was because there wasn't a textbook." A few students laughed. "I don't think that was the only reason of course. Ricky liked history and was intrigued by authenticating artifacts."

Gabriela's eyes were on Emilie, her face cast downward, her dark hair sliding forward like a veil.

Emilie raised her eyes slowly, and Gabriela saw her tears. "He loved the Traitor's Map," she said softly. "He really thought we could authenticate it—prove what it was."

"I want to talk to you all about the final assignment," Gabriela continued. "As you know, the Traitor's Map was tied to an execution. Then Ricky was shot and killed. While these incidents are nearly 250 years apart, I am concerned this assignment may be too traumatic for some of you."

"For who?" Emilie interrupted. "I'm the one who found him. And if I want to keep up this assignment—to do it *for Ricky*—then why should anyone else want to stop?"

Gabriela scanned the room. Every murmur and gesture indicated agreement. "If anyone wants to withdraw from the final project, please see me privately. There will be no pressure or penalty. Your grade will be based on your work thus far."

"It's okay," one of the students said. "If Emilie wants to keep going, we'll do it."

From the back of the room, Charmaine gave a slight nod.

"Okay," Gabriela said. "But let's work together. Every class period, we'll come up with ideas about who we would interview, questions we would ask. Maybe we'll even bring in a few guest speakers. Then you'll take the last week of class to write your reports. Sound good?"

Emilie swiveled in her chair to address Charmaine. "Can't you tell us who donated the Traitor's Map to the maritime museum? You have to know."

Charmaine clasped and unclasped her hands. "The museum was contacted about three months ago by the family that had owned the map for generations. They didn't want any fuss when they donated it."

"So, what'd they tell you?" a student with purple streaks in her hair asked.

"Will they talk to us?" another added.

"I don't know," Charmaine said. "It wasn't exactly an anonymous donation, but it was done quietly."

The student with the purple streaks spoke up. "But if they won't talk to us, then this whole class project is just made up."

"Not exactly. This is a genuine artifact," Gabriela corrected, hoping the educational value of the authentication exercise hadn't been lost on the students.

"I can't make any promises, but I will ask a member of the family," Charmaine said. "I see this person fairly regularly."

Someone on the faculty? Gabriela wondered. Maybe even someone within the history department. "We'll find out more soon," she told the students. "But in the meantime, keep talking to one another. Reach out if you need any help or support."

With ten minutes remaining in the class period, Gabriela let the students leave early, but several of them lingered. Emilie was the last one in the classroom with Gabriela and Charmaine.

"Have you talked to one of the counselors?" Charmaine asked.

Emilie shrugged. "Yeah. It helped a little. But this is better. Gives me something to think about other than…" Her voice trailed off.

"I'm a phone call or an email away," Gabriela told her and accepted a hug as Emilie left the classroom.

"Were Ricky and Emilie in love?" Charmaine asked.

"I think so. They were also best friends, which makes it even harder." Gabriela snapped off the lights in the classroom and closed the door as they left.

Back at her desk at the library, Gabriela tried to dive into her work, but every little thing distracted her—Delmina talking to herself as she tried to fix a paper jam in the printer, a bird landing on the windowsill and peeking through the glass. When softness brushed her ankles, Gabriela picked up Nathaniel, the black tomcat with the white-tipped tail who made his home between the library, City Hall, and the police station. He settled into her lap, purring loudly as she gave him a thorough back rub.

"Who's a good boy?" she said as Nathaniel rolled over, exposing his soft belly, and batted at one of her curls.

A throat cleared.

Gabriela sat up, and the cat jumped from her lap and streaked out of the office.

A man all in gray, from his hair to his coat and baggy trousers, stood in front of her desk. His bright blue eyes were his most distinguishing feature, magnified by the lenses of his silver wireframe glasses. It took a few seconds for Gabriela to place him—Clayton Brooks, the pharmacist at Ohnita Harbor Drugs.

"I understand you want to see me," he began.

Gabriela had no idea why he would assume that. Perhaps Mayor Phillips had suggested he serve on the citizens' committee. "Are you here about the beautification grant?"

Clayton's eyes widened behind his glasses. "No. The map. It belonged to my family."

"Oh!" Gabriela said, shocked at how quickly Charmaine had acted on this. Her class had ended only two hours ago.

In one smooth motion, Gabriela got to her feet, asked Clayton to wait just a moment, and called out her door for Delmina to join them and bring her stenographer's notebook. In her experience, when people were ready to tell a long story, it was best to capture it the first time.

Delmina wheeled her office chair through the doorway. Taking a seat, she had her pen and notebook at the ready.

Clayton took off his glasses and wiped the lenses with a white handkerchief extracted from his pocket. "The map was in my family for many generations. My father, Hubert Brooks, was the last to have it in a private collection. He died last fall at age ninety-two. I wanted to donate the map. My brother, Everett, disagreed. He thinks it's a bunch of nonsense, but I think it's an important part of local history."

His mouth tightened. "It's not the only thing my brother and I disagree on." Clayton sat back, one hand resting atop the other.

Gabriela waited for the next detail but suspected little would be forthcoming without prompting. "How did your family come to own the map? Are you descended from the Thorsens?"

Clayton shifted in his chair. "Direct descendants. On my father's side."

"I assume you mean from Colonel Thorsen—Jacob Elijah Thorsen," Gabriela continued.

Clayton bowed his head and seemed to examine the stitching along the cuff of his coat. "He's the best known of our ancestors, yes."

"But Henry is the most colorful," Gabriela added, hoping to spark a little more interest.

A grin transformed Clayton's face, and his serious air that had bordered on dourness morphed into joviality. "My father certainly thought so," he said with a chuckle. "He searched for years to find any trace of what happened to Henry. I think he was a little obsessed with him."

"Tell me," Gabriela invited, and Clayton launched into a story. In 1756 Jacob Thorsen, then only sixteen years old, had inherited all of their father's landholdings around Ohnita Settlement, while Henry Thorsen was given only a small stipend and sent out into the world to make his way. When Jacob served as a commander in the Continental Army during the Revolution, Henry had been his aide-de-camp.

"Henry must have resented Jacob enough to betray him," Clayton said. "He spied for the British, including with that map, though it's hard to tell how useful it was—given all of its mistakes."

"Any idea why it's so inaccurate?" Gabriela asked.

Clayton shrugged. "Henry was an amateur cartographer and would have been well acquainted with the shoreline. But I guess we'll never know. After all this time, I can't imagine anyone would really care one way or the other."

Gabriela didn't believe that for an instant and told him so. Historians loved nothing better than debating all sorts of obscure points.

"Will you talk to my class?" she asked. "They'd love to learn more about the map." Gabriela held her breath, hoping Clayton wouldn't lose his nerve. "It's so important for young people to get excited about history," she added. "If they don't understand the past, how will they find their way into the future? Don't you agree?"

Clayton made a noncommittal but positive-sounding response.

"People need to know about the Thorsen family history," Gabriela pressed.

"Preserving that history is a lot more than just some housing development. My brother is trying to capitalize on the family name—not that I haven't tried to stop him." Clayton shook his head. "I donated the map so people would know about Jacob and Henry, and not just think about a bunch of overpriced houses and a marina."

Gabriela heard the bite in his voice but resisted the urge to ask how his brother had taken over the family property and not him. "My class meets every Wednesday and Friday mornings, eleven to twelve thirty," she pushed on. "Any chance you might be able to come next week?"

"I-I suppose," he began. "Fridays are always busy with people getting prescription refills before the weekend. So, Wednesday, I guess."

"May I email you the details?" Gabriela offered, but Delmina thrust a sheet of paper from her notebook between them. The date, time, room number, and Gabriela's contact information had been put down in Delmina's careful handwriting.

Clayton folded the paper and slipped it into his pocket.

"Until Wednesday," Gabriela said, and the man in gray nodded and left her office.

She sent a text to Charmaine, informing her that Clayton Brooks would speak to the class, and received a thumbs-up emoji in reply. When the phone buzzed again, Gabriela expected more from Charmaine but instead saw Mary Jo's name.

Just saying hi.

Mary Jo Hinson had been executive director of the Ohnita Harbor Public Library until moving to Binghamton, New York, with her husband the previous August. She and Gabriela were close friends, but distance and circumstances had a way of elongating the time between their conversations. They hadn't seen each other in three months.

Gabriela sent a response, saying they had a lot to catch up on and asking when they could talk. Her phone rang almost immediately. Bypassing the small talk, they dove into the latest news for both of them—Mary Jo's new job at the Binghamton University library and Gabriela's class project on the Traitor's Map, Ricky's death, and Emilie finding the body.

Sorrow tinged Mary Jo's voice as she asked how everyone was coping. Gabriela assured her that Emilie had the support of her family, and the college offered counseling services to any of the students.

"What about you?" Mary Jo asked.

Gabriela knew her friend would never accept a perfunctory assurance of being fine. "It's hard sometimes. Brings me back to what happened at Still Waters Chasm. As long as I live, I'll never forget those two bodies." She pressed her eyes shut as if that could block the images flashing in her memory. "But this doesn't have anything to do with me. Emilie is the one who needs my support. I find it inconceivable that someone shot Ricky."

Pulling herself back from a spiral of worry about what had happened to Ricky and why, Gabriela got up from her desk and shut the door.

"I need to tell you something else," she told Mary Jo. Aiming her phone at her right hand, she took a photo of the turquoise ring and texted it.

"Beautiful!" Mary Jo exclaimed.

"Daniel says it's a placeholder."

"Hmm, and what do you say about that?"

Gabriela fiddled with the too-big ring that slid around her finger. "I have no idea where we're going to live."

"Oh, my dear friend," Mary Jo said. "You're afraid to be happy."

"That's not..." Gabriela felt strangled by the words that caught in her throat, and her eyes burned. "I've never trusted happiness. I've had my moments of course. But it always seemed like something other people had."

"Well, maybe it's time to change that. I've got my calendar open. What are you doing Friday? I'll come up and we'll have dinner."

"This Friday? In two days?" Gabriela wanted to make sure she understood.

"Too soon?"

"No, it's great. And you'll stay at my house."

"I intend to." Mary Jo laughed. "Get Daniel to hang out with Ben so we can have some one-on-one time. If he's going to be a stepfather, he needs to know that this comes with the territory."

Gabriela got an idea. "Any chance you can come early and speak to my class? I'd love for you to tell them about returning artifacts to their place of origin."

"It's not like I'm an expert," Mary Jo said, but she sounded pleased by the invitation. "I only did it once."

Gabriela would never forget that one time. With a million-dollar deal on the table to sell a medieval cross donated to the library, Mary Jo had decided to put principles over money and return the artifact to its original home in Italy.

"Once is plenty. Class starts at eleven. Can't wait."

Gabriela put down the phone, pleased at how much she'd accomplished—a guest speaker for each of her next two class sessions and time to hang out with Mary Jo. After she texted Charmaine with the latest updates, her phone rang.

"Dinner, my house—Friday night?" Charmaine offered. "I'd love to see Mary Jo again."

Chewing the side of her mouth, Gabriela contemplated how to turn down Charmaine without offending her. "I can't commit for Mary Jo."

"Okay, I get it. The two of you need to catch up. How about swinging by after dinner for a glass of wine?"

That, Gabriela decided, was the best compromise.

Chapter Seven

By nine thirty Friday morning Gabriela had abandoned her desk and any pretense of being able to concentrate on her work. Downstairs at the library she pushed around the cart filled with returned books to be put back into circulation. It gave her something to do while being near the front door when Mary Jo walked in. While putting a novel back on the shelf, Gabriela noticed several others out of order. She pulled down six volumes, put four back on the shelf in their rightful places, and set two others—one that belonged in *C* and the other in *P*—on the cart. Rounding the corner, she heard Mary Jo's low, melodious voice and saw her friend standing just inside the front door talking with Francine Clarke, who worked on the circulation desk.

At five-foot-ten, Mary Jo projected a presence that seemed to fill the room. Seeing her again, Gabriela thought back with pride on Mary Jo's tenure as the library's executive director and the only African American woman associated with Ohnita Harbor's municipal government. Treated like an outsider by the previous city adminis-tration, Mary Jo had used that to her advantage as she stood up to the former mayor who, in the end, had gone to jail for corruption and misuse of public funds. In comparison, Gabriela knew she had it so much easier working with the current mayor, who emphasized cooperation above all else.

"There she is!" Mary Jo opened her arms, and Gabriela stepped into the hug.

Francine fluttered around them. "I just told Mary Jo it felt like old times having her back here. I wish she'd never left." Francine's forehead puckered in a look of embarrassment. "Oh, I didn't mean—it's not that you're not a good executive director, Gabriela. I, uh—it's just nice to see you, Mary Jo."

Mary Jo smirked. "It's nice to be missed, Francine."

As she walked with Mary Jo across the main floor of the library toward the stairs to the second floor, Gabriela felt as if they'd slipped back in time. Less than a year ago, Mary Jo had been executive director, while Gabriela had overseen circulation and programming. Now, because of chronic budget issues, Gabriela assumed the executive director role but had kept all her former duties as well.

Halfway up the stairs, Mary Jo stopped and took Gabriela's hand. "Let me see this ring."

"Daniel says we're going to shop for an engagement ring, but I don't need all that fuss."

"Yeah, you do," Mary Jo said, continuing their climb.

"We're not kids," Gabriela protested. "It's only a piece of jewelry."

Mary Jo paused one step from the top. "How much of what you just said is really what you believe? And how much is you trying to make things easy for everybody else?"

Gabriela drew in a long breath and let it out slowly. "It's an old habit. My parents never had much money, so I always knew better than to ask for something. Jim and I struggled financially in New York. He spent money we didn't have, and I went without."

Mary Jo paused outside the administration suite and lowered her voice. "And how has that been working for you? There's some worthiness stuff going on, my friend."

Before Gabriela could answer, Mary Jo stepped through the doorway to greet Delmina. Gabriela walked past them and into her office, where she picked up materials for class then returned to Delmina's desk. The two women were locked in conversation, and Gabriela hated to interrupt; but if they didn't leave now, they'd be late for class. She slipped her car keys out of her purse and glanced once more at her phone for the time.

"I guess that means we'd better go," Mary Jo said. "But I'll be back."

As they crossed the community college campus, Mary Jo reminisced about being back where her husband, Clem, had taught before accepting a job in the Binghamton University history department. As fondly as Mary Jo spoke, Gabriela knew her friend had found a home in Binghamton, a larger city and a four-year university.

Snapping on the lights in her classroom, Gabriela noticed the desks had been arranged in a circle by the last class and set about putting them back into rows. Mary Jo stopped her. "Let's leave it like this. I'll do a discussion in the round."

Together they enlarged the circle to accommodate two dozen students, with Mary Jo at the front. Gabriela pulled a desk for herself behind the circle. As the students filed in, they noticed the new configuration and paused before choosing a seat. At the start of class, Gabriela introduced Mary Jo and described for the students the day a tiny cross with colorful designs on the front had been found in the donations to the library's rummage sale. She had dismissed it as a decoration, while Mary Jo had been the first to suspect that it was old and valuable. It turned out to be a medieval artifact worth at least a million dollars. That set off a rumble of gasps and comments about finding treasure.

Gabriela smiled. "But instead of selling this artifact to benefit the library—which could use the money, believe me—Mary Jo decided to return it to its original home in Siena, Italy." With that, she turned the program over to her friend and guest lecturer.

"Not everything that comes into our hands belongs to us," Mary Jo began. "Sometimes things are simply passing through, and it's our job to move them to their rightful place."

At the end of her presentation, the students jumped in with questions about how she'd known where to return the cross after seven hundred years.

"Thanks to Gabriela's expertise in authentication and contacts in New York City, we pieced it all together," Mary Jo said.

"It was a group effort," Gabriela interjected.

"But you knew who to ask," Mary Jo countered. "Without your connections, we wouldn't have gotten anywhere."

A student in the back raised his hand. "Professor Domenici, didn't somebody try to kill you over that cross?"

A one-inch scar below her jaw would always remind Gabriela of the man—of all people, the library board president at the time—who had wielded the knife that almost ended her life. Back then she'd seen him almost every working day and never suspected that he could be capable of killing someone.

"Yes, that's true," Gabriela said. "Desperate people do desperate things. Someone wanted to steal the cross. I stood in his way."

"That really sucks," the student said.

Glancing at Emilie and noticing her troubled expression, Gabriela wanted to move this discussion off the topic of murder and death. "Well, who says a librarian's life is boring?" she joked.

The mood lifted and the discussion returned to establishing a provenance—where something came from, its authenticity, its age and value.

"How do you know if someone is telling you the truth?" Emilie piped up. "Maybe they want to make you think something is worth a lot of money. Or maybe they don't have the right information."

"Happens all the time," Gabriela said. "That's what makes the Traitor's Map so interesting. We're told that it dates to the American Revolution, and there is no question that the parchment is old. But was it really made by Henry Thorsen? Could it be a fake—even a very old one? Fortunately, you're going to have a chance to ask those questions next Wednesday."

The students pressed her for details about the upcoming guest speaker, but to keep up the suspense, Gabriela purposefully remained vague. She also wanted to prevent a crowd of students from pouncing on Clayton Brooks at the pharmacy.

Several students lingered after class, hoping to get a hint about who would be at class the next week.

"You'll have to be here to find out," Gabriela said.

Charmaine Odele entered the classroom but stood back until the last student left. "Half your class choosing to stay late? You're showing up the rest of us, Gabriela," she said with a grin.

Gabriela tried to duck the compliment, explaining that Mary Jo had been the star attraction. "Now they can't wait for Wednesday," Gabriela explained. "I feel like I should warn Clayton before he comes that they'll probably want to cross-examine him."

"I'm thinking maybe you should ask the students to go a little easy on him," Charmaine replied.

The comment took Gabriela aback. "Is he having second thoughts?"

"It will go fine, I'm sure. Clayton will tell them whatever he's comfortable saying." Charmaine checked her phone. "I've got a class in fifteen minutes. I'll see you both tonight—how about seven?"

That evening, with Ben and Daniel out for burgers and bowling, Mary Jo and Gabriela had the house to themselves. They made an early dinner of pasta and salad, talking while they cooked. Afterward, they lingered at the table, feeling a little sleepy from the meal and a long day. Going over to Charmaine's house felt like an enormous effort, and Gabriela wondered if they could possibly call and cancel.

"Come on," Mary Jo said, getting up to clear their plates. "Charmaine's expecting us. And you need to stay on her good side."

Charmaine's big square Victorian sat back from the street with a landscaped front yard that appeared to be three times the size of Gabriela's modest lawn. Gabriela had been to Charmaine's home a few times before, but the age and beauty of the place still charmed and intimidated her a little. She couldn't imagine how much work it would take to keep up a place like this, not to mention the money.

Their footsteps on the brick walkway sounded a little like horses' hooves on cobblestones. Gabriela started to share the observation with Mary Jo, then noticed her friend's somber expression. "What's wrong?" she asked.

"I miss my house," Mary Jo said. "I doubt I'll ever live in anything like that again."

Gabriela recalled Mary Jo's one-hundred-year-old farmhouse on the western edge of town, furnished with antiques and eclectic artwork.

"Clem loves the condo we're in now—no yard, no maintenance," Mary Jo continued as they approached the front steps. "I hate it for all those same reasons. I promised to give it a year, but I won't last six months."

Before Gabriela could respond, the front door swung open and there stood Charmaine in jeans, an oversized sweater, and moccasin slippers. Welcoming them and taking the bottle of wine Gabriela brought, Charmaine beckoned them inside. As they followed her through the house, Gabriela peeked into the study where she'd met with Charmaine a few times and took in the cozy fireplace and built-in bookshelves that were original to the structure. It was her favorite room in this house.

Mary Jo groaned with pleasure when they entered the kitchen with its stainless-steel appliances, black granite countertops, and white cupboards. "Okay, that's it. When I get back to Binghamton, I'm telling Clem that we're looking for a house. If he wants to stay in the condo, he can be there by himself. I need these countertops."

Charmaine extracted the cork and poured wine for them. Gabriela asked for a decaf coffee instead, and their hostess began brewing a cup for one. With beverages in hand they went to the back of the house to a large living room dominated by a wide fireplace of brick painted white. Gabriela sank into an oversized armchair and fought the urge to curl her legs on the cushion. Mary Jo took the loveseat, and Charmaine settled on the sofa. In front of them stood a coffee table fashioned out of a wooden chest with brass fittings.

When Mary Jo asked several questions about the house, Charmaine obliged them with details from her research into its history all the way back to the original occupants in 1852. "The place was in pretty bad shape when I bought it ten years ago. Water damage upstairs. Plumbing a mess. And really awful paneling in here," Charmaine said. "I wanted to restore its former glory."

"All by yourself?" Gabriela asked.

Charmaine shook her head. "I was married when I started. When we divorced five years ago, I bought him out of his half of the house. So now it's just me."

Gabriela wondered how Charmaine could afford this place on a community college professor's salary, but of course she wouldn't dare ask.

"I guess I'll be looking for a new house at some point," Gabriela said.

"Oh?" Charmaine reached for a plate of cheese and crackers and passed it to both women.

"Mine is okay for Ben and me, but not if Daniel moves in." Gabriela bit into a cracker with a thin slice of cheddar on it.

"*When* he moves in," Mary Jo added.

"And there's my mother," Gabriela added.

"Back up." Charmaine uncrossed her legs and planted both feet on the floor. "I want to hear about Daniel moving in."

Gabriela had never shared much about her personal life with Charmaine, who was more boss than friend. But relaxing company and a fire snapping in the grate made her open up, and she told Charmaine about Daniel giving her his grandmother's ring.

"That's wonderful. I only met him once, but he seems like such a good guy. Your son likes him, right?" Charmaine said.

Mary Jo reached for a slice of cheese and a cracker. "Oh, it's a lovefest all the way around. Even Agnese is happy."

"Oh, please," Gabriela laughed. "My mother has been trying to get Daniel and me together from the moment she met him. But marriage is hard. Ben is a preteen. When he's fifteen or sixteen, he might resent Daniel."

"Count on it. He'll resent you too." Mary Jo sipped her wine. "My kids drove me nuts at that age. Never got into any real trouble, but they pushed the boundaries, believe me."

Gabriela clutched her coffee cup. "What if Daniel can't handle that? He and his wife never had kids. I don't even know if they wanted them." Looking up, she caught the look exchanged between Mary Jo and Charmaine. "What?"

Charmaine set her wineglass down on a side table with curlicue legs. "I'm on the outside, looking in. But it seems you're more worried about what Ben wants and what Daniel wants. What do you want? What makes *you* happy?"

Letting her eyes wander around the room with its high ceiling and decorative crown molding, Gabriela wished they could go back to talking about houses. "My family, being with Daniel—that's what makes me happy."

Mary Jo raised her glass. "Well, hallelujah! I've been waiting for you to say that. What about you, Charmaine? You gonna stay in this big old place by yourself forever?"

Gabriela almost choked on a cracker crumb. As she looked over for Charmaine's reaction to that blunt question, she caught a coy smile. "There is someone in my life these days. We're an unlikely couple, but it's good."

Gabriela tried to think of anyone she'd seen Charmaine with before or after the library board meetings or at the college. No one came to mind.

"Clayton Brooks," Charmaine said.

"You're kidding," Gabriela blurted out, then caught herself. She never would have paired the quiet pharmacist all in gray with vivacious and colorful Charmaine.

"It started when he approached the museum about donating the Traitor's Map. We met a few times, then he asked me to dinner. That night we talked for four hours," Charmaine said. "He's such a good man. And he is very interested in local history, especially the Thorsen connection."

Mary Jo looked between Gabriela and Charmaine. "What am I missing here?"

Gabriela explained briefly that Colonel Thorsen had been a local hero of the American Revolution and the War of 1812, while his brother, Henry, had been tried and convicted as a spy and traitor.

"Happens in the best of families," Mary Jo quipped.

Charmaine's smile broadened. "I find all that intrigue romantic. Clayton thinks so too. We're both sort of obsessed with genealogy at the moment."

Now Gabriela knew why Clayton had agreed to talk to her class. He had wanted to please Charmaine. She also knew how that felt— knowing that Daniel would do anything for her, just as she would for him.

Chapter Eight

On Saturday morning Gabriela got up early to make coffee. Mary Jo joined her a short while later, her overnight bag packed and set by the door. They sat at her kitchen table, as they had done so many times before as colleagues and as friends. With a 120-mile drive ahead, Mary Jo would have to leave soon to be home around lunchtime, as she'd promised Clem. Gabriela hated to see her go.

Ben's footsteps sounded overhead, and he came downstairs, dressed but unwashed, his hair standing on end. He and Daniel had stayed out until nine thirty the night before, and Ben hadn't gotten to bed until after ten. He slumped at the table as if he might fall asleep at any moment.

Mary Jo patted him lightly on the back. "Oh, I remember these days. Now mine are in college."

Gabriela set a toaster pastry and a hot chocolate in front of her son. He sat up and started eating. "Can I go over to Ryan's today?"

"We'll see. I've got to get some things done around here," Gabriela said. "And you need to pick up your room."

Ben groaned with complaints about it being Saturday and not fair.

"I think this is my cue to leave," Mary Jo said. "You've got your hands full. Can I get a hug?" Mary Jo stretched out her arms and, to Gabriela's surprise, her son allowed himself to be embraced. "Next time, you, your mom, and Daniel will come to see us. Bones misses you."

At the mention of the old basset hound, Ben brightened. "I want to get a dog. Daniel says I can when we move."

"Oh really?" Gabriela raised an eyebrow, wondering how much plotting and negotiating was going on unbeknownst to her.

"Let it go, let it flow," Mary Jo said in a little singsong. "Some things are not worth fighting over. Believe me."

Gabriela walked Mary Jo to her car, where the two friends clung to each other in a long hug with promises not to let so much time go by before seeing each other again. Standing in her driveway, she waved as Mary Jo backed out, beeped the horn twice, then drove off.

Already feeling her friend's absence, Gabriela went inside the house and started a load of laundry. As she ran the vacuum cleaner in the living room, Ben approached her and shouted something over the noise about his room being clean and going to a friend's house. She switched off the machine to hear the details, then gave him permission to ride his bicycle to Ryan's.

After Ben left, Gabriela told herself she could get so much more done with everyone gone. But as she transferred wet clothes into the dryer and started another load of laundry, the quietness of the house weighed on her. She should go somewhere—shopping, maybe get a pedicure, but neither of those things interested her. The restlessness that she blamed on boredom had nothing to do with feeling idle. She was lonely.

Picking up the phone, Gabriela called Daniel, fully expecting to get his voicemail since he was working. Instead, she heard road noise.

"Hey, I was just thinking about you," he said. "Did Mary Jo leave?"

"Yes, a little while ago. Ben's over at Ryan's. Where are you?"

"I'm going to see about a possible job. Someplace that might interest you."

Gabriela held her phone between her shoulder and her ear to free up her hands as she wiped the kitchen counter. Daniel related his call about a half hour ago with the developer of Thorsen Manor. He was headed up there to discuss the project. "The guy is only going to be onsite for the next few hours. You wanna come with me?"

Looking down at her baggy jeans and sweatshirt, Gabriela wondered if she'd have time to change. "Give me five minutes?"

"Be there in three."

Racing upstairs, Gabriela decided the jeans would be okay but shucked off the sweatshirt and put on a blouse and sweater. Taming her curly hair as best as she could, Gabriela slipped on a headband made of twisted copper like a double helix. When Daniel's blue DRD Roofing pickup truck pulled in the driveway, she grabbed her jacket and headed out the front door.

As they drove out of town, Daniel told her about the developer's vision for the property, with a first phase of fifty custom-built homes on half-acre lots. The old farmhouse would be rehabbed into a community space for entertainment. "That's where I come in," Daniel explained. "As long as the basic structure is sound, we can renovate."

Gabriela thought back to the previous night's conversation and told Daniel about Charmaine's house restoration.

"I'd love to see what she's done," Daniel said. "Might give me some ideas. Everett says the old farmhouse is a wreck, except for the fireplace. It's massive—the kind you could stand up in."

"Everett?" Gabriela repeated.

"Everett Brooks. He's the EB in EBR Properties. The *R* stands for *realty*." The name clicked from her conversation with Clayton Brooks. "I know Everett's brother. He's speaking to my class next week." She filled Daniel in on the basic details about Clayton's connection with the Traitor's Map and with Charmaine. "I wonder if Everett can tell us about Penelope Thorsen and her grave."

Daniel reached over and took her hand. "Do me a favor? Let me ask him about this construction project first. He's really pressed for time. If I get this job, you can find out all you want about the family tree."

"Got it. I'll look, not talk."

Grinning, Daniel shook his head. "As if."

The access road to Thorsen Manor seemed smoother, or maybe the DRD pickup truck could handle the ruts better than Daniel's small SUV they'd driven there the first time. As they neared the construction site, they saw a sleek black vehicle parked in front of the tumbledown farmhouse.

Daniel got out, slipping a quilted navy blue vest over the denim shirt he wore. When he reached for his DRD Roofing baseball cap, Gabriela wondered if he would tuck his ponytail inside and was glad when he didn't. If someone didn't hire him because of his long hair gathered back in a leather tie, she couldn't imagine Daniel wanting to work with them.

As they started toward the old farmhouse, Gabriela grabbed Daniel's arm. "Maybe I should wait in the truck. It might not be professional to have your girlfriend with you."

"Fiancée," Daniel corrected. "And you're an expert on historic artifacts."

"Yes, but not houses."

Daniel took her hand. "I want you here."

Climbing the old house's broken porch steps challenged them to find solid footing without breaking through rotted wood. They skirted a large hole in the porch and made it to the door that stood ajar.

"Everett?" Daniel called out.

"In here," a man's voice answered. "The floor inside isn't as bad as that porch. But you should still watch where you walk."

Daniel yanked the door open the rest of the way, and he and Gabriela stepped into a small entranceway. They passed through an archway into a great room dominated by a massive fireplace covering an entire wall. It had a fieldstone front and a slab of limestone for the mantel. Gabriela ran her fingertips over the stones, feeling both rounded smoothness and rough edges.

"Impressive, isn't it?"

Gabriela turned to see a man about fifty, slim built and an inch or two shorter than Daniel, with salt-and-pepper hair and a suntanned face. Her first thought was she never would have picked him out of a lineup as the brother of Clayton Brooks, the gray-clad pharmacist. Then she looked closer at Everett and saw the family resemblance in his bright blue eyes.

"First time I saw that fireplace, I had to have this house," Everett said.

He explained that his great-grandfather had sold the farm to someone outside the family. Over the years, it had changed hands several times, and much of the acreage had been sold off. "I've spent the better part of the last five years reassembling the parcel. Now I own the original house and seventy-eight acres, and I hope to acquire another fifty-six. I'll need that for a nine-hole golf course that's going to take about eighty acres total. That'll be my phase two after the fifty custom homes in phase one."

"If ever there was a time to launch a project like this, it's now," Daniel said. "People are buying up houses in Ohnita Harbor. If remote working lets people be anywhere these days, why not here?"

Everett grinned. "Exactly. And here they'll get the best of both worlds. Rural living with all the amenities—golf course, dock, marina." Searching on his phone, he showed them a document. "My wife designed this marketing brochure. She has twenty-five years with an agency in New York." He rattled off several big-name brands for which she'd designed campaigns.

"Very nice," Gabriela said, even as her mind returned to Clayton's comment about his brother capitalizing on the Thorsen name and history. It was hard to connect luxury living with a Revolutionary War hero and his brother who spied for the British.

"We still live in Westchester," Everett continued. "Two kids in college and one finishing high school. As soon as Thorsen Manor gets underway, we'll move up here."

Gabriela looked beyond the broken windows, peeling plaster, and warped floorboards and saw the beauty this house once possessed and could again. "I'm so glad you're not going to knock this down."

"Never. This house is more than just our family's heritage. It's local history that needs to be preserved." Everett beckoned them over to the far corner of the fireplace. "I'm told George Washington sat right here and smoked a pipe while visiting his good friend Colonel Thorsen."

And there it was, Gabriela thought to herself—the claim to fame for just about every colonial-era house and inn: *George Washington slept here.* "Do you have any letters or other documentation of that visit?" she asked.

Everett shook his head. "Just family stories." He pressed his hand against the fireplace. "If only these old stones could talk."

Watching Everett, Gabriela's opinion of him softened beyond being a born promoter who wouldn't mind bending the facts into myths and legends to sell his vision of Thorsen Manor. She could understand why that would irk Clayton, who was committed to unearthing the family story through genealogical research. Yet seeing the rapt look on Everett's face as he put both hands on the fireplace, she also couldn't deny his passion for this place.

Daniel joined them at the fireplace, pointing out how the stones had been meticulously matched by size and shape. Gabriela spotted recesses on the sides of the chimney and speculated that they could have been used as warming ovens or for baking bread. The giant opening where the fire would have burned no longer held an iron hook for hanging stewpots, but when she reached inside, her fingers traced grooves where bolts had once anchored it to the stone. "There's a small ironworks out in Ohnita County," she said. "They might be able to make a replacement."

"Do you work with Daniel?" Everett asked.

"No," Gabriela said. "I'm a librarian and an authenticator, and Daniel's fiancée. And insatiably curious about historic places."

"Glad you came along," Everett said.

Gabriela wandered around the room while Daniel presented Everett with a folder that included photos of recent roofing jobs, some with rebuilt attics and crawl spaces, and a few rehabilitation projects, including his own farmhouse conversion.

"You live there?" Everett asked. He sounded impressed.

"For now. But I'm going to be selling it as soon as I put some of the interior walls back up."

"Don't you dare change it. And make sure you tell me first before you put it on the market," Everett said. "I'd buy it for myself as is."

Gabriela kept her back to the men to hide her excitement over the prospect of Daniel getting this huge job and selling his house. Directly in front of her and at a right angle to the fireplace was an archway and a narrow hallway leading into the interior of the house. To the left of that archway, at about eye level, a carved stone medallion was set into the wall.

At closer range, Gabriela took in the design of a tree with two birds roosting in its branches and a deer standing beside the trunk. A doe, she corrected, noticing the slender body and no antlers. Raised letters along the curved bottom spelled out *Pro Patre*.

"The family coat of arms, or so I'm told," Everett said.

She googled a translation of the Latin phrase and read it aloud to the others: "For the father."

"God and country," Everett said. "The Thorsen family lived by that motto."

Except for traitorous Henry Thorsen, Gabriela added silently.

"How bad is the upstairs?" Daniel asked. "Given the condition of the roof, I'd suggest repairing the upstairs as quickly as possible. That'll prevent more water damage inside."

Everett led the way up the old staircase, but Gabriela chose to stay behind on the ground floor. She could not get enough of this fireplace. Running her hand over the large, rounded stones, she imagined them being gathered from a nearby field or even the shoreline.

On the far side of the fireplace, a small wooden door hung off a hinge. Gabriela resisted touching it for fear it would break off in her hand. Tapping the flashlight app on her phone, she peered inside but saw only dust and bits of plaster. She took a picture of the door with her phone, then enlarged the screen to examine the details. The faint outlines of a tree and a deer etched the wood, the same design as the crest on the stone in the wall.

"Everett here?"

Gabriela swung around. "He's upstairs."

The man entered the room wearing a stained camouflage jacket that gave off an odor of sweat and motor oil. His black rubber boots flapped at the top. One of them, Gabriela noticed, bore the silver stripe of a duct tape patch. When the man pulled off a brown knitted hat, it sent his shaggy gray hair in all directions.

Gabriela smiled at the old-fashioned politeness of a man taking off his hat indoors, something her father would have done.

"You doin' something with the house?" the man asked.

"My fiancé is. Daniel Red Deer." She pointed out the open doorway toward the truck parked in front. "He's the DRD of DRD Roofing." She noticed the rusted pickup truck beside it, its red paint faded to a faint crimson. "I'm Gabriela Domenici."

"Clawson, ma'am."

Noticing how he clenched his knitted hat, Gabriela discerned he might be shy and decided not to offer a handshake.

Footsteps sounded, and Daniel and Everett came down the stairs talking about joists and plasterwork. At the ground floor Everett greeted the man warmly. "Clawson, good to see you. And you met Gabriela."

"Yes, sir." Clawson nodded in her direction.

"Fish biting today?" Everett asked.

"Got some yellow perch yesterday. Fileted and frozen. I'll bring you some next time," Clawson said. "So, what you doin' here?"

Everett clapped Daniel on the back. "This man is going to help me restore the farmhouse."

"Ain't too far gone for that?" Clawson asked.

"Almost," Everett agreed. "But Daniel thinks we can save it."

Gabriela showed the three men what she'd discovered about the cupboard built into the side of the fireplace. Enlarging the image on her phone, she suggested this motif likely would have been featured throughout the house. "In the corners of the lintels, for example," she said, pointing to a plain squared-off doorway. "Maybe a carving over the fireplace itself."

Everett's eyes misted. "What I wouldn't give to bring that all back."

Gabriela gave him a sympathetic look, recognizing in him a fellow conservator. "Well, you can. Daniel is an artist. Did he tell you?"

"You're kidding," Everett replied.

Scrolling through his phone, Daniel showed Everett several photos of his watercolors, charcoal sketches, and a large wood carving.

Clawson stepped closer for a glimpse, then turned to leave. "I'll be around," he said. When Everett didn't respond, Gabriela piped up, "Nice to meet you." But Clawson had already descended the porch steps. Watching him amble toward his rusted pickup, Gabriela thought about how he resembled an Adirondack black bear, big but mostly harmless.

She returned her attention to Everett, who was praising everything he'd seen of Daniel's work. "We'll iron out the details later," he said. "But I want you to manage the reconstruction of this house. Your crew can replace the joists and do the roof, tuckpoint the chimneys, and all that. But I want you, personally, to oversee the restoration of the interior. This is your project, Daniel. I hope you'll say yes."

Gabriela beamed as the men shook hands. Daniel promised to come back with his crew in a day or so for measurements and to make proper estimates. "I'll break it all down for you," he told Everett. "And if you want, I'll hire the subcontractors to do the rest of the work that we can't. I'll charge you a small fee as the general contractor, but the subcontractors' costs will be passed through to you with no additional charge."

As Everett walked them out, Gabriela waited until a pause in their conversation to ask about Penelope Thorsen's grave. "I saw it the other day when we came to take a look at the site."

"Really? I knew there was a small cemetery here, but didn't really investigate it," Everett said.

Gabriela couldn't imagine letting something like that go unnoticed. Then again, Everett's entire focus was the house, not the grounds. She led the way around the back to the three plots ringed by a low wrought-iron fence. She pointed out the larger stone for Penelope, the one marked *Infant* beside her, and the third that had broken into pieces.

"We'll have to take care of this cemetery," Everett said. "Make sure nothing here is disturbed."

Gabriela swallowed a lump and cleared her throat, suddenly overcome with emotion that this place seemed to trigger.

Watching Everett as he examined Penelope's gravestone, Gabriela suddenly felt brave enough to ask the one question that had been on her mind since she first met Everett. "I teach a class on artifacts and authentication at the community college. We're studying the Traitor's

Map at the maritime museum. I'm sure you know the story about Henry and the map—"

"A hoax," Everett interrupted. "Henry Thorsen was the family ne'er-do-well, that much is true, but he died as a young man. Smallpox or pneumonia or some such thing."

"So Henry didn't draw the map and pass it to the British? That's the story I read in a local history book."

"People make up stories all the time and pass it off as truth," Everett said. "If your class wants to study something authentic, bring them up here anytime."

"That's very kind. Your brother is speaking to them on Wednesday."

Everett wheeled around to face her. "Clayton knows nothing about any of this. If you want to know the history of the Thorsen family, you ask me."

Jacob and Henry weren't the only brothers with bad blood, Gabriela realized. Everett and Clayton seemed to have their share as well. "That would be amazing," she said quickly. "My class would be thrilled to hear from you about Colonel Thorsen, his association with George Washington, and the restoration of this place."

Everett gave her a slight nod, almost like a bow. "I would be honored." He returned his attention to Penelope's marker. "She and Jacob had four or five children—or so my father told me. The youngest son, Alden Thorsen, was my great-great-great-great-grandfather. Give or take a couple of greats."

Leaning down, Gabriela felt drawn to touch the inscription, and her fingertips tingled. "I wonder why she wasn't buried in the Old Post Cemetery along with her husband. Colonel Thorsen's grave is quite the monument."

Everett shrugged. "She died after he did. I suspect she wanted to be near her home."

Patting the stone, Gabriela thought of all the stories associated with this property. Beyond the custom homes and the golf course and the rest of the development, Thorsen Manor would bring this history back to life.

On their way back to Ohnita Harbor, Gabriela and Daniel talked excitedly about Thorsen Manor, the scope of the project, and how quickly he could get started. DRD Roofing's current jobs and commitments would take several weeks. After that, Daniel could devote all his time and energy to the Thorsen farmhouse restoration.

"I'll get him a proposal and cost estimates by the end of the week," Daniel said. "I'm not letting this opportunity pass me by." He glanced at her. "This could be really good for us."

As much as Daniel relished having a project of this scope, it was his artistic contribution that excited Gabriela the most. She could imagine him sketching out designs for woodwork and molding featuring the family crest. It would be subtle, tasteful, but with a continuity that carried the motif. *Pro Patre*—for all the forefathers and ancestors who had lived on that land.

Chapter Nine

A light rain started on Sunday morning and by early afternoon had increased to a steady drizzle. Watching the spatters turn into streaks across the windows, Gabriela knew the weather might discourage some of the students from coming out for Ricky's memorial, but the somberness of the day felt appropriate.

Upstairs in her room, Gabriela put a gray blazer over a white blouse worn with black slacks. Glancing at the clock, she knew Daniel would arrive at any moment. Downstairs she found Ben sitting on the sofa and watching television while Agnese napped in an armchair. When Daniel opened the front door and stepped inside, Gabriela touched her mother's shoulder to rouse her, told her they would be back soon, and gave Ben a kiss on the cheek.

As they turned to leave, Ben rushed over to Daniel and hugged him around the waist. Daniel ran his hand over the boy's shoulders. "We're coming back soon. Then we can hang out for a while, okay?"

Ben shoved his hands into his jeans pockets and nodded.

Gabriela's throat tightened and she blinked back tears, moved by her son's affection for Daniel. She also suspected Ricky's memorial had something to do with it, a reminder of life's fragility and uncertainty. Such thoughts also explained her own emotional turmoil.

Picking her way around the puddles forming in the cracks of the front walk, Gabriela reached over and slipped her arm around Daniel. "Thank you for coming with me today."

"Where else would I be?" He touched her face lightly then opened the passenger door of his SUV for her to get in.

They rode mostly in silence to the college campus and parked in a designated lot for the service. As they approached the campus center, Gabriela spotted two of her students, who recognized her and waved. Inside, she estimated the crowd at close to a hundred people, mostly students but also some faculty. The turnout pleased her.

On a screen that descended from the ceiling, a slideshow rotated through photos of Ricky. Gabriela stood in the center of the room watching the display—a few baby pictures, a toddler held by a dark-haired woman, a little boy sitting on his father's lap, a group picture from elementary school, his senior high school portrait. Her breath caught at the next images of Ricky posing in front of Fort Ohnita, clowning for the camera with two other students from class. The next photo was of him standing beside Emilie at Colonel Thorsen's monument at the Old Post Cemetery. So few images to document nineteen years of life, with four of them from the class field trip.

Aware of someone standing beside her, Gabriela turned to see Emilie, her face pale and half-moons smudged under her eyes. Gabriela hugged the young woman, feeling the thinness of her frame.

"Ricky loved going to the Old Post Cemetery," Emilie said, pointing to the screen. "He told me he hadn't even known it was there. It was a real adventure for him."

"I'm glad," Gabriela said, though she wished her assignment had never taken Ricky anywhere near the lakefront and into whatever had ended his life.

When the college president stepped to the podium and asked them all to take their seats, Gabriela led Daniel to two places in the front row. She looked around for Walt Seymour and spotted him in the back of the room. Head down, Walt covered his face with his hands as he wept. Another man, who looked so much like Walt that he had to be his brother, steered him forward.

"The loss of one so young as Ricky Seymour is unfathomable to us," the college president said. "We all expect to grow up, grow old, and pass on after a long life. But sadly, that was not to be Ricky's path. He departed far too soon, and his family and friends mourn him."

The remarks were kind but impersonal because the college president had not known Ricky. She should have volunteered to speak, Gabriela realized, but hadn't wanted to insert herself.

Charmaine Odele took the podium, reading A. E. Housman's "To an Athlete Dying Young":

Smart lad, to slip betimes away
From fields where glory does not stay,
And early though the laurel grows
It withers quicker than the rose.

With each line the sniffles grew louder, and Charmaine's voice caught. At the end of the poem, the atmosphere in the campus center felt brittle, as if one loud noise or sharp movement would shatter it. Reaching over, Gabriela gripped Daniel's hand.

A stirring in the second row turned everyone's attention to Emilie getting to her feet. She looked down at her parents, who exchanged a glance then rose. A paper rattled in Emilie's hand as she placed it on the podium and adjusted the microphone. Her parents stood behind her.

"Ricky and I met this past fall, in our first class together. Me, the kid from Westchester County, new in town, and him, the local guy who knew everything about Ohnita Harbor." Pushing her dark hair out of her face, Emilie smiled at the crowd. "Porter's Pizza. Trudy's on the lake for hotdogs."

The shiny, straight cascade of Emilie's black hair caught the light as she looked out at the crowd. "We all remember how fun Ricky was. But he was serious too, especially about school. He really, really wanted to do something with his life. Go places, see things. He told me he was thinking of going to Syracuse University and studying archaeology. That's when I started calling him Indiana Jones—or, actually, Indiana Ricky."

A murmur of laughter rippled through the room.

"That dream started to feel real for Ricky with our last assignment," Emilie continued, describing how captivated he'd been by the Traitor's Map. "He wanted to be the one who authenticated it. I don't know how he planned to do that, but Ricky was determined. And once he got an idea in his head, he wouldn't let it go."

That's probably what got him killed, Gabriela thought. Relentlessly determined, he would have stopped at nothing to find a boat to explore the lakeshore. With no money or resources, he would have had to ask someone or do something that put him in harm's way. What that had been, she could not fathom. One thing she couldn't deny, no matter how coincidental or tangential, the Traitor's Map that had condemned Henry Thorsen to execution in 1777 had led to Ricky Seymour's death more than two centuries later. Not death, Gabriela reminded herself. Murder.

Emilie's voice began to shake, and Gabriela focused more intently on her words. "Now, Ricky won't see any of his dreams come true. I don't know why—nobody does. It seems so unfair that we all get to go on, but he doesn't. All we can do is our best and make the most of our lives because he didn't get a chance to live his."

Emilie left the podium flanked by her parents and walked to where Walt Seymour sat, his eyes cast to the floor. Gabriela watched Walt get to his feet, nod as Emilie said something, and then shake her parents' hands.

Charmaine Odele returned to the podium. "Mr. Seymour, would you like to say a few words?"

A stricken look crossed Walt's reddened face. "I can't."

Charmaine looked out into the audience, her eyes meeting Gabriela's. "I'd like to invite my colleague, Gabriela Domenici, to share her thoughts."

Gabriela stood and walked forward slowly as she tried to put together a few words. Adjusting the microphone, she bought herself a few more seconds, then began by introducing herself as the executive director of the Ohnita Harbor Public Library and explaining that this was her first semester as an adjunct in the history department. Gabriela paused, chided herself. *Too much about me and nothing about Ricky.*

"Teaching is a completely new experience for me," she went on. "One of the joys I discovered early on was having an intelligent, engaged student like Ricky. He and his classmates make teaching fun."

She scanned the audience as her thoughts gathered a second time. A familiar face gazed back at her—Thelma Tulowski in civilian clothes. Refocusing on her ad hoc remarks, Gabriela continued. "In a class like mine, we're always talking about some old dusty object. But as I tell my students, it's stories that bring them to life. Our current project is the Traitor's Map, as Emilie described a few minutes ago. Now that artifact will also contain Ricky's story. His enthusiasm, his imagination, his ideas."

Gabriela smiled in Walt Seymour's direction just as he looked up at her. "As sad as I am for his death, I am comforted by the fact that we will remember Ricky as the one who helped inspire our class. In everything we do on this final project and wherever that leads us, Ricky will be a part of it."

Returning to her seat, Gabriela threaded her arm through Daniel's, feeling the warmth of his body against the sudden chill she felt all the way to her bones.

Monday came and went with a balm of routine at work and at home. On Tuesday evening, Daniel stopped by for supper an hour after Gabriela and Ben had finished eating. He had been working late to complete two DRD Roofing projects so the crew would be ready to start on the Thorsen farmhouse reconstruction as soon as the contract was signed. Long after the dishes were done and Ben had gone upstairs to bed, Daniel sat at the kitchen table with Gabriela, going over the proposal and estimates.

As she listened, Gabriela thought of the slogan on Daniel's truck door: *Quality ~ Affordable*. More than a marketing tagline, it represented his work ethic. She had experienced that herself when he'd replaced the roof of her house because of storm damage. He'd been a stranger to her then, a name out of an online listing of local contractors. How she'd antagonized him over the cost, fearing he would turn out to be one of those contractors who kept finding more work that needed to be done at ever-increasing costs. She'd been wrong, pleasantly so. And now here they were, a couple.

At ten o'clock she took him by the hand. "Stay here tonight. You're too tired to drive to your place."

As Daniel headed up the stairs, Gabriela checked the back door, turned off the lights in the kitchen and the living room. Nothing could feel more natural.

Wednesday dawned under a sky so gloomy, no light pierced the eastern horizon. Daniel got up at six and left soon thereafter with a kiss and a promise to check in later. Turning on the television, Gabriela listened to the forecast—heavy rains and a severe thunderstorm warning. She hoped the weather wouldn't delay her guest speaker, but fortunately Clayton Brooks would not have far to travel from the pharmacy to the college.

By eight o'clock, as Gabriela drove Ben to school, the sky darkened to the point the streetlights came back on. At the drop-off for fifth graders, Gabriela reminded Ben that she would pick him up at 3:45. "No going to the park today," she told him. "Even if the rain stops, it will be a mudhole."

In the parking lot behind the library, pieces of paper and dried leaves swirled in a miniature cyclone. Shielding her eyes from airborne grit, Gabriela ran to the back entrance instead of walking around to the front as she usually did. A gust of wind slapped against the heavy metal door, and she needed both hands to yank it open. It slammed behind her.

Turning on the lights as she walked across the main floor, Gabriela tried to chase out the darkness that seeped through the windows like a cold draft. She called down the stairs to Mike Driskie, who came in early every morning to ensure the safety, security, and cleanliness of the place.

Mike emerged from the lower level wearing bright yellow rain gear. "I'm going out to get the book returns now before it starts pouring."

Gabriela peered through one of the arched windows to see the first heavy drops hitting the glass. "Maybe you should wait. The books will stay dry in the bin."

"This storm is going to get worse before it gets better." Mike raised the hood of his jacket and pulled the zipper up to his chin. "Just hold the door for me."

Putting her hand on the latch, Gabriela felt the rattle of the double doors with their heavy iron hinges. With Mike's help, she opened the first one and propped it with a door-stopper. Wind tunneled into the library. Mike pushed an empty bin with canvas sides down the sidewalk toward the book return on the front lawn. In the few minutes it took for him to unlock the receptacle, pull out the bin half full of returns, and put the empty one in its place, the rain intensified.

Gabriela strained to open the second of the double doors and held it with both hands as Mike ran up the ramp and pushed the bin over the threshold. Just as he stepped inside, a flash of lightning illuminated the yard with a burst of bluish light. A sharp crack of thunder shook the windows.

Rushing to the phone on the circulation desk, Gabriela called the staff and told them to stay home for now. She reached the circulation clerks, Francine and Pearl, at their homes and Eva, the new Children's Room director, on her cell phone while driving in. Gabriela urged her to pull off someplace safe until the rainstorm ended. When she called Delmina, Gabriela only reached her voicemail.

Knowing Delmina had to be on her way, Gabriela waited at the back door that led to the parking lot. "She's here," Gabriela yelled, and Mike ran out to help Delmina inside.

"What a tempest." Delmina stamped her feet on the mat at the back door. "They said thunderstorms, but I wasn't expecting this."

Gabriela suggested they stay together on the main level. The way the wind buffeted the second floor she didn't want to risk one of the windows being blown in by the storm. "You can help me process these returns," she told Delmina.

Side by side, they worked at the circulation desk—scanning books and setting them on the return cart, separating fiction and nonfiction. Overhead, the lights flickered then went out; the hum of the computers silenced.

Without electricity, Gabriela and Delmina pushed the half-filled return cart around the floor, using a flashlight to see in the stacks. They straightened the shelves and returned a half dozen misplaced books to their rightful positions. Although it amounted to busywork, Gabriela found it satisfying to bring more order to the library collection.

The fast-moving cold front that had brewed the storm over Lake Ontario swept through the town and off to the east. The lights came back on just before ten o'clock. The circulation computers whirled and hummed, and Gabriela resumed scanning in returns until Francine and Pearl arrived within five minutes of each other. Eva came in shortly thereafter with tales of having waited out the storm at a diner with her little Prius parked between two tractor trailers. Mike inspected tree damage on the library's expansive lawn and reported back that only a few limbs had fallen.

Climbing the stairs to her office, Gabriela looked down to see the first patrons arriving. Not much kept away the retirees who wanted to be the first to check out the new books, parents who looked forward to story hour as much as their toddlers, and an assortment of others who came in to check out materials or simply to sit in a warm place surrounded by other people.

At twenty minutes to eleven, Gabriela logged off her computer and told Delmina she would be back shortly before one o'clock. Rain had diminished to a light sprinkle, but damage from the torrent could be seen everywhere. Along Main Street a sign dangled from a storefront, and road cones from a street excavation scattered across the pavement like playing pieces from a board game.

On the college campus Gabriela parked in the spot reserved for her as an adjunct faculty member. She took a deep breath to quell the flutter in her chest, trying to discern between anxiety and excitement over Clayton's visit.

Students arrived early, and by five to eleven they occupied every desk in the circle. As they waited for Clayton Brooks, Gabriela checked her phone twice for a text, call, or email.

At one minute to eleven, she started class with some ground rules for questioning their guest speaker, as Charmaine had requested. "Understand that he is not a researcher. He's a private citizen who donated a family heirloom to a public institution and did so quietly. So let's listen first to what he has to say."

A knock sounded on the door and Clayton Brooks entered wearing a dark suit, white shirt, and blue tie. Gabriela did a double take at his transformation from the mousy man all in gray who had showed up at her office. Accompanying him was Charmaine, wearing a purple sheath dress and boots.

With a quick introduction, Gabriela turned the class over to Clayton, who took the chair in front of the room. Gabriela sat next to Charmaine behind the circle of students.

"Everything I know about the map is what my father, Hubert Brooks, told me," Clayton began. "It's the same story that had been passed down through the family. My father had no reason to lie to me, just like his father had no reason to lie to him. So I suspect that what I'm going to tell you is the truth. And that goes back a long time ago, to the early 1700s."

Hearing his words, Gabriela nearly squirmed with excitement. Authentication research didn't get better than this.

Clayton recounted his family history, starting with a young man named Arthur Thorsen, who ran away from a London workhouse and became a cabin boy on a merchant ship bound for the colonies. Landing in New York Harbor sometime around 1730, Arthur struck out on his own with little more than the clothes on his back. The city proved inhospitable, and the shopkeepers sized him up as a common thief. At the market he stole an apple, but the farmer who grabbed him by the ear heard the Yorkshire accent that reminded him of home. Taking Arthur back to his farm, the farmer promised him a meal, a bed in the barn, and a job.

Arthur stayed on that farm for a few years then set out on his own, ending up in Ohnita Settlement, where he opened what became the town's first mercantile. He married the daughter of a local farmer, and she bore him two sons: Jacob and Henry. As he made his way in the world, Arthur claimed to be a member of the English gentry, passing himself off as a third son who stood to inherit nothing and so had sought his fortune in the New World. "I wish he'd stuck to the truth. Being poor and making something of yourself is nothing to be ashamed of," Clayton said. "Arthur didn't see it that way."

A student raised her hand. "How did you find out about Arthur's lies?"

Gabriela straightened, ready to remind the students they should hold questions until the end, but Clayton didn't seem bothered by the interruption. "Arthur apparently confided the truth to his wife. It became the family secret."

Clayton continued, explaining to the students that although Arthur had been a commoner and not an English gentleman, he followed the rules of primogeniture—the rights of succession of property to the first-born son. While Jacob grew up with the knowledge that everything his father owned would be his one day, Henry heard a much different story. His lot in life would be to make his own way in the world. It drove a wedge between the brothers, and when Arthur died, that rift deepened.

"You know about the attack on Fort Ohnita in 1756, right?" Clayton asked, and the students nodded in near unison. "Arthur was a member of the colonial militia, and he'd brought Jacob with him to the fort. But when the French attacked, Arthur wanted to save Jacob, who was only sixteen at the time. He volunteered Jacob as a runner to sneak out of the fort and warn the settlers. Arthur was killed in that battle, but Jacob was spared. He inherited his father's property. At thirteen, Henry was beholden to his brother."

During the American Revolution, Jacob was both a wealthy land-owner and an officer reporting directly to General George Washington, while Henry was his brother's aide-de-camp. "But instead of treating Henry as a trusted confidante, Jacob made him into a servant," Clayton said.

That's why he made the map of the shoreline for the British, Gabriela surmised. Henry had wanted to get back at his tyrannical big brother. Unless he did it for money, she added. With no inheritance, Henry could have been desperate.

"There were a lot of Loyalists in those days," Clayton continued. "It doesn't take much to imagine one of them approaching Henry—maybe buying him a pint of ale at the tavern and feeding his resentment of Jacob. Spying for the British would have been a way of undermining his brother. At least, that's the way I've worked it out in my mind."

A hand rose slowly from the circle of students, and Gabriela was surprised to see it was someone who rarely participated in class. "Maybe Henry did want to stick it to his brother, but also not hurt his country. And that's why the map is, you know, so messed up."

Clayton gave a slow nod. "That's what I think too. The map has so many inaccuracies, it would have been useless to the British. But that didn't keep Henry from being convicted as a spy."

He told how two British spies who had been caught by the Continental Army gave up Henry's name as a co-conspirator. Tried and convicted, all three men were sentenced to death, but only two were executed. Henry Thorsen escaped from the stockade inside the fort, never to be seen again.

"I like to imagine Henry made it to Canada as a lot of Loyalists did during and immediately after the Revolution," Clayton said. "Maybe he made a new life for himself. I've been dabbling in genealogy to see what I can find, if anything."

A hand went up, then another. Students asked about why his family had kept the map a secret all these years and why Clayton had chosen to give it away. "It was an heirloom—something that belonged to one of our ancestors," Clayton said. "But I don't have any children, and my brother..." He looked down at his shoes. "Well, he never had much interest in the map. So I decided it should go to the maritime museum."

When class ended, none of the students made a move to leave. Gabriela walked to the front of the room and thanked Clayton for his time. The students began to file out, and Charmaine stood at Clayton's side as he spoke to the last ones to exit.

Checking her silenced phone, Gabriela was surprised to see a text from Inspector Thelma Tulowski. *Call me.* After declining Charmaine's invitation to join her and Clayton for lunch, Gabriela stayed behind in the empty classroom to return the call.

Thelma picked up on the second ring. "You'll never guess what the storm brought up," she said without preamble.

Gabriela sank into one of the desks. "I don't think I want to know."

"A boat," Thelma said.

Any number of rowboats, dinghies, and even larger boats probably got tossed around in that storm, loosed from docks and marinas. Gabriela wondered what made this boat significant but figured Thelma would tell her.

"It was one of two boats stolen about a month ago," Thelma said. "Coast Guard found it this morning."

The pieces clicked together in Gabriela's mind. "And you think this might have been Ricky's boat?"

"Why don't you stop by the station when you have a minute," Thelma said. "And bring your map."

Chapter Ten

Half an hour later, Gabriela's photographic copy of the Traitor's Map stretched across Thelma's bare desk. Gabriela stood back, trying to figure out what, if anything, the investigation into Ricky's murder and a stolen boat had to do with a Revolutionary War–era drawing of the shoreline, an inaccurate one at that. But she didn't want to interrupt Thelma's intensity as she examined the depiction of the shoreline.

"We're here." Thelma placed her right index finger on Ohnita Settlement. "And Fort Ohnita is here." Her middle finger marked the second place close by. "Ricky's body was found right near there." Her ring finger tapped a third place on the map.

She stretched her ring finger about an inch away. Based on what she knew about the map's scale, Gabriela guessed it to be about five miles outside of town. "That's where the boat washed up."

Gabriela thought about the boat Ben had found on her birthday in the marsh at Peninsula Point. But that boat had been much farther away—a good ten or twelve miles from where this craft had washed up. She also recalled the fisherman cruising the shoreline in what had looked like that boat in the marsh and decided against saying anything to Thelma.

"So, my question is, if someone was using this map as a guide, what would they be looking for?" Thelma asked.

"If it were me, I would be trying to find this big cave," Gabriela said. "But in reality, there is no cave there. It's one of the flaws in the map."

"Yeah, I know." Thelma retrieved a second map from her desk drawer, a modern schematic of the shoreline that showed every river, creek, marsh, road, and boat launch. She aligned the maps, one above the other. "But I'm trying to think like Ricky. You said it yourself at his memorial—he was completely captivated by this map. Everything he did up to the point of his murder was about unlocking its secrets."

Gabriela followed the logic but still struggled to get past the map's many inaccuracies.

Thelma shifted to the modern survey of the shoreline. "I'm guessing Ricky might have wanted to see what was there. If not a cave, then something else. Like, maybe, this." Thelma pointed to a thin blue line on the modern map. "There's a creek there. In the summer it's not much more than a mudhole and a trickle. But this time of year, with the snow runoff and the spring rains, it's pretty sizable."

"You think Ricky was exploring that creek?" Gabriela asked.

Thelma shook her head. "I think that's where the boat he wanted to borrow was being stored, at least temporarily." She straightened from her hunched posture over the two maps. "A body and a boat wash up within a few days and not that far apart. That makes me think there's something going on around here."

"I assume you've searched the area," Gabriela said.

"We searched within our jurisdiction. State police combed the rest. Any footprints or vehicle tracks around there are long gone. But we did find this."

Thelma drew a plastic bag marked "Evidence" from a drawer. Inside was a rectangle the size of a business card. Thelma held the bag closer for Gabriela to get a good look inside. It was Ricky's college ID.

"How did—?" Gabriela pressed her fingertips to her lips, cutting off her question.

"Maybe he showed it to someone to prove who he was. Or maybe someone rifled through his pockets to get rid of any identification," Thelma added.

Gabriela studied the map. "Let's assume Ricky met someone at that creek to ask about the boat. Then how did his body get to the bluffs below Fort Ohnita?"

"You know my theory—he was shot somewhere else and his body was put in the boat to be disposed of in the lake. Maybe they wanted it to look like he was murdered in town," Thelma explained. "Focus the investigation away from where the boat was stashed."

"You said the boat was stolen," Gabriela prompted.

"Two were taken from a boatyard outside Cape Vincent, right where Lake Ontario meets the St. Lawrence River. What's curious is that those two boats were hardly the nicest ones there—not by a long shot. Completely nondescript," Thelma said.

"And I suppose nobody knows how one of those boats got from Cape Vincent all the way down here," Gabriela said. "That's got to be, what? Fifty miles?"

"Seventy-five," Thelma replied. "And somehow Ricky knew about those boats."

"Maybe he knew about the boat, but not that it was stolen," Gabriela said, though she was beginning to worry that Ricky had gotten involved in something illegal.

"You ever see where Ricky lived?" Thelma asked. "Down by the old papermill. There's a whole row of houses built in the 1930s that are literally on the wrong side of the tracks. Half of them have been condemned, but people still live in them. Squatters, some of them. A lot of stuff goes on there that you don't want to know about."

Drugs, Gabriela suspected, especially meth, the scourge of rural America. "It's still possible that Ricky crossed paths with the wrong person at the wrong time."

"How much does it cost to go to Syracuse University?" Thelma asked.

The question puzzled Gabriela; then she remembered Emilie mentioning Ricky's aspiration in her eulogy. "Sixty thousand a year, plus room and board and books. Why?"

"Even with a scholarship, Ricky would have been hard pressed to pay for it," Thelma added.

"So, he stole an old boat?" Gabriela made a face. "Ricky might have lived in a tough neighborhood, but that doesn't mean he was a criminal."

Thelma didn't reply, and Gabriela let it drop. But one more question remained that she just had to ask. "Why did you want to discuss this with me? I'm hardly part of the investigation."

Thelma scoffed. "You've been part of this since you showed up on your jog the day Emilie found the body." She turned her eyes toward Gabriela, her expression sobering. "But honestly? You see patterns. I think that's how you authenticate stuff."

Gabriela nodded. "It's a lot of comparison—handwriting samples, artistic techniques."

"Same thing in my business," Thelma said. "We look for patterns and connections that might point us to the next step."

Reaching across the desk, Thelma quickly rolled up the copy of the Traitor's Map and handed it to Gabriela.

"Why don't you keep it?" Gabriela suggested. "I've got other copies."

"Thanks." Thelma put a rubber band around the rolled-up map, then began carefully refolding the modern one. "There's one great thing about rivers and creeks. A leaf falls somewhere upstream, and it will eventually end up in the lake. All we need to do is keep our eye on the shoreline and, one of these days, we'll know a lot more."

———◇———

Her brain buzzing after the meeting with Thelma, Gabriela headed straight to her office and shut the door. She tried to focus on her mounting responsibilities: running the library, chairing the citizens' committee for the beautification grant, and her class at the community college. But she accomplished little.

At the end of the day, as she packed up to go home, Gabriela sent a text to Daniel. *Just checking in. XO.* An hour later, her phone chimed with a text response. *Working late. XO.*

With a sigh, Gabriela sent back a heart emoji. Another night of not seeing Daniel.

———◇———

When Daniel finally came over on Saturday night, dark circles ringing his eyes prompted Gabriela to cancel their plans to go out; she cooked dinner at home instead. They watched a film on Netflix, but twenty minutes into it, Daniel fell into a deep sleep on the sofa. Ben dozed on the floor, and Gabriela ended up watching the rest of the movie by herself.

The next morning, Daniel got up early and announced he was going back to Thorsen Manor to work on what he called site prep. Gabriela wanted to protest how much time and energy that project was consuming, and he hadn't even started the actual construction work yet. But she withheld comment as she listened to Daniel's complaints that Everett Brooks had questioned his bid and asked for more information about the cost of labor versus materials. It sounded to her like Everett's concerns went beyond cost control. From what Daniel said, Gabriela suspected the project had run into cash-flow issues.

Daniel left shortly after seven thirty. It was Easter Sunday, but Gabriela hadn't mentioned it. Instead, she called her mother and suggested that she and Ben take her to church at ten thirty.

"*Si, si.* We go then," Agnese agreed.

"We'll come back here and make a big lunch," Gabriela said. "You'd like that, Mama."

With Daniel busy all day, she might as well make her mother happy.

That evening she waited to hear whether Daniel would stop by. The call came after eight o'clock, Daniel sounding tired and distracted. "I'm going home," he said. "I'm beat."

Home—his house, not hers. Gabriela tried not to read too much into the comment. "Get some rest," she said. "See you tomorrow."

The following morning, while preparing for the usual Monday staff meeting, Gabriela received a text from Daniel. *Signed the contract. Work starts immediately!*

Resisting the urge to call, she texted him back a one-word reply: *Yes!!!!!!!!!!!!* Now that the business end of things had been settled, Daniel could focus on restoring that old house. No matter how hard the work he would be in his element.

Dinner tonight to celebrate? Lasagna—your fav. She added a kiss emoji.

His reply came fifteen minutes later: *Meeting EB after work. Will try to be there by 8.*

This would be their life for a while, Gabriela told herself but vowed not to complain. *Whenever you get here is fine.*

That evening, sitting in her home office doing more staring out the window than at her computer screen, Gabriela noticed the headlights hitting the garage door. Jumping to her feet, she opened the kitchen door before Daniel reached the back deck.

"You must be starved," she said as she hugged and kissed him. It was quarter to nine.

"Ravenous." He washed his hands in the sink. "But we got everything hashed out—the scope of the project, the budget, how much DRD Roofing will take on, and how much we'll have to subcontract. We'll be having weekly progress meetings. And, I have this." He waved a check made out to DRD Roofing. "A down payment so we can buy materials and get the crew working."

"When?" Gabriela asked excitedly.

"Immediately. We'll start demolition of the roof and attic in a few days. Everett agrees it has to be a complete rebuild."

Gabriela took a slab of lasagna out of the microwave and set the plate on the table. She watched as Daniel took a forkful, blew his breath to cool the steaming food, then popped it in his mouth. His face relaxed as he chewed.

"This is so good." He took another bite. "We're not going to make much money on this project. Everett has been funding this himself. He's got a lot of debt and needs to keep expenses down. But the exposure will be good for us. I'm even thinking of renaming the company—DRD Construction. This is a good time for us to be expanding."

Gabriela grappled with two opposing thoughts—excitement over future prospects for DRD and worry over what Daniel had just said about not making much money. "I'm glad things are coming together. But your crew has to get paid for this work, and you do too."

Daniel plunged his fork into the lasagna again. "If I can work along with the crew, it will keep my cost down, since I don't pay myself overtime."

Gabriela reached for Daniel's free hand. "I'm sure you'll make this work."

"I like Everett," Daniel said. "He's so passionate about restoring this property and reclaiming the history of the place. It's really a mission for him."

And that, Gabriela knew, appealed to Daniel even more than the chance to make a profit.

------◆------

The next morning Gabriela pulled out her roster for the citizens' committee and took Daniel's name off the list. Although disappointed that they could not serve together, she knew the decision made the most sense for all involved. Daniel worked too many hours, and the committee needed dedicated members. When she considered who to ask to be a co-chair, only one name came to mind—Charmaine. Gabriela's phone call to her received an enthusiastic response with one caveat: Charmaine wanted to add Clayton Brooks to the committee.

"He's well respected in the business community, and he's become consumed by local history," Charmaine said.

And they wanted to work together, Gabriela added silently, knowing she had hoped for the same arrangement for herself and Daniel. To prevent personal preferences and conflicts of interest from infecting the citizens' committee, Gabriela had asked the mayor to approve every member. She felt sure, though, that he'd agree with the amended roster.

Excited by this new project, Charmaine suggested they get together for lunch. Citing a mounting to-do list, Gabriela countered with meeting at the library instead. "I'll bring the lattes," Charmaine promised, and she showed up precisely at one o'clock that afternoon.

As they reviewed the agenda for the upcoming committee meeting, the first priority was the library ceiling restoration project, which would begin soon. That topic of discussion led to a short tangent about Charmaine's latest projects at home; then talk turned to Thorsen Manor.

Wanting to get everything out in the open, Gabriela told Charmaine that Daniel was working with Everett. "He's thrilled about restoring the old farmhouse. Once Daniel makes some progress, perhaps we can all go out and see it."

Charmaine grimaced. "Don't get me started on that place."

Taking the last sip of her latte, Gabriela inhaled quickly at Charmaine's reaction. A tiny droplet slipped into her windpipe, and she started coughing. Unable to stop, Gabriela grabbed her water bottle and took three long swallows. "You can't imagine the fireplace," she began, her voice a little ragged from the coughing. "The fireplace fills an entire wall."

"I have no interest—and you couldn't drag Clayton there. Thorsen Manor—what a joke to call it that." Charmaine sat back with her arms folded tightly across her chest.

"But it's their family legacy," Gabriela insisted. "Jacob Thorsen bought the land before the Revolution. He built the original farmhouse in 1770."

"And what's Everett going to do with it? Turn it into a museum? No, he's going to make a clubhouse for people living in his overpriced homes. And from what Clayton tells me, Everett is in serious trouble on this. Up to his neck in debt, and interest rates are rising. I won't be surprised if he goes bankrupt. And not for the first time."

Gabriela couldn't believe the smugness of Charmaine's comment, with no thought of what might happen to Daniel if Everett ran out of money. If Everett failed at Thorsen Manor, Clayton would probably be glad—maybe Charmaine too.

She took another sip of water and cleared her throat. They needed to get off this subject, and fast. "Speaking of money, what do you think about putting a referendum back on the ballot to increase the library's operating budget? The last time, we came so close to getting it passed."

Charmaine loosened her arms and leaned forward. "I think it's too soon. People know the library just received grant money from the state."

"But only for beautification," Gabriela interjected. "Surely people understand we can't use it for operations. And with property values going up and more people moving into the community, there's a bigger tax base."

"New property assessments are giving everybody sticker shock on their tax bills. I couldn't believe how much my taxes are going up. We can't add to that by asking for more funding."

It did not seem fair that with all the new money coming into Ohnita Harbor, the fate of the library still hung by the fraying thread of their budget. One of these days, Gabriela vowed, they would have to put the funding referendum back on the ballot. Until then, they would find a way to keep going with the little they had.

Later that afternoon, Gabriela called a staff meeting. They met in a corner of the Reference section that received little traffic but still allowed access to the circulation desk and the front door. "Our traffic numbers were down over the winter," Gabriela added. "We have to think of everything we can do to increase our patronage."

Francine and Pearl exchanged a glance. "We have an idea," Francine began.

"It's gonna bring down the house," Pearl added.

"Well, maybe," Francine replied.

"Why don't you tell us about it," Gabriela said, trying to head off the long-running antagonism between the two circulation clerks that had become something of a library legend.

"We're calling it the 'Freak Show.'" Pearl laughed at her own joke.

"No, we're not." Francine shook her head. Tiny cross earrings dangling from her earlobes caught the light. "We're calling it 'Curiosities of the Collection.'"

"I like mine better," Pearl said. "More accurate too."

Francine sighed. "There are about a dozen really bizarre books in this collection. Nothing racy, of course."

"Too bad," Pearl interjected.

"But—" Francine shot a look at Pearl. "There are some really quirky titles. Like a 1928 field study of aphids. Just aphids, with photos."

"My favorite is *Homemaking for the Bride-to-Be*, written in 1951. Gloria Steinem would puke if she read it," Pearl said.

Listening to this back-and-forth, Gabriela wondered how these two had ever agreed on doing a program together and whether they could pull it off.

"We're thinking of a tour of the collection. Maybe get people interested in doing something besides surfing the internet and staring at their phones," Francine said.

"Love it," Gabriela said and meant it. The more strangled the library's budget, the more creative the staff needed to become in creating programs. If nothing else, these two were setting an example.

Movement attracted Gabriela's attention, and she saw a young woman walk into the library. "Please excuse me for a moment," she told the staff and greeted Emilie at the circulation desk.

"Nice to see you. I'm just finishing up a staff meeting over there." Gabriela pointed toward Reference. "If you can hang out for a few minutes, I'll be free."

Emilie gave her a smile that didn't reach her eyes, which seemed tired and dull. "I'll be in Fiction."

The meeting wrapped up in fifteen minutes, with Gabriela's profuse thanks to everyone for their ideas. She asked for summaries by the end of the next day so Delmina could begin promoting the programs in email blasts.

Eva, the Children's Room director, stopped Gabriela after the meeting with questions about any additional funding for art supplies for her summer reading program. "So sorry," Gabriela told her. "We're really running close to the bone these days."

"But that grant?" Eva asked.

"For beautification of the building only—that was the requirement from the state. So if you wanted ceiling tiles or a decorative railing, I could get that for you. Art supplies for the kids—no." Gabriela made a sympathetic face. "Let me talk to Friends of the Library. They can usually get a donation out of their network."

Gabriela found Emilie browsing the Fiction section, scanning titles but not taking any books from the shelves. "Who's your favorite author?" she asked.

"Impossible to say. I love the Brontë sisters and Jane Austen. And Jodi Picoult and Margaret Atwood and about a million others." Emilie brightened, then her expression returned to neutral. "Can I talk to you for a minute?"

Gabriela gestured toward the stairs. "Come up to my office."

"Here is fine." Emilie walked over to a round table at the end of the Fiction section, and Gabriela took a chair across from her.

"The police called me back for questioning. My mom was working, so I went by myself."

"Why would they do that?" She'd talk to Thelma, explain that this constant questioning was traumatizing Emilie.

"I already told them everything I know or could think of. But they keep asking me about the boat. Did Ricky mention anything about who owned it? Did he say his father was helping him?" Emilie looked up, her eyes tear-filled. "If I hadn't been so excited about going out on the boat, Ricky wouldn't have tried to get it. I should have told him no."

"You can't blame yourself. And we still don't know why Ricky was killed," Gabriela said. "You're grieving, Emilie. You need to be gentle with yourself and find some support. Have you gone to the counseling center?"

"A few times. Mom wants me to keep going. It really helps to talk to you." She looked around. "You know, I've never been in this library before."

Another reminder of just how new Emilie and her family were to Ohnita Harbor, Gabriela thought. "Well, then, let's take a tour."

Walking Emilie through the building, Gabriela briefly described its 160 years of history back to the founder, Josiah Wollis, an abolitionist who had rewarded the town for its role in the Underground Railroad, as people escaping slavery made their way from Ohnita Harbor to freedom in Canada. She explained the Norman Revivalist architecture, giving the library its distinct castle design. In the foyer, Gabriela unfastened a velvet rope that cordoned off a narrow staircase and led Emilie up to the unfinished third floor. Their footsteps thudded dully on the dusty floor.

Emilie made her way to one of the filmy windows at the top of the library. The view stretched across the rooftops of the town, all the way to the lake.

"This level has never been finished," Gabriela explained. "My dream is to one day get a grant from the state that will extend the elevator to the third floor and convert this into usable space for meetings and presentations. One day—I hope."

"You're so lucky, working here every day," Emilie said.

Her comment gave Gabriela an idea. "Do you have a job?"

As they descended the stairs to the lower level, Gabriela explained the beautification grant and the library's restoration projects, starting with removing the acoustic tiles and refurbishing the original plaster ceiling. There was money in the grant for a temporary part-time position, helping Mike Driskie, the custodian, with light work such as moving books and shelves as the ceiling restoration began. They had already advertised the position, but only two applicants had expressed interest, and both wanted a full-time job. Earning minimum wage to push around furniture for a few weeks probably did not sound that appealing to most people.

"I'd love it," Emilie said, sounding more enthusiastic than she had thus far in their conversation. "And I don't mind getting my hands dirty."

"That's inevitable in an old place like this." Gabriela grinned. "Let's go find Mike."

After making introductions, Gabriela stepped away to let Mike and Emilie speak privately, but didn't go far. At the end of the conversation, she saw Mike reach over the circulation desk for a notepad and write something down. Emilie took the paper, shook his hand, and headed over to Gabriela.

"I am going to work on this immediately. If Mr. Driskie likes what I write, he'll invite me in for an interview," Emilie said. She thanked them both and left with a wave.

"And what is she writing, Mr. Driskie?" Gabriela asked in a teasing tone.

"An essay on library restoration," Mike added. "I figure if she does the assignment, then she really wants the job."

"You know every applicant will be asked to do that," Gabriela said.

"Yep. But I bet she'll be only one who will."

Chapter Eleven

A cold front moved in that turned mid-April rain to wet, sticky snow, and Gabriela had to spread rock salt on her driveway before leaving for work in the morning. The inclement weather set back Daniel's schedule for roofing jobs both in Ohnita Harbor and at Thorsen Manor. Gabriela understood the situation, but it bothered her that Daniel had no time for her and Ben during the week. At least he called each night on the way to his own house, which was a shorter distance to the Thorsen project. Every time they spoke, he sounded so tired from the long hours, Gabriela hesitated to ask him for any updates, even to show her interest in what he was doing.

By the weekend, the weather improved—bright sunshine and temperatures flirting with sixty degrees. After working ten days straight, Daniel arrived at Gabriela's just before noon on Sunday with a plan to take her, Ben, and Agnese on a ride to see the progress they'd made on the old farmhouse. By two o'clock, the four of them rode in Daniel's SUV along country roads, past woodlands greened to a shade of emerald and fields where cows and new calves grazed in a pastoral scene. Apple trees showed their first bursts of pale blossoms, and tulips and daffodils bobbed bright heads on tall stems.

"I could drive this in my sleep," Daniel muttered as they passed the sign advertising Thorsen Manor, just before he turned onto the access road. "Sometimes I think I do."

Heavy blue tarps covered the upper story of the farmhouse. As they walked the perimeter, Daniel explained what they could not see under the covering—the attic framed with new lumber and crowned with strong joists. Over the years, leaks caused some water damage to the interior, but the building's basic structure remained sound. The foundation needed to be shored up in a few places, but otherwise it held up surprisingly well. "Cellar's got stone walls three feet thick," Daniel explained. "Nothing short of an earthquake could disturb them."

Gabriela wanted to take another look at the fireplace and the carved stone inside the farmhouse, but before she got to the front steps, Ben darted toward the back of the property. Trotting after him, Gabriela called out to her son, but he kept running.

"There's a path," he yelled, and headed toward it.

Agnese picked her way over, clutching Daniel's arm. "Where does he go?"

"Down to the beach," Daniel said. "I'll catch up with him."

Planting her hands on her hips, Gabriela watched him set off after Ben. She felt her mother's tiny hand at the crook of her elbow.

"*Va bene.* We go see too."

Walking slowly, Gabriela led Agnese away from the house. As they passed the small cemetery and its low wrought-iron fence, Gabriela pointed out Penelope Thorsen's grave from 1832 and the tiny marker beside it that very faintly read *Infant*.

"Her husband is there?" Agnese pointed to the crumbled stone at the third grave.

"No, he's buried at Fort Ohnita. There's a big monument for him."

"He leaves her behind." Agnese frowned.

"Penelope died after he did. Maybe she wanted to be on her own land." A picture flashed in Gabriela's mind, as vivid as recalling a photograph—a white house with black shutters and smoke curling from its chimneys, surrounded by beautiful, well-tended gardens and a grape arbor and farmland and woods that stretched to the lake. She blinked, and the image faded.

"I think she's here because she doesn't want to leave the baby." Agnese pointed to the tiny marker beside Penelope's stone and crossed herself. "What will happen to them? You don't plow them under. They are people, not old potatoes."

"The developer wants to restore the cemetery," Gabriela said. "These graves are part of the history that makes this place interesting." *And valuable*, she thought, remembering Charmaine's criticism.

At the edge of the overgrown backyard, they reached the narrow path hemmed in by trees on both sides. As they took their first steps, Gabriela was surprised to see bare ground and the tall grass beaten down on both sides, as if the path were used regularly. Anglers, she decided, and remembered Clawson talking about catching perch when he'd showed up at the house at Daniel's first meeting with Everett.

Thick tree roots cut across the path, and patches of mud marked where puddles had stood after the rain. "This is going to be difficult for you, Mama," Gabriela said. "I don't know how far we can go."

"*Avanti*." Agnese tugged on her arm. "We see."

As they made their steady progress, Gabriela held back branches adorned with swelling leaf buds and pushed against a new profusion of brush that crowded the path. From up ahead, she heard Ben's voice raised in excitement and Daniel calling after him. The wind carried their laughter.

Sound traveled far here, Gabriela thought, recalling a long-ago Earth Science lesson about how cool air over water caused sound waves to bend. Someone on the shore could hear something in the distance as if it were much closer. She had noticed the same phenomenon at Peninsula Point, which probably explained why those two soldiers from the Continental Army had been able to eavesdrop on the British planning an attack on Fort Ohnita.

Although she could not see them, Gabriela heard Ben and Daniel as if they were just five feet ahead. The rumble of the waves seemed close and, if she didn't know differently, Gabriela would have expected that she and Agnese would soon reach the beach that had to be at least another half mile away.

The women kept walking, skirting puddles and avoiding a few slick patches of mud. Keenly attuned to her mother, Gabriela listened for any hint of wheezing or labored breathing.

A man shouted.

Tensing, Gabriela wondered if Ben had gotten too close to the water and Daniel had to drag him back. Then she heard the voice again and knew it didn't belong to Daniel. A second person yelled, but Gabriela could not make out the words.

"Who is that?" her mother asked.

Gabriela shushed her, knowing their voices carried as well.

Then silence, the argument apparently over as quickly as it had erupted. But there was no question that they weren't alone here, though it was hard to tell how far away the men might be.

Agnese raised her chin and started to turn around. "Maybe we go back."

Walking even more slowly this time, they headed back toward the old farmhouse, Gabriela chiding herself for allowing her mother to walk so far. They passed a large tree, its trunk divided into a deep V. As they paused to rest, Gabriela pointed out how two trees had grown together into one, probably a hundred years before—maybe longer.

A sharp crack broke the silence, then another. *Gunfire!*

Gabriela's head swiveled, trying to pinpoint the source of the sound, and guessed that it had come from the east, though she couldn't be sure. She thought of Ben and Daniel along the lake, but she couldn't leave her mother. Taking Agnese's arm, Gabriela urged her along. Branches snapped behind them, and she turned to see Ben burst through a thicket along the path, pursued by Daniel—both laughing.

Gabriela relaxed. They were safe. "Did you hear something? Shots?"

Daniel shrugged. "Just somebody shooting at a target. You hear that a lot out in the country." He reached for her free hand and squeezed it. "Nothing to worry about, okay?"

Ben snuck up behind them and tagged Daniel, sending them both off down the path. Gabriela laughed as she watched Ben stay just out of reach, until Daniel lunged forward and looped one long arm around the boy's middle. "Gotcha!" Daniel yelled.

"You see how he wants to be with Daniel? That's good," Agnese said. "No problem when you get married."

The same thought had occurred to her, but she didn't want to get into a discussion with her mother—the when and where of the wedding. Instead, Gabriela made a wish for them all to be as happy as they were at this moment.

On Wednesday evening, with Daniel working late, Agnese stayed with Ben while Gabriela returned to the library for "Curiosities of the Collection." A week's worth of email blasts, website announcements, and flyers at the circulation desk had attracted twenty-eight people, not counting the staff, including Emilie, who had been hired by Mike as his assistant.

Watching the crowd settle into the chairs arranged in rows, Gabriela took a seat in the back. Francine welcomed them, reading from notes as she explained their program. "Tonight we'll be exploring some of the library's oddities."

"And not just the people," Pearl interrupted. "We've got some weird books too."

Francine sighed loudly, and Gabriela began to worry that their antagonism would derail this program. Then it dawned on her: This was the main event, and both women knew it.

"My favorite is *Aphids of the World*." Francine held up the book. "I didn't know that an entire book could be dedicated to an insect no bigger than an eighth of an inch."

"I'm not surprised," Pearl deadpanned. "I bug you so much, I could fill an entire library with stuff I've said to annoy you."

Even Gabriela had to chuckle.

"But none of what you say is worth writing down," Francine shot back. Laughter broke out, and a couple of people clapped.

The two women took turns presenting books on offbeat and obscure subjects. Pearl read "ten ways to your man's heart" from *Homemaking for the Bride-to-Be*. "Never complain about cooking or cleaning. A spotless home will make your husband happy every time he walks in the door." Pearl tossed the book aside. "I've been married for forty-one years, and I can tell you housecleaning isn't the secret to a happy husband." She wiggled her eyebrows. "It's a pound of Velveeta and a six-pack."

Just as Gabriela thought they should videorecord the program, she saw Emilie holding up her phone. Putting a clip on the library website would probably triple the traffic.

Pearl made the last presentation: a book called *My Favorite Graves—Ohnita Harbor's Best Headstones*. Printed by the Ohnita Harbor Historical Society in the 1960s, the glossy pamphlet contained photos of what it called interesting and attractive grave markers. "Didn't know a cemetery was supposed to be a beauty pageant," she said. "Personally, I like them old and mossy, a little broken down and creepy."

"Sort of like you," Francine added.

The crowd roared with approval, and both women took a bow. Gabriela thanked Pearl and Francine, calling them Ohnita Harbor's answer to *Saturday Night Live*. She invited people to stay for refreshments and reminded them that the circulation desk was open for any checkouts.

As Gabriela chatted with patrons, she noticed Emilie trying to get her attention by holding up the booklet on Ohnita Harbor graves. She made her way over, waylaid several times by people who gushed over how much they'd enjoyed the program and asked when the next one would be held.

Emilie's eyes bright with excitement widened Gabriela's smile. "What did you find?"

"Colonel Thorsen's gravestone is in here," Emilie said.

No surprise there, Gabriela thought, given the size of that obelisk and the fact that half the members of the Ohnita Harbor Historical Society probably belonged to the Daughters of the American Revolution. Then she remembered that the obelisk had been erected in the 1980s and this pamphlet had been printed twenty years earlier.

She stepped closer and saw a full-page photo of what had been Thorsen's original stone. Lichens dotted the slab and obscured part of the name, but the inscription remained legible: *He Served His Country to the End.* Below that simple tribute, an ornate pattern had been carved into the stone. Much of the detail had been lost to erosion, but Gabriela recognized the same crest she'd seen at the farmhouse: the tree, the deer, and enough letters of the motto for her to discern *Pro Patre*—for the father.

"What happened to this stone? Did they just throw it away?" Emilie asked.

"Oh, I doubt that," Gabriela said. "Tomorrow morning we'll call Fort Ohnita and see what we can find out." Spotting Thelma Tulowski just inside the entrance, she excused herself and left Emilie huddled over the pamphlet.

Thelma wore street clothes, which made Gabriela wonder if she'd come for the program. But when she asked, Thelma shook her head. "I came here to see you." The frown on the police inspector's face told Gabriela this visit wasn't social.

"Let's go to my office." Gabriela headed toward the stairs, Thelma a step behind her. A few years ago, she couldn't have imagined having these conversations with the police—questions asked, others avoided, theories batted around—now it was all so familiar. If Thelma showed up now, after hours, it had to be connected to Ricky's death. Gabriela vowed to do whatever she could to help solve the nagging question of what had happened to him. And exonerate him, she added to herself, refusing to believe the swirl of rumors that hadn't died down, that getting shot the way Ricky had—one bullet in the back of the skull—labeled him a drug dealer.

Gabriela unlocked her office door and shut it behind them.

"I got a call a little while ago from the state police—Trooper Doug Morrison." Thelma cocked an eyebrow.

Gabriela kept her expression neutral, trying not to betray her memories from when Trooper Morrison had investigated the deaths at Still Waters Chasm. He'd accused her of getting in the way of police business, then told her how much he admired her. *If you weren't with Daniel*, he'd said. She pushed that recollection away.

"He called the station about an hour ago," Thelma began. "He was on a call at Peninsula Point. You know where that is, right?"

Gabriela nodded, recalling her birthday weekend and the fun she'd had there with Daniel and Ben. "What's going on there?"

"Fishermen found a gun," Thelma said and began rattling off specifics: a Smith & Wesson .357 Magnum. "The kind of gun used to kill Ricky."

"You think that's the murder weapon?"

Thelma raised one shoulder in a half shrug. "We'll know soon. But given where it was found—in a thick marsh—it's possible somebody tried to dispose of the gun there. But it's just a possibility. Could be a different gun entirely."

Gabriela's mind clicked. "On Sunday, we heard gunshots."

Thelma leaned forward. "Where?"

She told Thelma everything she could remember from the moment they arrived at Thorsen Manor that day. She recalled Ben and Daniel running down the path toward the lake; she and Agnese making their way slowly; the shots echoing across the water, which they'd dismissed as someone shooting at targets.

"And you didn't report it?" Thelma went on.

"Why?" Gabriela widened her eyes. "We didn't see anything suspicious. Sounded far away. You know how sound travels over water."

Thelma asked a few more questions, then Gabriela remembered something else. "The marsh area where the gun was found, was that by the footbridge at Peninsula Point? The one that leads to the little island where the historical marker is?"

"No, it wasn't found at the park—but close by. There are a lot of marshes around there," Thelma said. "You have your Traitor's Map?"

Gabriela retrieved her copy and unrolled it across her desk. It bore a few creases and ink marks from use in class discussions and her own musings.

"Right about here." Thelma tapped a place close to Peninsula Point, then left her finger on the map. "Never thought about this before. Peninsula Point is one of the places clearly marked on this map. So maybe that had been Ricky's destination with Emilie."

A chill made a spidery crawl down Gabriela's spine. "We found a boat at Peninsula Point."

"And you're just telling me now?" Thelma snapped.

"I didn't think it was connected. We'd gone to Peninsula Point on my birthday, a couple of days after Ricky was killed," Gabriela explained. "I figured someone had just parked it there or maybe it got lose from a dock and drifted there. I didn't think it was relevant."

Taking out her phone, Gabriela scrolled through the photos she'd taken that day of Ben sitting inside the boat in the tall grass of the marsh. Part of the registration number showed on the side.

"Send me those photos," Thelma said, and Gabriela texted them.

Chapter Twelve

As tired as she was, sleep eluded Gabriela after her conversation with Thelma. Sitting up in bed, she read for an hour, hoping it would make her drowsy, but kept checking her phone to see if Daniel had responded to her text and her missed call from earlier in the evening. The screen remained frustratingly blank.

When her eyes burned and watered, Gabriela turned off the light and tried to get comfortable. The last time she looked at the clock, it read 2:46. When her eyes snapped open again, it was 5:03. Staying in bed would be futile, she knew. Better to get up and start the day.

After dropping Ben off at school, Gabriela went straight to the library in hopes of losing herself in a backlog of work. At ten o'clock that morning, someone tapped on her door. Looking up, Gabriela saw Emilie. "You're here early," she said. Emilie normally didn't come in until the afternoon to work with Mike.

Emilie took a seat opposite her desk. "I don't have class until later, so I thought we might call the fort now."

It took Gabriela's sleep-short brain a moment to process what she was saying. *The original Thorsen gravestone.* "Of course. Good idea."

She set Emilie up at the small conference table outside her office not far from Delmina's desk. "Tell them you're calling from the library and that you work for me," Gabriela instructed her. "That might help you get an answer more quickly."

At another tap on her door, she raised her eyes to Emilie, smiling broadly as she related the conversation she'd just had with the fort director. "They have the original stone. Not on display, but since this is research, we can go anytime. I thought maybe we could go soon. Then I can work with Mike before my class at four o'clock. Is that okay?"

"Sounds great. I just need about an hour to finish up here."

"Oh, we can go another time," Emilie said.

Delmina appeared in the doorway, no doubt having heard the entire exchange. "I have a little job while you wait for Gabriela. I need to send out a flyer for some programs, and I can't figure out the best design."

"I can do that," Emilie said.

Gabriela watched the two of them leave her office—Emilie, who craved the balm of activity, and Delmina, who had never before asked for or needed help with a flyer.

After about an hour of triaging the most urgent items on her to-do list, Gabriela suggested that they get a little exercise and walk to Fort Ohnita, hoping the extra time together would encourage the young woman to talk. But instead of discussing how she was processing Ricky's death, Emilie spoke only of the library and looking forward to spending more time there that summer. "I'll volunteer—you don't need to pay me any extra," she said.

Listening, nodding every so often, Gabriela recognized Emilie's chatter as an attempt to compartmentalize, pushing back feelings too overwhelming to deal with in the moment. She knew it all too well.

They crossed Main Street Bridge from the west side of town to the east, then turned left. A few blocks later they headed up the access road toward the fort. Déjà vu swept over Gabriela as she retraced her steps from that Saturday afternoon jog, about a month ago.

The road rose and Gabriela leaned into the steep grade. "You doing okay?" she asked Emilie, her words punctuated by a puff of breath.

"Yeah, fine." Emilie looked around. "Doing this makes me think of Ricky—in a good way. I never met anybody who loved history so much. If he were here, he'd be all over Thorsen's gravestone. And he'd figure it all out too."

"Maybe you can be the one," Gabriela said.

Emilie raised her chin. "I'll do it for him."

Wallace Kersey, Director of Fort Ohnita, met Gabriela and Emilie at his office in what had been the old guardhouse. Short with a graying reddish beard, Wallace wore a quilted vest over a sweater, even though the outside temperature hovered near 60 degrees. Inside the fort the thick stone walls and thin glass panes made the place damp and drafty.

Like most Ohnitans, Gabriela had visited the old fort many times, from field trips as an elementary school student to taking Ben there just a few months ago. She felt hometown pride for this place that captured three centuries of history, from the first fortresses that had protected Ohnita Settlement to the barracks used by the military through the Second World War. But never had she been invited behind the scenes into the inner workings of the fort as a museum.

They followed Wallace along corridors used only by staff, then stopped outside a wooden door to his office. Inside, Gabriela placed her hand against the stone walls and contemplated all that had happened on this site. "Is it like going back in time whenever you come in here?"

Wallace chuckled. "Sometimes. All I need is a ghost—hopefully a friendly one." He flipped a switch, and soon the red coils of a space heater began to warm the air.

As they sat around a small wooden table, Gabriela asked Emilie to explain the Traitor's Map project for their class at the community college.

"So where does Colonel Thorsen's gravestone work into that?" Wallace asked. "His brother made the map, not him."

"It doesn't—not exactly," Emilie said, and looked over at Gabriela.

"We saw a photograph of Colonel Thorsen's original gravestone. It matches a design in the old Thorsen farmhouse." Gabriela gave a quick explanation of the Thorsen Manor project being managed by her fiancé. "It seems to be a family crest or coat of arms: a tree, a deer, and two nesting birds."

Taking out her phone, Gabriela scrolled to a photo of the stone in the farmhouse wall and enlarged it for Wallace to see the details.

"Quite lovely," he murmured. "Well, let's go take a look."

He led them down the hall to an unmarked door, explaining that the space had originally been used to store provisions. "There would have been sacks of flour and cornmeal, barrels of apples, and bins of carrots and turnips in here." Pointing toward the ceiling, he pointed out a couple of iron hooks. "Smoked hams and cured meats probably hung from them."

Now cabinets and shelves lined the walls, holding artifacts from rotating exhibits and props from the reenactments staged on the fort grounds, Wallace explained. "Occasionally we add something to our collection. We get donations from time to time. And then there's this." He slid open a shallow drawer in a cabinet. "Just last week the grounds crew noticed something metal poking out of the ground. Turned out to be a button from a British uniform."

Small and round, the object bore faint etchings of what had undoubtedly been an ornate design. "Maybe it goes all the way back to that attack on Fort Ohnita in 1777," Gabriela mused. "A lot more than buttons were lost that day."

Wallace nodded. "Heavy casualties on both sides. Colonel Thorsen was gravely wounded in that attack. Shot in the leg, facing certain amputation and probably death from infection and blood loss. But he survived and came back to fight another day—literally, in the War of 1812."

He opened another narrow drawer at the bottom of the cabinet and stood back. Arranged inside were the fragments of a gravestone, pieced together like a puzzle.

"This old marker stood on Colonel Thorsen's grave from his death in 1818 until 1987, when it crumpled," Wallace said. "Vandalism was blamed at first. But this is limestone. Water got into the crevices, and after one too many freezes and thaws, it shattered like glass."

Up close, they could read the muted letters that spelled out his name and rank and his birth and death dates that attested to a long life. Below the simple epitaph—*He Served His Country to the End*—a circle about the size of a salad plate had been carved into the stone. Had she not seen the family crest on the wall in the farmhouse, Gabriela probably would not have been able to pick out many of the details in the worn and broken stone. But having seen the design, she could make out the tree in the center, although the roosting birds were indiscernible. Beside it stood a deer and, from the look of it, it bore a rack of antlers.

Taking out her phone, Gabriela studied the picture she'd taken of the crest at the farmhouse. The deer in that design had been a doe, smaller, with no antlers. This etching depicted a large buck.

"It's different." She showed Emilie and Wallace the image so they could compare for themselves.

"Maybe it's a buck because Colonel Thorsen was this big military guy," Emilie said. "They wanted an obviously male symbol."

"But a family crest shouldn't change like that, right?" Gabriela said.

"Not necessarily," Wallace replied. "The royal coat of arms in Britian has the Scottish unicorn on one side and the English lion on the other. Historically, they faced each other, one on each side of a shield. But one of the royals I think turned them facing outward, as if watching everybody. A not-so-subtle reminder, 'I've got eyes on you.'" Chuckling, Wallace pointed two fingers toward his own eyes and then out at Emilie and Gabriela.

"So I guess the change in the deer does convey something—the buck for Colonel Thorsen's military career and the doe for Penelope's hearth and home," Gabriela said. It softened her opinion of Jacob Thorsen, that he'd paid tribute to his wife.

"Can we do a rubbing—if we come back sometime?" Emilie asked.

Wallace shook his head. "I'm sorry, but this stone is so fragile. Any extra pressure could damage it further. But you can have all the photos you want."

As Emilie took out her phone to photograph the stone, Gabriela thanked Wallace for making the time for them. "This really isn't library business. But Emilie has been so taken with the Traitor's Map research, I don't want to discourage her."

"Completely agree. I'm a curator at heart and by background. I could show off artifacts all day long." Wallace leaned over and whispered, "And it beats what's been going on here. Police crawling all over the grounds." He grimaced. "Ever since that body washed up on the shoreline here."

Glancing back, Gabriela made certain Emilie was engrossed in taking photos.

"The young man—he was one of my students," she whispered.

Wallace's jaw slackened. "I'm sorry—I had no idea."

"Emilie was the one who found his body. They were friends."

The fort director widened his eyes. "Geez, that's rough."

Emilie approached them. "I took a gazillion photos."

Gabriela turned to Wallace. "Thank you for letting us come by."

"Happy to help," Wallace told them. "Come back anytime. If you discover anything about Colonel Thorsen, I'd love to hear it."

As they left the fort, Emilie suggested they walk across the grounds to the bluffs. Gabriela chatted about the gravestone and the crest in the farmhouse and how they complemented each other. "It would be nice to have side-by-side photos of the images," she said.

Emilie stopped walking. "I heard what you and Wallace were talking about. You know, about the police crawling all over here."

Gabriela dropped her eyes toward the ground. "I'm sorry. I hope that didn't upset you."

Emilie sighed deeply. "It's all everyone talks about."

When she looked over, Gabriela saw the tears collecting against Emilie's dark lashes. "That's the way small towns are."

"I had a hard time when we first moved here. Ricky knew that; it's why we became friends," Emilie went on. "My parents wanted to live someplace quieter—less expensive and not so many people. Now I think it was a huge mistake, coming here. People stick their noses into everybody's business. They keep asking why Ricky died—what was he into? Somebody asked me if he was a drug dealer!"

Gabriela groaned. "That's hard. Are you getting the support you need? Do you think you should give the counseling center another try?"

"I went again last week," Emilie said. "It helps a little."

They stopped at the fence along the bluffs where the land sloped downward then dropped off sharply. Gabriela looked out over the lake and a steady line of waves rolling unbroken toward shore, thinking of how they brought with them driftwood and plastic, bits of fishing gear, and anything else dropped overboard. *And bodies.* Ricky had been found almost directly below their feet. She wondered if that's what drew Emilie here.

Beside her, Emilie clutched the railing, her fingers curling over the wood. "When we came here for class, Ricky told me it was one of the best days of his life. He felt like he was doing something interesting and important."

A class assignment had meant that much to him, Gabriela thought sadly, and suddenly got a glimpse of Ricky as a lonely and isolated young man. "I'm glad he had that day. It's a wonderful memory for us."

When Emilie let go of the railing, Gabriela turned and took two steps toward the fort and the general direction of town, but Emilie faced another direction. "Can we?" She pointed toward the Old Post Cemetery.

They passed through the archway where the two flags, one American and one British, fluttered in a light wind and headed toward Colonel Thorsen's grave. Running her hand over the highly polished stone, Gabriela remarked how sterile it seemed compared to the old lichen-covered marker. The original inscription seemed more personal too, not the encyclopedic listing of his military accomplishments on this monument.

"I like the old one better," Emilie agreed. "It gives me a sense of who Colonel Thorsen was."

Gabriela hummed a low, deep sound—half agreement, half appreciation. "That's what artifacts do. They convey story and emotion. We feel the people they belonged to. Whoever made the first grave marker knew Jacob Thorsen and admired him."

Her thoughts turned back to the crest at the farmhouse and the design on the original grave marker, which linked husband and wife in symbols, not words. On an impulse, she picked up her cell phone and called Daniel.

"What's up?" he asked.

"I'm at the fort with Emilie. We saw Colonel Thorsen's original gravestone. It has the family crest on it, but it's different than the stone at the farmhouse. Have you come across any more of them? I'm wondering—"

"I can't do this now," Daniel interrupted.

His tone stung. "Oh, sorry," she said. "I'll tell you later."

"Gotta go."

Back at the library, Emilie began working with Mike downstairs while Gabriela sifted through a stack of messages from Delmina. None of those calls to return, though, were the one she wanted to make—to Daniel. She knew he was busy, working unbearably long hours, and calling him on impulse had not been a great idea. But did she have to censor herself? Grabbing her purse, Gabriela announced that she'd be back shortly, as if she had an errand to run. What she needed was space.

Her heels beat an angry rhythm down the hill from the library, past City Hall and the police station, and into downtown Ohnita Harbor. As she walked, Gabriela recalled numerous times she and Daniel had let each other's calls go to voicemail or when they simply said, "I'll have to get back to you." But this conversation, if she could even call it that, had revealed a different side of Daniel. He had been impatient to the point of rudeness.

She understood that every big project inevitably took more time and more money than expected. The dilapidated condition of the Thorsen farmhouse made a problem out of every solution. Daniel had told her they'd had to shore up the walls before doing the joists. To stabilize the upstairs, they'd had to reinforce the downstairs. The way he'd described the work, Gabriela pictured a house of cards, ready to tumble.

Still, every time they talked about the project, Daniel always sounded upbeat. "We'll get there," he'd always say. "This project is just taking a little longer to sort out."

The last time she saw him—Gabriela thought back; it had been four days ago—he'd looked thinner, and stubble dotted his normally clean-shaven cheeks. In those sparse whiskers, he'd shown his tiredness. She remembered the circles that looked like bruises under Daniel's eyes and softened her judgment over one ill-timed phone call.

She understood, she always did.

Your father, he works hard—he's tired. Don't bother your mother— she's upset today.

Those echoes reverberated deep in her memory. Gabriela had heard them often enough in childhood so that, even as a young girl, she could anticipate when she should and should not speak with her parents. She would sense her father's exhaustion when he came home from a double shift at the factory. She would overhear her mother on the phone with Aunt Cecelia, speaking rapidly in Italian and crying about something that had happened long ago. Then she'd tuck the test paper or the book report marked with an A+ into her book bag. Shutting her door, she'd sit alone in her room, whispering aloud to herself, *Clever girl. Smart girl. I'm so proud of you.*

Those long-ago moments of needing to stay quiet, to be small, had diminished her. In keeping both her accomplishments and problems to herself, she meted them out only in portions others could swallow. And now, Gabriela realized, she was doing the same thing with Daniel.

This had to stop. Their future, their relationship, depended on it.

Chapter Thirteen

Calmer now, Gabriela looped back toward the library. Instead of walking up Main Street, where she'd probably run into a half dozen patrons wanting a moment of her time, she decided to take the paved path along the Ohnita River. Spring rains had elevated the level of the river running swiftly toward the lake. Seagulls dipped and soared; at the edge of the embankment, one solitary fisherman cast a line.

Rounding a curve, Gabriela saw a man on a bench. The way his shoulders curved and his head dropped forward, she thought he might be napping. When he shifted and looked in her direction, she recognized him. Gabriela considered walking past with only a nod, but his eyes met hers.

"You're the teacher," Walt Seymour said.

"Yes." She stopped. "Gabriela Domenici."

Walt slid down to the opposite end of the bench, and Gabriela perched at the edge of the seat. She could think of nothing to say to this man and reverted to the obvious. "I'm so sorry about Ricky. How are you holding up?"

Walt's shoulders rose and fell. "My boy's dead. That ain't supposed to happen."

"No, it's not." Gabriela folded her hands.

Walt looked at her with watery, bloodshot eyes. As he straightened, his movements stirred up the smell of sweat and alcohol. The odor of grief, Gabriela thought.

"I shouldn't have gone into your library like that the other day. I was pissed off and wanted to blame somebody. Not your fault," he said.

Gabriela shook her head. "I understand. I have a son too."

Walt turned back toward the river. Silence stretched for a minute.

"Police keep asking me questions. They ain't got a clue," he said. "People won't look at what they don't want to see."

"What aren't they seeing?" she asked.

Walt swiveled his stare to her. "That Ricky was a good boy."

"Yes, he was. Teachers aren't supposed to have favorites, but Ricky was one of mine."

She waited for Walt to say more, but after another minute of silence she got up from the bench. She bade Walt goodbye and walked the rest of the way to the library.

———◆———

In the late afternoon, with Ben playing at the park after school, Gabriela drove home by herself. With the longer days of spring, she could head out for a short jog as soon as her son came home. Then a hot shower and a quick dinner together.

Daniel's truck was parked at the curb.

The realization made her excited and a little nervous because she had to voice the thoughts churning in her mind all day—that no matter how busy they were, they had to make time for each other.

Parking her car in the garage, she glanced at the back door, expecting it to open any second, but it stayed shut. When she tried the knob, the door swung inward, but the house held only silence.

"Daniel?" she called out.

In the living room, she found him stretched out on the sofa. Gabriela studied him, his body relaxed, though his face still showed deep furrows between his eyebrows. Tiptoeing across the floor, she retrieved a throw from an armchair, spread it over him, then headed upstairs to change into her jogging clothes. Leaving a note on the kitchen counter, Gabriela closed the back door. After a few blocks, she wanted to turn back to be there when Daniel woke up but made herself keep going. She had to take care of herself.

Thirty-five minutes later, she found him still asleep on the sofa, though he'd shifted from his back to his side. After a quick shower, when she came out of the bathroom, Daniel was sitting on the bed.

"Ben's downstairs," he said, "watching TV."

Gabriela opened her chest of drawers and retrieved a pair of socks. "You hungry? We can eat early."

When she turned, Daniel slumped forward, elbows on knees and his hands dangling toward the floor. "I don't know how to tell you this."

Her thumb found the smooth band of the turquoise ring she'd gotten used to wearing and rubbed the satiny surface. "Whatever it is, just say it."

"Thorsen Manor is going bankrupt."

"What?" Gabriela dropped the socks on the floor.

"Everett told me today."

Sitting down on the bed, she took Daniel's right hand between both of hers. Gabriela listened without interrupting as he related mounting problems at Thorsen Manor—damage to the farmhouse beyond what had first been assessed, a plumbing subcontractor who had walked off the job after EBR's latest check bounced. "Everett finally admitted he is completely out of cash. I can't work there if we're not getting paid."

"So, the project's over?" Her first thought was that Daniel could stop working so hard, especially since he wasn't getting paid. The bigger loss for him, though, was the dream of doing this restoration project.

"About a week ago I had to put the guys on other jobs so I could keep paying them. I can't lose my crew. I've been doing most of the farmhouse work by myself. Damn near fell off a ladder yesterday I was so tired."

"You should have told me. I knew you were busy, but I had no idea. When I called today I thought you were just distracted."

"I'm so sorry about that. Everett had just dropped the bomb on me. He was standing right there."

Gabriela groaned. No wonder he had sounded so upset.

Daniel took his hand out of her grasp and stood. He paced across the room. "Everett kept telling me things would turn around, and I believed him. I swear to God, when he told me today that Thorsen Manor was out of money, I wanted to punch him."

Gabriela sucked in her breath. She'd never heard Daniel say anything like that before.

"And let's not forget Everett wanted to buy my house too." Daniel turned toward her, and Gabriela saw the tears in his eyes. "Told me how much he loved it—sleeping loft and all. And I believed that too. I'm so sorry."

"Honey, don't worry. There will be other jobs. You said the guys are working—"

"Those jobs pay my crew. Not me." He swore, an expletive hissed between teeth. "I've never been in a hole like this before. *Never.*"

Gabriela thought of what Charmaine had told her—Everett up to his neck in debt at high interest rates, how he'd gone bankrupt before. *Clayton doing nothing to help his brother*, she added to herself. She could imagine them both gloating over Everett's misfortune or maybe sweeping in to buy the land from Everett at a fire sale price. One brother's disaster, the other one's opportunity.

Daniel sank back onto the bed. "I should have walked away when that first check bounced, but then Everett made it good. I'll never trust that bastard again. You know what I hate the most? That I let you down. I thought this job would change things for us. I'd have bigger projects, more money. I wanted to start a college fund for Ben."

Gabriela reached for him, pulling him down to the bed. She scooted over to make room, and he stretched out across the mattress. "You never let me down. This is a setback—a disappointment. But you're here and I'm here. We'll figure it out."

He gave a short groan, and Gabriela watched his face cloud over with sadness. She touched his arm with a wordless inquiry.

"You know what I promised Ben, right? That when we got a new house, he could get a dog."

Gabriela rose up on one elbow. "Well, one of these days we will get a new house and a dog. Or we'll find a way to shove everybody in here. Just as long as we're together."

Daniel leaned over and she expected a kiss. Instead, he cupped her cheek with his hand. "It really doesn't matter to you, does it?"

"We matter—nothing else." She closed the gap and kissed him.

Early the next morning, before the sun had warmed the horizon, Gabriela stirred awake, her thoughts churning. It was Friday, and after being out with Emilie at the fort most of Thursday afternoon, she had so much to catch up on.

Downstairs, the cold kitchen tile shocked her bare feet as she made coffee. Sitting down on the living room sofa, Gabriela tucked her feet under herself and wrapped her hands around the yellow ceramic mug emblazoned with the words *I'm a morning person!*—a gift from the library staff last Christmas. She tried to focus on the positive. Her job remained secure, and Daniel could always take on more roofing projects. They'd find a way through this.

A short while later, her phone chimed with an incoming text from Daniel. *You up?*

Smiling, she texted back. *On my second cup of coffee.*

Her cell phone rang. "Start looking for a new house and tell Ben he's getting a dog," Daniel announced.

Gabriela's head snapped back as if whiplashed. "What?"

"Thorsen Manor is back on. Everett just called me."

"But you said..." She ran her tongue over dry lips. "I thought Everett was out of money."

"A big investor came through at the last minute. I don't know any of the details other than Everett wants to see me ASAP. I'm going back there this morning."

Gabriela couldn't believe what she was hearing, not after last night. "Are you sure? You said you'd never trust him again."

"I know, but Everett promises to pay me everything he owes me today. If the check clears, we're back in business."

Gabriela fisted one hand and pressed it into her abdomen to keep her gut from churning.

"You can tell me more over dinner tonight."

"Why don't I take you and Ben out. I'll be there around seven," Daniel promised.

"Let's stay in. I promised Ben that Ryan could come for pizza tonight. Might as well invite Mama too."

"Whatever you want. I love you, Gabriela."

"Love you too," she said then disconnected the call.

At seven in the morning, she dialed her mother, always an early riser, to check in.

Agnese answered without saying hello. "Why you up? You don't sleep?"

"Just getting an early start on the day." Gabriela opened a cupboard and started putting away the plates and cups in the dishrack on the counter. "I wanted to invite you for dinner tonight with Daniel and me. I'm going to let Ben invite Ryan. I'm thinking pizza and minestrone."

"You gonna make?" Agnese asked.

"I gonna order," Gabriela teased.

"*Bah*, that's no good. You take me to the store later, and I make the minestrone."

"You've got a deal, Mama."

Gabriela worked at the library until three o'clock without a break, then picked up her mother for a trip to the grocery store. Agnese strolled through the brightly lit produce displays, picking up a red onion here, smelling a tomato there. Gabriela tried to hurry her along by fetching three small zucchini and two bulbs of garlic, only to have Agnese frown and say, "I find better." Finally, they left with four bags of groceries, including an eggplant, a bunch of bananas, and a package of fresh mushrooms that hadn't been on the list, just because of the expediency of giving in to Agnese's whims.

With her mother busy in the kitchen, Gabriela logged into her work email from her home computer to triage her inbox: Delete, reply, or forward to Delmina.

Soon the pungent smell of sautéed garlic and the tang of tomatoes drifted through the small house. With it came a happy memory of her childhood home, of doing homework at the kitchen table while her mother made dinner. She could still picture her father coming through the back door and stopping at the stove, inspecting the pots and pans, lifting lids, stealing a taste.

Smiling, she returned to her screen and approved a request from the Children's Room director for twenty-five dollars from petty cash to buy punch and cups for a story hour with a local author. At five o'clock, Gabriela picked Ryan and Ben up at the park, where they'd been playing with a group of kids from school.

"When are we eating?" her son whined as the boys got in the car.

"When Daniel gets here. Won't be too long," Gabriela told him.

At five thirty, with no replies to her texts, Gabriela went ahead and ordered an extra-large pizza, half cheese and half pepperoni. When the delivery came, she gave two slices each to Ben and Ryan. The boys devoured them quickly, asked for more, then retreated to the living room and the video game paused on the one and only TV in the house.

Gabriela ladled two bowls of minestrone and sprinkled Parmesan on top. Seated at the kitchen table with Agnese, she spooned up cubes of zucchini and potato with a small round of carrot in tomato broth. Before she could taste it, her stomach clenched; she exhaled through her mouth as if cooling off the soup.

Agnese ripped a slice of Italian bread in two. "You worry too much. Everything will be fine—you see."

Putting her spoon down, Gabriela barked a laugh. "Really? This from the woman who thought being too happy invited the *malocchio*?"

"I know how to take care of that." Forking her index and pinky fingers, Agnese jabbed the air in the other direction. "You deserve happiness. Nobody takes it away from you."

Reaching across the table, Gabriela took her mother's hand, the one that only moments ago had cast a counter curse. "Thank you, Mama."

An hour later, Daniel arrived, hungry and tired, but talking excitedly about resuming the Thorsen project. As he washed up in the downstairs bathroom, Gabriela reheated pizza slices in the oven and set a bowl of soup at his place. Agnese fussed about going home now that Daniel had arrived, but Gabriela insisted she stay for a while.

Between mouthfuls, Daniel explained that Everett wanted to expedite the project, which would mean putting more crew on the job so they could finish the farmhouse restoration on an accelerated timeline.

"*Si, si.* This is good. We say a prayer to St. Joseph. Patron saint of workers," Agnese said.

"I'll take all the help I can get," Daniel said, leaning over to kiss her on the cheek.

Gabriela chuckled to see her mother blush. "So, who's this new investor?"

"Someone in the family," Daniel replied. "Everett said they were still working things out—ownership wise."

Clayton, Gabriela thought; it made sense, given his newfound interest in local history. *The Brooks Brothers, together again*, she added to herself—though the dirty work at the farmhouse couldn't compare with an exclusive clothing company.

"I even inherited a worker," Daniel said. "Remember Clawson? He's helping with the demolition, and Everett pays him, so I don't have to put him on my payroll.."

He got up and brought his empty soup bowl to the sink. "I have a surprise for you. On Monday, we're removing the stone crest so we can open the wall in the main room and check for water damage. If you'd like, you can come out to the site and watch."

"Oh, that's great! I'll bring Emilie with me," Gabriela said. "What time on Monday?"

"Hadn't really thought about it. What works for you?"

Gabriela scrolled mentally through her schedule. "Ten?" she suggested, then quickly sent a text message to Emilie, asking her to bring charcoal and paper to make a rubbing.

Chapter Fourteen

As they drove out of Ohnita Harbor on Monday morning, Gabriela could not tell who was more excited, Emilie or herself. She listened as Emilie explained what she'd learned from researching the meaning of each element in the Thorsen family crest: the deer, a symbol of devotion; the tree, which stood for strength and growth; nesting birds, a warm and safe home.

When they arrived at Thorsen Manor, Gabriela expected the construction site to be busier but saw only Daniel's DRD truck and Clawson's old pickup in front of the farmhouse. Daniel came out to greet them, handing them both hard hats and cautioning them to watch their step.

"Where is everybody?" Gabriela asked.

"My crew is finishing up a roof in town today. It's just me and Clawson."

Daniel put on safety glasses and a mask and went back inside. Gabriela and Emilie stood just outside the doorway to the house, so as not to get in the way or breathe in the plaster dust.

"How are you going to get the stone out without cracking it?" Gabriela called out to Daniel.

He ran a finger around the perimeter of the crest. "The mortar is loose. We can chip it out."

With a grunt, Clawson grabbed a chisel and a mallet and took the first swing. Gabriela gasped. "Stop! You'll smash it," she yelled, rushing into the house. Clawson kept swinging.

"I got it," Daniel said as he squatted down, hands planted against the front of the stone. He said something to Clawson, but Gabriela couldn't hear him clearly over the chisel strikes against the mortar.

Tears welled as Gabriela expected the crest to come out in pieces, but the stone tipped forward into Daniel's hands.

"Told you." Clawson took his safety glasses off with one hand and rubbed the cuff of his flannel shirt across his forehead with the other.

Getting to his feet, Daniel carried the crest over to Gabriela and Emilie. "This thing's got to weigh thirty pounds."

Gabriela followed Daniel outside to the porch. "Does he know what he's doing?"

Daniel laid the stone in a corner, away from the doorway. "He's a bit of a loose cannon, but I need the help right now," he said quietly. "He works for Everett, so he can't be all bad."

Gabriela heard the shuffling of boots and turned to the doorway where Clawson stood, mallet in one hand and a chisel in the other. Ignoring him, Gabriela knelt beside the stone, running her fingers over the design. She noticed three braided lines ringing the perimeter like a frame, which she hadn't seen before. Emilie took several photos of the carving and close-ups of each individual element: the tree, the birds, the doe.

Resting her palm against the crest, Gabriela felt a frisson rip through her body—impatience mingled with something else that made her want to put the stone in the back of her car and drive off.

"I don't suppose Everett would loan this out—you know, while you guys are working on the house?"

"You feeling a little possessive?" Daniel gave her a smile.

Gabriela shrugged. "Just an authenticator's passion."

"Is it okay if I start doing this?" Emilie held up a sheet of onionskin and a piece of charcoal.

"Rub away." Gabriela stepped back to make room for Emilie to work but didn't want to go too far. Mesmerized, she watched the crest materialize on the paper.

"Hey, there's somethin' else in here," Clawson called from inside the house.

Daniel dusted the legs of his jeans with a swipe of his work gloves. "Probably two centuries of mouse droppings. Make sure you wear your mask."

"No. Take a look at this." Clawson stepped through the doorway with what looked like parchment in his hands. "It was in the wall, behind that stone."

Unrolling it, Clawson held the parchment up for the others to see. "Wonder how much this is worth."

"Oh, my God." Gabriela rushed forward toward the document, taking in every marking: Ohnita Settlement, Fort Ohnita, and an undulating shoreline marked with marshes, streams, and coves. This was a copy of the Traitor's Map. *Or was it?*

Gabriela searched for the biggest inaccuracy on the Traitor's Map—the large cave, but it wasn't on this one. "I think this is a *real* map of the shoreline."

Emilie left her rubbing on the porch, where the breeze caught a corner and skittered it away. Daniel retrieved the thin paper before it sailed off.

Extending her hands to take the parchment, Gabriela met Clawson's narrowed eyes. One side of his mouth curled into a sly grin. "You want this, don't ya?"

"I'd like to take a closer look," she replied. "I think this is the work of Henry Thorsen, a cartographer during the Revolution."

"That so? Well, I think this is a case of look, don't touch," Clawson said. "I'm the one who found it in the wall."

Gabriela felt Daniel's hand on her shoulder, then a slight pressure that drew her back a step.

"Let's lay it down on some of that rubbing paper." Daniel led everybody toward the corner of the porch, where Emilie spread out several sheets of onionskin. When Daniel reached for the map, Clawson handed it to him.

"Wait!" Emilie cried. "Look at the other side. It's all drawings."

Daniel flipped the map over, and Gabriela drew in a sharp breath. Sketches covered the entire surface: two birds roosting in the bare branches of a tree; a solitary tree in full leaf with no birds at all; a single deer standing beside the tree; a doe and buck flanking the trunk of another tree.... Each was a variation of the Thorsen family crest.

Parchment had been very expensive in the eighteenth century, Gabriela knew, so using both sides would have been common practice. But a map on one side and sketches on the other pointed to the likelihood that Henry had drawn all of it. But that hint of a provenance raised an even bigger question. "Jacob wanted to *execute* Henry. Why would he keep this map? And why take Henry's design and make it into the family crest?"

"And put it on Jacob's grave," Emilie added.

It defied logic, Gabriela thought. Surely Jacob would have banished any reminder of his brother, but here was evidence of a tie that remained between them.

Emilie took more photos, and Gabriela did the same with her phone. She'd text the images to Charmaine as soon as she got a strong cell signal. "This needs to be in a museum, under climate-controlled conditions."

"No, we need to notify Everett about what's been found on his property." Daniel rolled the map up slowly.

Gabriela tugged at his forearm. "This is a significant discovery. We can't just pretend we didn't find it."

The thud of a sledgehammer against a wall inside the house interrupted her. Daniel went inside, taking the map with him. Gabriela trailed a step behind, with Emilie at her heels. From the doorway, through a cloud of plaster dust that smarted Gabriela's eyes, she saw Clawson slide a long box from inside the wall.

"If there's money in here, don't forget I was the one who found it," Clawson said, his voice a low growl.

"This is Everett's property," Daniel said. He reached for the box, but Clawson clutched it to his body and made a half-turn away. Daniel extended his hand and unfastened the clasp. "Let's just take a look. Might be something, might be nothing."

The hinged lid opened easily. Gabriela took a step forward and saw what looked like a stack of paper. Her conservator side wanted to slow things down—if nothing else, to close the lid and keep the contents from being exposed to light and air and moisture. But another part of her just wanted to get her hands on that box.

Clawson reached in and drew out several sheets of paper, sending a shower of shards adrift.

"Don't!" Gabriela yelled. "That paper is too fragile to be touched like that."

"You act like you own this," Clawson said. "It ain't yours."

"No, but I *do* know about handling old documents. You're ruining them."

Daniel raised his voice. "Take it easy. This is old and falling apart. Maybe it's nothing."

"Then why is she getting so worked up?" Clawson jutted his chin in Gabriela's direction.

She took a step forward, her expression neutral. "I'd just like to see it, that's all."

Clawson snorted a laugh, and Daniel shot him a look. "Don't be a jerk," Daniel said. Clawson held the box out toward her.

A woman's spidery handwriting covered the brittle paper, and Gabriela knew it had to be Penelope's. Perhaps letters written to Jacob while he was away, fighting in the American Revolution or the War of 1812. Her fingers itched to examine them, but she knew the paper could crumple at the slightest touch.

"You see this?" Clawson grabbed a small leather-bound book beside the stack of paper.

"Oh!" Gabriela groaned, as if feeling the roughness of his clasp on her own body.

"It ain't gonna break." Clawson opened the cover to reveal an ornate signature: *Penelope Stanton Thorsen.*

Gabriela recognized the round-hand style of writing popular during the late 1700s and early 1800s, with elaborate curlicues at the start of the capital letters and flourishes at the end of the names. It spoke of a woman trained in penmanship for social duties. Against her better judgment, Gabriela turned a page of the journal, her fingers grazing Clawson's hand. She fought the instinct to recoil from the touch.

My husband builds a house for us.

Gabriela laughed with excitement. "It's her daily diary. This is an amazing resource for studying colonial life." She flipped through a few more entries, and lines jumped out from the pages—the purchase of a milking cow, the birth of a first child, the mention of visitors.

Then, toward the middle of the book, on a page dated 3rd October 1781, Penelope had written one line.

Henry came back.

Gabriela gasped. "Henry?"

Emilie took two photos of the page.

"Henry came back," Gabriela read aloud. "So he and Jacob reconciled? But the date on the page shows this was written in the middle of the Revolutionary War."

Clawson closed the book. "I think that's enough. Like Daniel said, this belongs to Everett."

"This is a cultural and historical record. I have to call Charmaine." Gabriela pulled her phone from her pocket. "I'm sure the maritime museum would store it."

Clawson wagged his head slowly. "That's for Everett to say. Not you."

"We can't just leave this here," Gabriela protested.

Daniel took out his phone and punched in a number. "Hey, Everett, got a minute?" He took a step away, and Gabriela listened to Daniel's description of the wall demolition, removing the crest in one piece, and finding the map and the metal box in the wall. "Gabriela thinks the map might have been drawn by Jacob's brother."

"It looks like the Traitor's Map, but it doesn't appear to have the same inaccuracies," Gabriela said loudly, hoping Everett could hear her. "And there's a diary and a stack of letters that belonged to Penelope Thorsen."

Daniel plugged his free ear with a finger and asked Everett to repeat what he'd just said.

"Let me speak with him," Gabriela whispered.

Daniel put the phone on speaker.

"Hi, Everett. This is primary research material, the kind that historians will be salivating over." She grinned at Daniel. "And I suspect it will answer a lot of questions about the Thorsen brothers. Penelope clearly wrote, 'Henry came back.' Not Jacob—Henry! And her letters could reveal so much about life in and around Ohnita Settlement. You might even find your visit from George Washington in there."

Taking a breath, Gabriela heard only silence on the phone. "The paper and parchment need to be preserved and handled very carefully," she added. "We can bring it to the Ohnita Harbor Maritime Museum. I'm sure Charmaine would see that it's stored for you under—"

"You have no right to take anything off my property," Everett interrupted.

"Of course not. But you'll want to preserve this. I mean, it's probably valuable." She thought of Clawson standing a few steps away. "Not monetarily. But historically."

"Charmaine and Clayton will never put their hands on anything from my property," Everett said. "Clawson, you there?"

"Yep." Clawson stepped forward and leaned down toward the phone. "I found that stuff in the wall—just so you know."

"You put it aside for me. All of it. I'll be up on the weekend," Everett said.

"Will do." Clawson stepped back, and the phone screen went blank as the call ended. He slammed the lid back down on the metal box, sending bits of browned paper into the air like dust motes. When he stuck out his hand, Daniel handed over the map.

Gabriela made a small, strangled noise. She followed Clawson as he walked toward his truck, giving him directions to keep everything away from dampness, but also heat or direct light. "A dry, dark closet would do for now."

Clawson opened the passenger door of his old pickup truck and put everything on the floor. He started the engine and drove down the dirt road.

Tears burned in Gabriela's eyes. "That's rare primary source material. It will be ruined. Why is Everett doing this?"

Daniel came up beside her and laid a hand gently on her shoulder. "He probably doesn't want Clayton to have any of it."

Gabriela squeezed her eyelids shut. "This is my fault. I'm the one who mentioned him and Charmaine."

"You didn't know Everett would react like that," Daniel said.

Emilie touched her arm. "Don't forget we have the pictures."

Gabriela gave her a weak smile then turned back to Daniel. "Whatever you do, don't let Clawson touch that stone. We've got to put it somewhere safe. That design tells a story, and we need to figure out what it's saying."

"Nothing will happen to it," Daniel said. "Everett will see to that. It's the centerpiece of this restoration."

"I don't trust Clawson not to smash it," Gabriela said. "Just to spite me."

"Clawson won't do anything. He knows it belongs to Everett." Daniel started back toward the house. "Remember that old garden shed in the back? I'll put it in there."

Gabriela imagined the little outbuilding covered with vines near the family cemetery. *Penelope would keep it safe*, she thought.

She waited outside while Daniel retrieved the stone from the house and carried it with both hands down the front steps. She and Emilie accompanied him across the yard and past the overgrown tangle of a feral garden. When they reached the shed, Gabriela tugged open the moisture-swollen door. A musty cloud expelled from the interior piled high with junk. She could make out the metal frame of a baby stroller, an old bicycle with flattened tires, a rake with curled tines. Gabriela pushed aside a stack of broken clay flowerpots on a shelf, and Daniel set the stone on it.

"Should we put something on top—you know, to keep someone from seeing it?" Emilie asked.

An old burlap sack with a large hole in the bottom, as if it had been chewed, and a black plastic tray that probably once held plants from a nursery covered the stone. Gabriela burrowed her fingers into the pile, feeling the rim of the crest. The touch soothed her, but when she withdrew her hand, the ache of loss lodged in her chest.

"You better go," Daniel said softly. "I'll handle Clawson. He won't get the stone. I promise. But you need to do something for me."

"Anything," Gabriela assured him.

"You need to keep what we found here a secret. No telling Charmaine, because the first person she'll tell is Clayton."

"But this is his family history too," Gabriela said.

"Uh-huh, and Everett's property."

Gabriela looked away, remembering how close she'd come to texting photos to Charmaine. "Okay," she agreed. The excitement of discovery crumpled like the fragile pages of Penelope's letters, leaving only the dust of disappointment that what had been found that day might never come to light again.

Chapter Fifteen

On Friday afternoon, Gabriela headed over to City Hall for the first meeting of the citizens' committee. Open windows in the large conference room let in a mild breeze scented with freshly mowed grass and flowering trees. As chair of the citizens' committee, she sat just to the right of the head of the table but saved the place of honor for Mayor Duncan Phillips. Like her, the mayor had grown up in Ohnita Harbor. But he was only in his early thirties, and the difference in their ages meant she had no memory of him from childhood. She admired him now for having stepped in during the darkest days of the city's municipal government after a disgraced mayor had gone to jail for siphoning city funds. Duncan had restored trust by emphasizing transparency and collaboration.

Duncan bustled in, greeting everybody by name. "I just want to extend my personal thanks to all of you for serving on the committee. I don't have to tell you how important it is to ask questions, speak up, and speak out."

"No problem here," Charmaine said. As co-chair of the committee, she sat at the other corner of the table, opposite Gabriela. "I'm known for not keeping my mouth shut on anything."

A light round of laughter arose from the table. Clayton Brooks, seated next to Charmaine, leaned toward her, his shoulder brushing hers.

The committee members already knew one another, so Gabriela dispensed with introductions and got down to business with the first item on the agenda—an update on the library ceiling renovation. She reviewed the bidding process, the city attorney's approval of the accepted bid, and told the committee work would begin soon.

"How many bids?" Clayton asked, looking at her over his reading glasses.

"We advertised in the local paper and received two bids," Gabriela explained. "Removal of the drop ceiling is fairly straightforward, but restoration of the plaster will take some expertise. Of the two companies, the local contractor came in significantly lower. Copies of both bids are in your packet."

"Just to clarify," Duncan interjected, "the committee's role is not to review bids. The city attorney's office will do that. The committee is to make sure that procedures are followed. On that, the library renovation has set the standard for those procedures."

Discussion moved on to the city's beautification plans: new planters and trees for the downtown area, additional benches and playground equipment in the city's two biggest parks, and the first phase of an expanded walkway along the river. Two hours and several tangents later—including what they could spend money on if they got another grant in the future—the meeting concluded. After sitting so long, Gabriela felt her leg stick to the chair as she got up.

"You drafted a great committee. They're really engaged," Charmaine said after the others left.

"Everybody asked good questions," Gabriela agreed, although far too many of them had come from Clayton, she added to herself.

"It's shocking how fast you can spend a million dollars," Clayton remarked. "Sprucing up downtown and fixing a few parks."

"There's always more work to be done than money to pay for it," Gabriela agreed.

Clayton tucked his papers into a small briefcase and zipped it shut. "Just ask my brother."

Heat rose in her face, and Gabriela kept her eyes on the conference table.

"I think I would like to see Thorsen Manor one of these days," Charmaine said to Clayton. "Gabriela tells me that old farmhouse is really something."

Clayton shook his head. "Trust me, there's nothing there to see except the shell of what was once a beautiful old home. Everett is chasing a dream, and he's going to ruin himself in the process."

Charmaine got up from her chair. "You're too hard on your brother."

"Everett hasn't lived here since he left for college thirty years ago. He has no emotional stakes at all. It's all money to him."

Gabriela thought of how easy it would be to take out her phone and show Clayton and Charmaine photos of what had been found at the old farmhouse. She could imagine Charmaine's excitement and Clayton's disbelief. The Traitor's Map was nothing compared to Henry's original sketch of the shore, the drawings of the family crest, and the biggest treasure of all—Penelope's letters and diary. But she'd made a promise to Daniel. It wasn't her property, and the story wasn't hers to tell. Thorsen Manor and all it contained belonged to Everett. Whatever the conflict between these two brothers, she would not get in the middle of it.

Monday morning brought the first week of May, the start of the renovation project at the library. When Gabriela arrived, heavy plastic had already cordoned off the back corner of the main room to contain the dust as the ceiling tile was removed. When work started, the noise sent patrons scurrying away after checking out books. Others came as far as the front entrance, then retreated.

Delmina shut the door to the administration offices, but the rumble of power tools penetrated their space. At eleven o'clock, Gabriela went downstairs to see how things were progressing. Something streaked out from under the plastic draped from ceiling to floor and ran past her. It was Nathaniel, the stray tomcat who always started his morning at City Hall for a breakfast of kibble, moved on to the library where he spent much of the day, then prowled around the neighborhood before moving on to the police station, where he got a second meal and endless petting. Now, meowing loudly at the library's front door, Nathaniel made it known he couldn't stand it there.

Gabriela opened the door, and Nathaniel bolted toward City Hall, the white tip of his tail flashing like a laser light.

"Smart cat," Pearl grumbled from the circulation desk. "If I could get out of here, I would."

Approaching the source of the din, Gabriela looked for Mike to ask his opinion about whether they should close the library during the tile removal. But as soon as she started to call out for him, a power drill whined long and loud. She gave up and went back upstairs.

Her office phone rang and Gabriela picked it up before Delmina could intercept and answer the call. "You got a minute?" Thelma Tulowski asked.

"Want me to come over?" Gabriela asked, just as the drilling resumed.

"You tearing the place down?" Thelma asked.

"Just the ceiling. I'll be there in five minutes."

"I wouldn't say no to one of those lattes," Thelma replied, and Gabriela promised to make a detour to A Better Bean before coming to the police station.

When she arrived, the desk sergeant told Gabriela that Thelma was waiting in her office. Holding a coffee in each hand, Gabriela rapped a knuckle on the door that stood ajar, then pushed it open.

"Delivery," she joked and handed over a latte.

Thelma took a long sip. "This is a hundred times better than what we make around here. How much do I owe you?"

"You can buy next time." Gabriela took the now-familiar seat opposite Thelma's desk.

Thelma opened a folder and held up a report. "Ballistics analysis on the gun. It's not the one used to kill Ricky."

"Oh." Gabriela wasn't sure what to feel about that—disappointment that so much remained unsolved about his murder or relief that his killing hadn't taken place so close to Thorsen Manor where Daniel worked every day.

Thelma took a photo out of the folder and held it up. Gabriela recognized it as the one she'd taken of Ben sitting in the boat he'd found in the marsh.

"This shows only part of the registration number, but it's enough to confirm it was one of the stolen boats out of Cape Vincent."

"Really?" Gabriela set her latte down. "It wasn't exactly well hidden. Ben found it in the marsh."

"That's why the state police think kids took the boats to go joyriding along the lake. Ran out of fuel and then ditched it," Thelma said.

"Then someone came back for it," Gabriela added, finishing the hypothesis.

"Maybe," Thelma said.

Gabriela waited to hear more, but when Thelma didn't offer any details, she prodded with a question. "What's your theory?"

Thelma studied the photo. "I think there's something going on along the lakeshore. Not just here, but all the way up to the St. Lawrence."

"What?" Gabriela asked, even though she doubted Thelma would elaborate.

"Something," Thelma repeated. "We need to see what else turns up."

Leaving the police station, Gabriela mulled the history of the Lake Ontario shoreline—from invasions out of Canada to battles fought during the American Revolution and the War of 1812. Rumrunners had plied that same shoreline from the islands of the St. Lawrence River to the coves and marshes closer to Ohnita Harbor. Today boats carried anglers, including charters for salmon fishing, along with pleasure craft and sailboats. But none of that explained anything about Ricky's murder or anything else that had been going on.

All they could do was wait to see what else the lake revealed.

Chapter Sixteen

Gabriela spent the first hour of the workday at home, avoiding the construction din, before leaving for a midmorning North Country Library Association meeting at a county library about forty minutes away from Ohnita Harbor. Passing through the kitchen, she got an idea and texted Daniel.

How about I bring u lunch? 1230ish after my meeting?

Daniel replied with a thumbs-up.

The meeting lasted until noon, with good discussions about programming, budgets, and New York State Department of Education grants for libraries. Gabriela had done a short presentation on the Traitor's Map, using it as an example of local history that could be turned into community programming. After the meeting, several librarians asked to look at the photographic copy of the map she'd brought with her.

She texted Daniel, letting him know she was on her way to Thorsen Manor. She stopped at a small grocery store and ordered a turkey sandwich for Daniel and a soup for herself, plus two coffees. Thinking about Clawson and anyone else who might be working that afternoon, she ordered two more sandwiches, one ham-and-cheese and one roast beef.

Ten minutes later, she reached the access road to Thorsen Manor. Driving slowly along the dirt and gravel, she looked for signs of progress and noticed a few more building lots had been surveyed and staked off.

Daniel's blue DRD Roofing truck angled in front of the old farmhouse; otherwise the parking lot was empty. Gabriela parked beside Daniel's truck and strode up the steps that had been replaced with new wood. At the doorway she called for Daniel but heard only the staccato rap of hammering upstairs. She waited for the noise to cease, then announced, "Lunch is served!"

Daniel descended the staircase, grinning at her. Raising her face, she kissed him lightly.

Two sawhorses and a sheet of plywood provided a makeshift worktable. Daniel brushed off the sawdust, and Gabriela set out their lunch. "I brought three sandwiches just in case your guys were hungry too."

Daniel explained that two of his guys had just left to help with a roofing project in Ohnita Harbor but would probably be back later. "I'm framing walls, which is easy for me to do solo." He selected the turkey sandwich and took a bite.

"Clawson here?" Gabriela asked as she removed the lid from the chicken noodle soup.

"He must be out fishing today," Daniel said. "He works for Everett, so I don't have any say in his schedule."

A few minutes later a black SUV pulled into the yard. Gabriela peered out the window. "Expecting someone?"

Daniel joined her at the window. "Everett," he said, as a man stepped out of the driver's side door.

Gabriela tensed. She doubted Everett would be all that thrilled to find her at his property.

Wiping his hands on a paper napkin, Daniel left the house. Gabriela stayed behind but remained at the window to observe. She watched as Daniel greeted Everett and an older man who got out of the passenger side of the SUV. Stepping back from the window as the three men approached the house, Gabriela put the lid back on her half-eaten soup. She wouldn't stay.

The conversation sounded friendly enough as the three men entered the house. "You remember Gabriela, my fiancée," Daniel said to Everett.

"Of course," Everett said. "Good to see you again."

Gabriela gave a polite smile but kept her distance. "I was just leaving."

"Nonsense. We just got here," the older man beside Everett said. He introduced himself as William Bulcher, Everett's father-in-law. "Call me Billy—everybody does." He reached for her hand.

Gabriela took in his Florida tan that offset his silver hair and guessed him to be in his mid-seventies. He wore black trousers and a black shirt with a pale gray linen blazer. On his feet were expensive-looking loafers, the soft, gleaming leather completely unsuited for a construction site.

Everett stepped toward her, his expression contrite. "I need to apologize for the other day. You caught me off guard. Finding some old map and a diary and letters in the wall—well, let's just say that's the last thing I expected."

Gabriela wanted to pounce on that statement and correct Everett's dismissal of what they'd found: *Henry's* map, *Penelope's* diary. Instead, she decided to appeal to his ego.

"You know, with a discovery like this, you could really attract some attention to Thorsen Manor. Not just historians but also media.

I can imagine the Syracuse TV stations running a feature on this," Gabriela said.

"Once we have a chance to examine everything, I'm sure we'll know what to do with it," Everett said.

"It's a miracle the water damage was limited to the outer walls. Thankfully nothing got into the inside walls. The metal box protected the letters and the diary, and the map is on parchment. But still, they need to be handled carefully; ideally, in climate-controlled conditions."

Everett turned to his father-in-law. "Gabriela used to work for a big museum in New York City."

"It was Archives and Documents at the New York Public Library," she corrected. "I spent my days researching and cataloging materials just like the ones we found here."

"So why aren't you listening to her?" Billy asked. "She'd know what to do with those old documents."

Everett gave a slight nod, then bobbed his head more vigorously. He left the farmhouse, and through the window Gabriela could see him heading toward his SUV. He opened the rear and extracted a large cardboard box with a lid and carried it to the house. She met him at the door.

"I have two conditions," Everett said, still holding the box. "One, don't go public with these documents or put them on display. Two—and most important—you don't show them to Clayton. I don't want him to know these exist."

"I understand," Gabriela said. "I'll keep everything safe and secure until you know what you wish to do with them." As she brought the box out to her car, she formulated a plan for storing the artifacts. They would be far safer with her than handled by people who did not understand how easily two-hundred-year-old paper could disintegrate under the wrong conditions. That also meant she could not go through the papers herself until she could be sure they wouldn't be damaged by handling.

Gabriela met Daniel's gaze when she returned to the house, and he gave her a smile. Everett, though, looked somber. "So, where are you taking it?" he asked.

"I'll need acid-free archival paper to create a barrier between the documents and the environment," she said. "I'll store it all in a large, locked cabinet in my office—cool, dry, and dark. It's the best solution I can think of. Temporarily, of course."

"Where's your office?" Billy asked.

Gabriela explained her current role as executive director of the Ohnita Harbor Public Library, then briefly gave its history back to the 1860s while noting the challenges of managing a building on the National Register of Historic Places. "We have our own restoration project going on," she added. "Behind acoustic tile on the main floor of the library is a gorgeous plaster ceiling. We got a state beautification grant to pay for it."

"Gabriela's expertise is far more impressive than she lets on," Daniel said, stepping up beside her. "She's even teaching now at the community college."

"One course—as an adjunct," Gabriela corrected him. "But I love teaching it."

Billy nudged Everett with his elbow. "We need to listen to this lady. She knows about getting grants. I'm telling you—the state would probably give us money to help with the farmhouse."

Gabriela seriously doubted that New York State would fork over money for a commercial project, no matter its historic connection. *Unless Billy Bulcher had political strings he could pull to make that happen*, she added to herself.

"We should stop by your library and see this ceiling project and find out more about the grant," Billy said.

"You'd be most welcome. It's probably the only library you'll see that looks like a Norman castle," she added.

Billy held out his cell phone. "Can you put your contact information in here? I've got to take a look at this place."

Gabriela entered her name, work email, and cell phone number into Billy's contacts. Then she gestured toward the makeshift table on sawhorses. "We have extra sandwiches if you'd care to join us for lunch."

Billy held half a ham-and-cheese in his hand as he strode toward the fireplace. "I had no idea what I bought into here. It seems like quite the treasure to me."

So, this was the investor Everett had brought in, Gabriela thought. "Are you in real estate development?"

"Me? No," Billy said. "Used to own a couple of businesses but mostly retired now. Then Everett came to me, needing my help. And I'm happy to be part of this." He clapped a hand on Everett's shoulder. "I think we can do some good here too."

"Expand the tax base, for sure," Gabriela agreed. Fifty homes on large building lots—the county assessor would be turning handsprings, she added to herself. "That tax revenue might help bring more services to the county." She chose her words carefully. "In the rural areas there's an undercurrent. Meth labs, drugs in general. A couple of fishermen found a .357 Magnum in a marsh not far from here."

"Here?" Billy said.

She glanced at Daniel, noticing his frown. Criminal activity wouldn't be good for business at Thorsen Manor, but anyone who read the newspaper knew about it. "Down the shoreline a mile or so. Police thought the gun might have been tied to a murder in Ohnita Harbor, but it wasn't."

"The police have Gabriela on speed dial for their investigations," Daniel joked.

"I just know the police investigator in Ohnita Harbor. She's a friend," Gabriela said. "And we had some unfortunate incidents at the library a year or so ago."

"Really?" Everett widened his eyes with concern and exchanged a glance with his father-in-law. "I thought this was a nice, quiet area."

"Our library troubles were due to some corruption at City Hall, but we have a new administration now," she said, keeping her tone light. "The murder a couple of months ago is probably an isolated incident." She dropped her voice, unwilling to shrug off Ricky's killing just to make Everett and Billy feel better. "It was one of my students, actually. A young man with a lot of promise who happened to be at the wrong place at the wrong time."

Billy made a low noise in his throat. "That's what happens when people think there's no other way. They get involved in something, thinking they'll do it just once or twice. Make a little money, get out of a hole. They never think they'll get caught—or end up on the wrong side of somebody."

"You give us a little time to get up and running. Then we'll all sit down and discuss what we can do," Everett said. "Create some jobs. Maybe a couple of summer internships. Anything to help the economy."

"That's awfully good of you," Gabriela said. She glanced at Daniel and caught his reassuring smile. "The library can also contribute some resources for research when it comes to grant writing." She thought of Emilie Hernandez and how this would be a wonderful internship for her.

Billy clapped his hands together. "Fantastic. Tell me more about this farmhouse. I want to hear everything."

Daniel explained the scope of the renovations—rebuilding the upstairs, repairing the outer walls downstairs because of years of water damage, and the need to update the plumbing and wiring. Everett interrupted with questions and clarifications, but as far as Gabriela could tell, he was completely onboard with Daniel's plan.

As they talked, Billy seemed captivated by the fireplace, running his hands over the stones, inspecting the mantel, and even leaning down to peer into the cavernous opening and up into the chimney.

"It's my favorite part of the house too," Gabriela said, stepping up beside the older man. "It was the heart of the home and still is."

Billy extended his hands toward the gaping cavity, as if feeling the warmth of a fire. "Won't it be something to see this in use again. A big roaring blaze."

Rumbling down the access road away from Thorsen Manor after lunch, Gabriela replayed her plan to preserve Penelope's papers and Henry's map. She couldn't wait to get started. As she rounded a curve, her tote bag slipped off the front seat and dumped onto the floor of the car. Pulling over just before she reached the county highway that would take her back toward Ohnita Harbor, Gabriela righted the bag and its contents. She picked up her photographic copy of the Traitor's Map.

Unrolling the map she'd studied so many times, Gabriela examined the features near Peninsula Point. Just to the east, a faint line had been drawn from inland to the lakeshore. Most likely a stream, she thought, although a path wouldn't be out of the question. Of course it could also be just one of the many inaccuracies on the Traitor's Map.

She thought of Henry's original map in the back of her car but didn't dare open the box. Instead, she retrieved the photos she'd taken the day it was found. Scrolling through close-ups, she found an image of Peninsula Point, and there, just to the east, was the same marking. This match told her that whatever Henry had drawn had to be significant. Perhaps a hiding place for the Continental Army and its boats, or maybe an encampment used by the British and their loyalists.

She decided to look for it on the off chance that it might still exist. A quarter mile later, she neared an intersection with an unmarked road and pulled to the shoulder. Looking at the map again, she couldn't be sure if this road corresponded with the faint line Henry had drawn nearly 250 years ago, but she couldn't rule it out either.

After she made the turn, broken pavement soon gave way to dirt and gravel. Ruts slowed her down to a crawl, and she wondered how far she should keep going. She looked for a place to turn around, but the narrow track had no shoulders—only grass, weeds, and mud from rains over the past two nights. Gabriela hoped she wouldn't have to back out all the way to the county highway.

Up the next rise, she spotted vehicular tracks cutting into a field to the right. She braked, then backed up for a closer look, thinking it could be a turnoff.

Deep grooves in the rain-soaked ground and clear imprints of tread made the tracks appear fairly recent. Curious, Gabriela cut the engine and got out of the car. She walked in new green grass that poked out of last year's browned hummocks. The sun warmed her shoulders, though a cool lake breeze drifted across her bare forearms.

The tracks widened to two distinct sets. Somebody out four-wheeling most likely, Gabriela told herself, although the tracks looked wide enough to belong to a couple of cars. At the edge of the marsh, one set of tracks seemed to head straight in, while another traced elaborate loops and headed another way. Probably kids, she decided, and started to turn away from the marsh.

Sunlight glinted on something. A taillight, Gabriela realized, and pushed back the cattails to reveal the back end of an old red pickup truck. Rust had eaten holes in the tailgate and burnished the paint. But Gabriela instantly recognized Clawson's old truck.

Her heart raced at the thought of him losing control and driving into the swamp, but her fear eased when she realized that the pickup had not submerged. Clawson, or whoever had been driving, had obviously gotten out and left the pickup behind.

She looked down, examining the sodden earth for footprints that would indicate Clawson had left the truck. The only markings she saw had been made by her own feet.

Two tentative steps brought her to the corner of the tailgate. Pushing back the tall marsh grass, she stepped to the side of the truck and got a clear look through the grimy rear windshield. A man's head lolled against the driver's side window, a dark starburst of blood on the glass.

A scream tore at her throat. Stumbling backward, Gabriela entangled her feet and hit the ground, her tailbone making hard contact. Her purse spilled and out came her phone. Three times she picked it up and dropped it until she finally managed to dial Daniel's number.

Breathing too fast, Gabriela panted out a few details—the road, the ruts, and Clawson dead in his truck. "Come, please."

"Call the police."

"I can't—please." The sky and the trees began to rotate; feeling faint, Gabriela stretched out on the ground, her eyes closed.

Chapter Seventeen

Hearing a vehicle approaching fast, Gabriela slowly sat up. Her stomach lurched, and she breathed through her open mouth to keep from retching. Getting to her feet, she saw Daniel exiting his truck and running toward her, a hat flying off his head. A black SUV followed a few seconds later, but she paid no attention. Her eyes stayed on Daniel as he neared, then enveloped her in a hug.

Her face buried in Daniel's shoulder, she was aware of Everett Brooks and Billy Bulcher but did not break the embrace. She heard Everett say, "Oh, Jesus. Clawson," as he walked past them. Then Billy came closer, his voice nearly in her ear. "She okay?"

"Pretty shaken up," Daniel replied.

Gabriela raised her face and pushed out a long exhale. "It's the last thing I expected."

"State police are on their way," Everett said.

Billy kept asking why she'd come down this road, but Daniel interrupted. "Give her a minute."

Gabriela read the concern on Daniel's face and tried to assure him she was fine.

Her explanation spilled out in stops and starts—the faint line she'd found on both the Traitor's Map and on the original, wanting to see if this road might have been what Henry had drawn. "Then I saw the ruts, and I got curious."

As Daniel held Gabriela, Everett and Billy both examined the truck. They spoke in low voices, their words barely reaching her ears. When they turned, Billy wore a grieved expression, while Everett buried his nose and mouth in the crook of his raised arm.

"He's been there a few days, I'd guess," Billy said. "Must have hit his head pretty hard when he crashed."

Gabriela swallowed hard to keep her lunch down. "There's too much blood for that. I think somebody shot him."

"Clawson? He's just some old fisherman," Everett sputtered. "And it's not like somebody would want to steal that truck."

Gabriela thought of the shots they'd heard on their Sunday excursion to Thorsen Manor and the gun that had been found in the marsh, but the timing didn't match Clawson's death. Still, someone out here had been shooting and not just at targets.

Billy blew out his cheeks. "Makes you wonder what the hell is going on around here." He shook his head. "This kind of publicity is going to be bad for the manor."

The comment struck Gabriela as callous—a man was dead, possibly murdered. Then she thought of the repercussions for Daniel and felt the same fear that Billy had just voiced. It shamed her.

Several minutes later, a state police cruiser thundered along the rutted road and came to a stop. As the state trooper approached, Gabriela recognized him—Trooper Douglas Morrison.

She steeled herself for what he might say—that every time a dead body turned up somewhere in the county, she could be found in the vicinity.

"Start from the beginning," Trooper Morrison instructed.

As Gabriela spoke, Trooper Morrison nodded, as if it made all the sense in the world to follow a Revolutionary War–era map down an unmarked road and find a corpse in a truck.

When she paused, Everett offered the name of the victim. "Lionel Clawson. Local guy, liked to fish along the shoreline behind Thorsen Manor. I'd see him from time to time, so I gave him some odd jobs to do."

"When was the last time you saw him?" Trooper Morrison asked.

"A couple of days ago," Daniel said.

As Trooper Morrison headed toward the pickup in the marsh, Gabriela overheard him on his radio confirming a body inside. "Happened a few days ago from the looks of it. Given the amount of blood inside the truck cab, my guess is he was shot."

The world seemed to spin. While Daniel's arm stayed around her, Gabriela's body and mind separated, as if she hovered over the scene. She let out a soft cry, and her consciousness slammed back into her body. "Take me away from here," she told Daniel. "I just can't take this anymore."

⁘

Daniel drove her car, while Everett Brooks followed in the DRD pickup truck and Billy Bulcher brought up the rear in the black SUV. Her head against the window, Gabriela closed her eyes against a lingering dizziness. Daniel pulled into the garage and helped Gabriela out of the front seat and into her house. He removed her shoes, and she stretched out on the sofa.

Gabriela overheard voices in the kitchen—Billy suggesting they take her to the hospital, and Everett's agreement.

"She'll be okay," Daniel said. "Gabriela's faced a lot worse than this, unfortunately."

Gabriela fingered the scar on her neck from the knife that had nearly taken her life a year ago. That attack had been the first. Then, last fall, she and Agnese had been locked in a shed in the woods at Still Waters Chasm. Whether karma or curiosity, something about her seemed to attract these near-fatal experiences, each one a terrifying echo of the one before.

Gabriela put both feet on the floor and headed to the kitchen, where she offered them all coffee.

Daniel pulled out a chair at the table for her and leaned down to her eye level. "I have to go back. Just for a little while. I left tools all over the place."

Everett put his hand on Daniel's shoulder. "No, stay here with Gabriela. I'll lock everything up."

Billy approached Gabriela. "I know how stubborn an *Italiana* can be. But you need to take care of yourself. A terrible thing happened to you." He touched her cheek with a gesture that recalled her own father, except Billy's hand felt soft and warm, while her father's had been rough from hard work.

"We're going to need your help on the project—you and Daniel both," Billy said. "You get better."

—◆—

Daniel spent the night with his arms wrapped protectively around her. Gabriela heard his breathing slow and felt his muscles relax, but sleep eluded her. Slipping out of his embrace, she went downstairs and sat on the sofa. In the cocoon of her darkened home, she replayed everything that had happened that day, from leaving Thorsen Manor to discovering Clawson's body in the front seat of his pickup, his bloodied head resting against the window. She'd had no reason to turn down that road, yet she'd felt a pull, as if something had drawn her.

She'd experienced it before, especially during her days at Archives and Documents when something about a handwritten note compelled her to compare it to an authenticated document. It came down to some recognizable similarity. Thelma had said the same thing about her not long ago—she saw patterns. Having memorized every feature on the Traitor's Map, she had paid special attention to a road close to Peninsula Point and the Thorsen farmhouse, especially because it was on both the original drawing and the erroneous Traitor's Map. Gabriela could see the logic in what she'd done.

Now the question in her mind was what had led Clawson down that road. Had he been heading to a favorite fishing spot, or did he have a camp nearby? Then, remembering the second set of tire marks, she pondered the possibility of Clawson trying to evade someone pursuing him. Whatever his reasons, Clawson had been heading toward the lake when someone shot him in the head. The similarity to Ricky's death felt far too close to be a coincidence, though Gabriela couldn't see an obvious connection between a college student wanting to borrow a boat and a man driving a pickup truck. Not the victims, she decided; they were too dissimilar. Rather, the commonalities must point to the perpetrator, someone prowling the lakeshore with something to protect or to hide.

Her first thought was for Daniel and the danger he could face just by going to work every day on the Thorsen project. She thought of Billy, a well-dressed older man, and Everett, driving a shiny black SUV; both could look like easy targets if they crossed the wrong person in the wrong place. She needed to warn all of them.

Exhausted from a lack of sleep and nursing her third cup of coffee that morning, Gabriela walked into the library a half hour later than usual. Even though she'd been gone only one day, she marveled at the progress the contractor had made in removing ceiling tiles from the rear half of the main room. Now work had shifted to a different spot, which meant moving more books and shelves.

Gabriela wondered if they should take advantage of the temporary chaos to rethink the library layout. It had always struck her that fiction and nonfiction books should be on either side of the main floor toward the front, nearest the circulation desk. Reference, which received far less traffic than the more popular sections, should be toward the back and condensed. Pleased with the idea, she climbed the stairs to her office to sketch out a plan for Mike and get his input.

In the early afternoon, Delmina tapped on Gabriela's office door and announced someone had come to see her. Before she had a chance to contemplate who it might be, Gabriela saw Trooper Douglas Morrison in full uniform standing behind Delmina.

Delmina stepped back, let the state trooper enter the office, then shut the door as she exited.

Removing his Smokey Bear hat with the wide brim and dimpled crown, he set it on the edge of her desk. "How are you doing?"

"As well as can be expected." Gabriela pointed to the chair opposite her desk for him to sit.

"I wanted to ask you about Lionel Clawson and thought it would be better to do this in person. If that's okay with you."

"Sure, it's fine."

When he asked how well she knew Clawson, Gabriela explained that she had met him twice at Thorsen Manor. "He was helping Daniel on some demolition at the old farmhouse."

Without waiting for the question of why she'd been on the site a few times, Gabriela explained about the stone crest in the wall and its significance. Then, deciding the stone needed context as well, her narrative jumped back to Colonel Jacob Thorsen and his brother, Henry, the spy.

Morrison's eyes widened. "That's a lot to digest. I wasn't expecting a history lesson."

"Well, that's why I was there when Daniel and Clawson took the stone out of the wall." Gabriela paused, waiting for the next question.

"What was your impression of Clawson?"

"Hardworking, rough around the edges," she replied. "He did odd jobs around the Thorsen Manor project for Everett."

That prompted another question from the state trooper about whether Daniel had been expecting Everett and Billy that day, and why Gabriela had brought lunch for all of them. She explained again that she'd made sure to have extra sandwiches just in case Clawson or someone else on the crew was at the house. Trooper Morrison seemed skeptical.

"It's an Italian thing, okay?" she told him. "You don't have food for everybody, it's like an insult."

"Even if you don't know they're coming?" Morrison added.

"Just ask my mother."

Picking up his hat from her desk, the state trooper got to his feet. "Maybe you'll have a sandwich waiting for me the next time I show up. Or at least a cup of coffee."

Gabriela snorted a short laugh. "Now it's my turn to ask a question. The gossip keeps speculating about Ricky Seymour's death. Drug deals, meth labs out in the county, that sort of thing. Ricky was a good kid. I can't imagine him getting involved in something like that. Then Clawson gets murdered the exact same way. Is there a connection here?"

Morrison stood and put his hat on. "Hard to say."

Gabriela got up from her desk to follow him out. "So that's it? You can ask me two dozen questions, but I ask one and you have to leave?"

Morrison wheeled around, and Gabriela stepped back to keep from colliding with him. "No, but you do have a bad habit of getting involved in things, endangering yourself and others. Stay out of this."

"There's nothing for me to stay out of." Gabriela really didn't like the tone or direction of this conversation.

Reaching for a piece of paper on her desk, he wrote two numbers on it. "My contact information—the dispatcher and my cell."

"I have both," Gabriela said, recalling the numbers she'd put in her contacts during the investigation at Still Waters Chasm.

"Good," he said. "If you think of something, contact me. But don't go poking around yourself." He paused. "Please."

The following week, Gabriela decided to close the library for three days to enable the contractor to remove the rest of the ceiling tiles in the front half of the main room and into the foyer. She wore jeans and sneakers to work and pitched in to help Mike and Emilie remove books and rearrange the shelves. By the third day, they could see all of the old plaster ceiling that crowned the main room, its condition far better than they'd hoped. Some replastering would be needed, but no damage or water leaks appeared. The room dimmed considerably with the removal of the old light panels that had been set into the ceiling tiles, but two of the new hanging lights already had been installed near the circulation desk.

Walking around the main floor, Gabriela took in what looked like garlands of laurel encircling the molding. She snapped photos and texted a couple to Daniel. He responded with a one-word answer: *Nice.*

She waited for the dots indicating another text being composed, but the screen remained idle. Scrolling through their exchanges over the last few days, Gabriela saw the increased brevity of the messages. She thumbed a reply quickly: *Take care of yourself—you're working too hard.*

Her finger hovered over Send, but she deleted the text instead. Daniel didn't need the extra pressure.

On Friday Gabriela went out to the community college for the last session of her course. Final projects needed to be turned in electronically by the following Wednesday, but most of the students had already made their submissions. Based on what she'd read thus far, they'd all done an outstanding job. As expected with a large group project, much of the research and discussion was similar. But their short essays on the meaning of authentication had produced several thoughtful reflections about making history relevant through the study of objects.

"I'm going to miss this class," Gabriela told them. "We've been through a lot together, and we've all grown because of it. I hope you'll stay in touch with one another and with me. I want to know what happens to you next."

Every student thanked her on the way out the door. Emilie was the last to leave.

"I'm awfully glad you're working at the library," Gabriela said. "I don't want to lose contact with you."

Emilie shook her head. "No chance of that. Not ever."

As Gabriela left the classroom for the last time that semester, she looked at the empty desks still arranged in a circle and thought of Ricky, who had enlivened so many of their early discussions. Two months had passed since his death, and no one seemed to know what had happened to him.

Gabriela switched off the lights and closed the classroom door.

The weekend did not change Daniel's work schedule, and Gabriela tried to hide her disappointment when he called at five thirty on Saturday to say he needed to stay for a few more hours. She could not remember a Saturday evening apart since they started dating, but did not make an issue of it. When she called him on Sunday morning, she could tell by the background noise that he was at it again.

"You can't keep working like this," she told him.

"We're behind. But if I put in extra hours this weekend, we'll catch up."

"Sure," she said. "I'll talk to you later."

To shake off the disappointment of not seeing each other, Gabriela told herself to get out of the house. Rounding up Ben, she decided to join the rest of Ohnita Harbor in an annual tradition—the reopening of Trudy's, a lakeside takeout on the edge of town.

At eleven o'clock in the morning, Gabriela and Ben took their place at the end of a long line of customers who welcomed Trudy's as a harbinger of summer. A light shower did not deter anyone, and umbrellas sprouted from the parking lot to the outside order window. Nearly an hour later, Gabriela and Ben reached the front of the line, where a red-faced woman scribbled on a pad and yelled to the cooks behind her: "Two dogs—one plain, one with the works. One fries."

Ben insisted on sitting at a picnic table, and Gabriela held an umbrella in one hand and a hotdog in the other. Finally, she gave up. The light shower had diminished to a sprinkle, and she put up the hood of her sweatshirt. When the sun came out, Ben headed for the rocky beach. Gabriela finished the last of the fries they'd shared and joined him. Watching her son skip a flat rock across the water, she remembered Daniel teaching him at Peninsula Point, and the memory saddened her. It seemed such a long time ago.

She took a picture of Ben atop a driftwood log, arms out for balance, and texted it to Daniel. No matter how busy, Daniel would know they had thought of him.

Later in the afternoon she stopped at Agnese's house to pick her up for Sunday-evening dinner. Her mother got in the car with a bowl of potato salad covered in aluminum foil. "Daniel, he likes this," Agnese said.

"Not sure he's coming for dinner tonight, Mama," Gabriela said. "He's working."

"Too much." Agnese frowned. "He can't work in the dark."

"Apparently, he can." Gabriela kept the rest of her thoughts to herself.

Mother and daughter cooked together in Gabriela's small kitchen, making fried chicken, Italian style—rolled in flour, dipped in egg and milk, then coated with breadcrumbs seasoned with oregano, parsley, and a shake of Parmesan cheese. Ben kept popping in, claiming to be starving and asking when it would be ready.

"Soon," Gabriela said the first time; "Almost" the second time. Finally she told him he could set the table, and that made him disappear for a while.

They sat at the kitchen table, just the three of them. When her phone rang, Gabriela sprang out of her chair to grab it, thinking it might be Daniel, but the caller ID read "Potential spam." Sitting back down at the table, she took a mouthful of potato salad but had a hard time swallowing.

As they cleared the table, Agnese began arranging four pieces of chicken on a plate and heaped a small bowl with potato salad. She covered both with foil and pushed them toward Gabriela. "You take this to Daniel."

"I don't think it's a good idea," she told her mother. "If I show up, I'll slow him down."

Agnese slapped her hand against the counter. "This man gonna be your husband. You feed him dinner."

Turning on the tap, Gabriela started to fill the sink. Not having a dishwasher turned out to be fortunate when she needed to keep herself busy. "Times have changed, Mama. Daniel can feed himself."

"I know this. You work. He works. But this is about you making sure he takes care of himself." Agnese reached into the silverware drawer, extracted a fork and a knife, and wrapped both in a couple of paper napkins. "You go. I stay here with Ben."

Gabriela shut off the water and dried her hands. "I should see if he's still at the manor."

"He doesn't call. He don't send a message. Where else is he? Working." Agnese gave her a gentle push.

Taking her jacket from the front closet, Gabriela told Ben she would be back soon. She kissed him on the forehead, gathered up her purse and keys, and took the food her mother had packed in a grocery bag.

In the garage she called Daniel's cell phone. It went to voicemail. The dashboard clock read 7:46. The possibility crossed her mind that Daniel might not be at the jobsite. He could have gone to his own house and fallen asleep. The more she thought about it, the more likely that scenario seemed, but first she needed to check.

She started her car, backed down the driveway, and set off for Thorsen Manor.

Chapter Eighteen

Darkness made the road unfamiliar, and Gabriela turned her headlights on bright, dimming them only when another vehicle approached. Up ahead, a small animal scurried across the road and she braked. Eyes glowed back at her from the opposite shoulder then disappeared into the tall grass.

She passed the turnoff for Peninsula Point and slowed as she approached the access road to Thorsen Manor. Ahead of her, the sky seemed brighter, and Gabriela imagined Daniel working under some kind of floodlight he'd rigged up.

Then she smelled smoke.

Lowering her window, she tried to discern whether the odor came from a campfire, but it intensified the closer she got. Rounding the bend, she saw an orange glow and hit the accelerator.

Flames shot out of the upper story of the house. She threw her car into park, not bothering to turn off the engine, and ran.

"Daniel!" she screamed, her eyes watering and her throat strangled by smoke.

Fumbling for her cell phone, she called 9-1-1. "Hurry," she begged the operator. "Oh, God, he must be inside."

"Stay away from the building," the operator instructed. Gabriela ignored the warning and pulled the neck of her shirt over her nose and mouth as she approached the front steps. Thick smoke drove her back.

"His truck is here. He has to be inside," Gabriela sobbed over the phone. *Move the truck*, she commanded herself. If it caught fire, it would explode.

"Stand back," the operator insisted. "The firefighters are on their way."

The door handle of the truck felt hot to the touch, but Gabriela managed to open it. Daniel's keys dangled from the ignition along with the twin charms he called his talismans—one a thunderbird and the other his name written in Hebrew letters. Sitting at the edge of the seat, she dropped the phone in the cupholder, not listening to whatever the 9-1-1 operator was saying, and started the engine. She backed up, unable to see clearly and not carrying if she hit anything. The headlights illuminated the front of the house, just as the wind shifted enough to lift a curtain of smoke. Lying near the front steps, face down on the ground, was Daniel.

She slammed on the brakes, and her body lurched into the steering wheel. The headlights lit the path to the house, but the smoke forced her eyes to close. Her lungs burned, and every inhalation hurt.

Eyes streaming with tears, she couldn't see Daniel. Her foot hit something solid. Grabbing Daniel's arm, she tried to pull him but couldn't budge his deadweight. Smoke and heat forced her back a few steps, then she rushed toward him again.

Crouched on the ground, she managed to roll him over. He stirred and coughed.

"Get up!" she screamed in his ear.

Daniel rose to his hands and knees, and she pulled him away from the worst of the smoke. He made it about ten feet before collapsing again. Gabriela covered him with her body, hoping to shield him from the smoke. In the distance, she heard the wail of sirens.

Firefighters and paramedics swarmed the yard. They carried Daniel away from the blaze and administered oxygen. Someone wrapped Gabriela in a blanket and handed her a bottle of water. The first sip scorched her throat, but she drank anyway, coughing and sputtering. Paramedics insisted on checking her over, but she refused oxygen.

"Take care of him," she croaked.

A gray uniform appeared in her field of vision, and a woman about her age began asking questions. Gabriela tried to respond, but her body started to shake uncontrollably.

"She's going into shock," she heard the state police officer say.

Paramedics reappeared, and tubing stretched across her face. A cool stream entered her nose, and she began to drift. Fighting against that tide, Gabriela willed herself to stay alert. She grabbed the paramedic's sleeve. "Daniel."

"He's being treated," the paramedic told her. "Right now, we're taking care of you."

She drifted again, and all the lights and sounds faded into the distance.

Someone said her name. Eyes fluttering, she tried to see, but it took too much effort to raise her lids.

"Gabriela," a woman's voice repeated.

Opening her eyes, she saw monitors and a metal pole that held a clear plastic bag. Her hand hurt a little. Raising it, she saw adhesive tape crisscrossed over a needle. She was in the back of an ambulance.

Struggling to sit up, Gabriela looked around for Daniel. Was he riding with her? A strong hand in a blue latex glove pressed her shoulder against the gurney. A strap held her in place.

"You're okay," the woman said.

Wide-eyed, Gabriela stared at her, taking in the EMT uniform, the surgical mask.

"We're taking you to Upstate Medical in Syracuse. You took in some smoke, but there are no burns."

"Daniel?" The sound ripped her raw throat like broken glass.

The paramedic patted her shoulder. "You lie back and rest. We're almost there."

Eyes rolling upward, she stared at the IV bag swinging slightly as the ambulance sped along the highway. It held her attention until she couldn't watch any longer. Her eyes closed.

From her bed in the emergency department, Gabriela peered out through a gap in the curtain to watch a small slice of the frantic world around her. Nurses rushed by. Paramedics pushed a stretcher. Doctors strode past purposefully, reading charts. In no danger and fully revived, she'd been taken off the IV and oxygen. Only a monitor clipped to her finger like an oversized clothespin tethered her to the equipment. Lying there, she could think only of seeing Daniel and going home.

None of the nurses who periodically stopped by would give her an answer to when those two things would happen, nor did the doctor who breezed in for a minute. And so she waited, straining her ears for any mention of Daniel's name and his condition. She suspected he'd been taken deeper into the hospital, most likely ICU. But no one would tell her anything.

The curtain moved, and Gabriela shifted her focus to the face of the nurse approaching her bed. "The doctor would like to keep you overnight for observation."

Gabriela shook her head—it hurt too much to speak. "Home," she whispered and began coughing.

The nurse frowned. "You'll need to discuss that with the doctor. But staying one night, just to be sure, is a good idea."

The nurse examined the screen beside the bed. "Your oximeter reading is better."

Tapping her hand on the bedrail, Gabriela got the nurse's attention. Forcing volume into her voice, she let out a raspy croak. "Daniel? Daniel Red Deer?"

The nurse shook her head. "I'm sorry, honey. I can't say anything."

Gabriela's eyes filled as she pointed to herself. "Fiancée."

A strong hand gripped hers. "I believe you. But without authorization, I can't disclose any information. I can tell you the doctors are taking excellent care of him."

Nodding, Gabriela let the tears fall. Being cared for meant Daniel was still alive. She held onto that fact as she clutched the handful of tissues the nurse gave her.

⸺⸺⸺

At one o'clock in the morning, the emergency department doctor agreed to release Gabriela. Improving oxygen levels and decreasing coughs had tipped the balance toward her going home. That and the fact Gabriela wanted out of the emergency department enough to go against medical orders if necessary.

As she dressed, Gabriela wondered who she could call at this hour to come get her. Pulling back the curtain, Gabriela could not believe who stood at the nurses' station: her mother and Charmaine Odele.

"How?" she began but ended the question when her mother stepped forward to give her a close look.

"*Va bene*," Agnese murmured. "I say two rosaries—one for you, one for Daniel."

Charmaine hugged Gabriela lightly and patted her back. "When Agnese called me, I was only too happy to help."

"The police, they come to your house," Agnese said. "They tell me you are in the hospital. Daniel too. I remember this lady and call her."

As she moved, Gabriela smelled the stench of smoke that clung to the fabric of her clothes, setting off a coughing spell that she tried to tame before the doctor made her stay.

"You take good care of her," a nurse said to Agnese as they passed the ER station.

"Of course," Agnese replied. "I'm her mother."

A thin arm wrapped around Gabriela's waist as Agnese led her toward the exit. Her tiny mother, so frail herself, exuded strength that Gabriela could feel in the marrow of her bones.

"Did they say anything about Daniel?" she asked.

"They wouldn't tell us much," Charmaine told her. "Agnese found out he's in ICU, but that's it. They've called his next of kin."

"Me!" Gabriela squeaked.

Agnese lifted her chin. "His sister."

"His sister?" Gabriela repeated, confused. How could the hospital staff know about this woman Daniel hadn't been in touch with for years?

She needed to go home, get some sleep, and call the state police. They would have more questions for her, and she had some of her own.

"Arson Suspected in Thorsen Manor Fire." The headline pierced her brain. Lying in her own bed, Gabriela tried to read the online article on her phone, but the sentences disintegrated into random words. Closing her eyes, Gabriela pressed her pounding head into the pillows.

It was 8:16 on Monday morning, and she'd been home for six hours.

Across the landing, Ben slept. He'd been up all night, waiting for her to come home. When Charmaine had picked up Agnese to bring her to Upstate Medical, they'd told Ben to keep the door locked and not answer the phone until they returned. Contemplating this now, Gabriela couldn't fathom how scared her son must have been to be left alone. The only other choice would have been to take Ben to the hospital, and she wouldn't have wanted that for him either.

Pushing off the covers, Gabriela stood slowly, testing her legs. She took a few steps toward her dresser, opened the drawers, and pulled out clothes for the day. In the bathroom, she turned on the shower and stepped into the clouds of steam that soothed her lungs as she soaped and scrubbed, trying to remove the lingering smoke smell. Wrapped in a towel, she brushed her teeth and moisturized her face, parsing out each action as a return to calmness and coherence.

Downstairs, Agnese sat at the kitchen table with her coffee and her rosary. "You up so soon?"

Gabriela kissed her mother's soft cheek. "I'm doing okay." Her voice sounded as if she had a mild sore throat. "I'm letting Ben sleep."

A mug of coffee appeared, then a bowl of oatmeal.

Gabriela accepted each offering as an expression of her mother's care and concern—Agnese's love language. Bolstered by the breakfast, Gabriela went into the living room with her cell phone.

The state police dispatcher answered her call to Trooper Doug Morrison and took a message. Ten minutes later, he phoned her.

"I want to know how Daniel is," she began. "The hospital wouldn't tell me."

"This is pretty complicated," Morrison replied.

She paced the tiny living room, believing his hesitancy could only mean one thing: Daniel was in serious condition, clinging to life.

"No," she moaned. "He can't die."

"He won't," Morrison said. "Last night they upgraded his condition from critical to serious."

Gabriela's knees bent, and her body sank into the sofa.

"Listen, this isn't my investigation," Morrison continued. "I've had to recuse myself. I know you and Daniel too well."

"But that's why I called you. You know Daniel and I are a couple. You know the hospital should give me information about him. I want to see him."

"I'll do what I can. They've contacted his sister in New Mexico. She was in his record from years ago as next of kin, along with his late wife," Morrison said. "His sister's name is Rose Red Deer. I'll see if I can get a number for her and ask that she call you."

"I would be so grateful," Gabriela said. "If she could tell the hospital I'm Daniel's fiancée."

"There's more," Morrison interrupted.

Scenarios ran through her mind—Daniel severely injured, maybe permanently disabled. She didn't care. The two of them would get through it together.

"The cause of the fire is arson."

"*Suspected* arson. I saw the news headline," Gabriela retorted. "But the fire must have been an accident—an electrical fire in an old house."

"Gabriela," Morrison began softly. "I don't want to tell you this, but maybe it's better you hear it from me than from someone else. Or, God forbid, you read it in the press."

The room seemed devoid of air, and Gabriela fought to inhale deeply enough. When she did, a cough shook her body.

"Daniel is suspected of setting the fire."

Gabriela scrambled to find mental footing, to land on some fact that would abolish all suspicion of Daniel. "That's impossible."

"He had a heated argument with Everett Brooks a few hours before—in front of several witnesses, including his own crew. Daniel stayed behind, saying he wanted to keep working. Everett told him to leave, but he refused."

"There's only one reason Daniel would keep working—because he loved that old farmhouse. It was his dream job to restore it," Gabriela interjected. "Everett knows that."

Her words spun, faster and faster, describing the day when Everett and his father-in-law, Billy Bulcher, had come to the site, and the four of them had talked about the importance of preserving the Thorsen homestead as a tribute to local history. "Daniel loved that old house as much as they did. They *know* that. If you talk to Everett and Billy, they'll vouch for Daniel's dedication."

She pushed herself to find something else to convince him, relying on her ability to see patterns, even if that meant connecting tangential dots. "Did you ever stop to think of what's been going on around there?"

"You mean Clawson's murder," Morrison replied. "We have witnesses who say he was arguing with someone at a bar just a few hours before he was killed."

"But it does show that there are other people who have—" Gabriela paused. "Bad intentions. And don't forget Ricky Seymour's murder."

When Gabriela took a breath, silence stretched over several seconds that felt like countless minutes.

"There's no connection between the shootings and the fire," Trooper Morrison said. "They found evidence of an accelerant. Daniel was the only one there."

Her body sagged as if all her bones had dissolved. Gabriela held the phone in her hand but away from her ear. She heard her name but did not respond. She had nothing to say to anyone.

Chapter Nineteen

Over the next hour the phone rang several times, and Gabriela scanned the caller ID as she waited for the hospital to call. One was from Delmina, another from Charmaine, and the third from a library trustee. The last call was from the state police. She let them all go to voicemail. She had nothing to say and even less to hear from them. Not their concern, not their pity, and definitely not their questions.

When Ben got up bleary-eyed and grumpy, Gabriela tried to coax him back to bed, but he claimed to be starving. Agnese fussed over the boy's breakfast while Gabriela stayed at her computer in the downstairs home office, scrolling through the news reports on the fire. With each detail panic swelled, catching under her ribs and making her breathing shallow. The more she tried to tell herself that everything would be okay, the harder it became to believe it. Daniel was still in ICU, under police suspicion, unable to get a message to her.

Gabriela twirled the silver and turquoise ring around her finger until the metal felt warm. When Daniel had given it to her, she'd believed in the hopes and promises, the possibility of a good life together. Now it was being taken away from her—from them. The Thorsen project was gone—that was obvious. And maybe so was his business. An arson charge, even if unproven, would damage his reputation beyond any repair.

Slipping the ring from her finger, Gabriela studied the tiny markings in the silver. It was the work of an artisan, Daniel's grandfather, and had been worn every day by the grandmother who'd raised him. This was far more than a placeholder, as Daniel called it—a piece of jewelry to wear until he bought her a ring of her own. It was an heirloom, a tangible piece of his history that he so rarely talked about. Holding the band between her thumb and forefinger, she closed one eye and focused on the satiny finish—a lifetime of minute scratches and scuffs.

She couldn't wait passively for someone to call. She needed to speak with Rose Red Deer.

With the ring back on her hand, Gabriela latched onto this one thing she could do and typed Rose's name into a Google search. A few hits turned up, but none with her contact information. An Albuquerque newsletter listed Rose as a longtime volunteer at a community food pantry. It showed her picture, a face that bore a strong resemblance to Daniel's.

It would be early in Albuquerque, just after eight in the morning, but Gabriela dialed the contact number expecting to reach voicemail. Someone answered.

Gabriela gave her name, explained that she needed to reach Rose Red Deer, and asked if she could have her phone number. The person knew Rose and offered to pass along a message but refused to share her number.

"It's about her brother. I'm his fiancée," Gabriela said. "I need to speak with Rose."

"Is he okay?" the person asked.

"I just need to speak with Rose. She won't know my name. But I beg you, please give her my information. It's urgent."

The person promised, and Gabriela could only hope.

When she entered the kitchen where her mother and son sat quietly, Gabriela felt their eyes on her every movement as she opened a cupboard, retrieved a mug, filled it with coffee, and leaned against the counter.

"What do you hear about Daniel?" Agnese asked.

Gabriela added milk and stirred her coffee, watching a small whirlpool form in the brown liquid. "I left a message for his sister. We'll know more soon."

Tears returned before Gabriela could check them. Turning her head, she wiped them with a napkin. "My eyes are still really sensitive. The smoke, you know."

Agnese clucked her tongue. "You see—everything be okay. Ben, you go play. Your mother needs to rest."

Ben balked, putting his head down on the table. Gabriela reached over and rubbed a slow circle onto his back. "Sure you don't want to go back upstairs and rest a little more?" she asked him quietly. Slowly, he dragged himself to his feet and left the room.

Agnese retrieved the boy's empty cereal bowl and began washing it in the sink. Seeing her mother, immovable as a mountain, Gabriela could no longer avoid sharing what she'd heard. "It's bad, Mama," she whispered. "The police think Daniel set that fire."

"What do you mean, set it?" Agnese said.

Gabriela flapped her hands downward, signaling for her mother to lower her voice. "They think he burned down that house on purpose."

"Bah, impossible." Agnese gripped the back of a chair and slammed it a little as she pulled it out and sat down. "Why would he destroy what he works so hard on?"

Too much talking raked her throat, and Gabriela took a long swallow of coffee, hoping to soothe it. "There was an argument between Daniel and Everett—over money."

"Daniel is a good man," Agnese said. "He never do something like this."

"No, of course not," Gabriela said, but doubts gnawed at her. He'd been so tired and distant, his anger sparking at times, though not at her. She remembered the night he had told her about Thorsen Manor being on the brink of bankruptcy, saying he'd wanted to punch Everett. Had Daniel been pushed to extract revenge, to take away from Everett the one thing he cherished—the family legacy of the old farmhouse?

Her mother's grip cinched her arm. "No, you don't doubt. You know the truth. Somebody else did this."

Gabriela nodded weakly, her resolve crumbling as she recalled what Trooper Morrison had told her. Daniel had been alone at the farmhouse, even his crew said he wouldn't leave.

Images flashed in her mind faster and faster as her thoughts spun out of control. She pictured Daniel dousing the place with kerosene or lighter fluid, then a match and a fireball. That old building would have gone up like a pile of straw. He could have been angry enough to do it—pushed to his limits by fatigue and constant worry over money.

And if he had done it, Daniel would go to jail. He would be ruined, and their life together would be over. Folding her arms on the table, Gabriela buried her face and cried.

Her mother's touch did little to soothe her, but she didn't shrug off the gentle pats on her back or the cooing in Italian like she'd heard as a child. It lulled her into numbness, and Gabriela let exhaustion pull her under like a tide.

"She's here." Her mother's voice snapped Gabriela awake. Raising her head from the kitchen table, she focused on Agnese holding her cell phone.

"Some lady from New Mexico," Agnese said.

Gabriela straightened in her chair, coughed once, and winced at the soreness in the back of her throat. "Hello?" she said, still groggy.

"This is Rose Red Deer. You wanted to reach me?"

"Thank you so much for calling," Gabriela began. "I've been trying to find out about Daniel, but the police won't tell me anything."

"Who *are* you?" Rose asked.

"Gabriela Domenici. I'm Daniel's fiancée."

"Fiancée, huh," Rose said with an edge that Gabriela didn't like, but she ignored it.

"I found Daniel at the fire," Gabriela continued. "They took me to the hospital, but I couldn't see him."

"Assholes," Rose said. "As soon as he comes around, he'll ask for you. As for me, I don't hear from my brother for years, and then I get a call from a hospital saying that he's in serious condition."

"Daniel mentioned you to me," Gabriela said, hoping that would help bridge the gap.

"A mention. That about sums it up." Rose let out a loud sigh. "I guess my brother had put down my name as one of his next of kin when he had an appendicitis attack years ago. Me and Vicki. Apparently the hospital has been trying to reach Vicki. That was the first thing they asked me. How can they get in touch with her? She was treated at that goddamn hospital, and I had to be the one to remind them she died."

Gabriela murmured her commiseration, then pushed for information. "What have they told you? Is he—will Daniel be all right?"

"He took in a lot of smoke. And he's got some bad burns on his leg. They're starting skin grafts."

That information landed like a punch to the gut, and Gabriela grunted. "When?"

"Today, I guess. They needed to stabilize him first. What the hell was he doing at that place?"

"Construction, working day and night," Gabriela said. "It's an old house—really old. He loved restoring it."

"Yeah, and now the cops say he torched it."

Squeezing her eyes closed, Gabriela willed the tears to stop. She couldn't cry anymore. "I can't believe that. I won't believe that."

Rose's laugh rang with irony. "Well, I wouldn't think so either. I hope he didn't do something stupid. My brother comes across as Mister Sensitive—the artist. But he grew up pretty tough. We both did. Got in trouble as a kid. Vicki smoothed out those rough edges."

The first wife, Gabriela thought yet again. Maybe the love of his life.

"I'm coming in for a few days," Rose said. "See what I can do."

"Stay here if you'd like," Gabriela offered. "I know we don't know each other. But it's just my son and me. My mother on occasion."

"That's nice of you, but I want to be near the hospital. If I need to be there longer, I'll stay at Daniel's. I would like to meet, of course. That is, if you're going to stick with him."

The accusation slapped, and Gabriela stiffened. "Yes, of course I am."

"Good. He's going to need help."

One tear escaped, and Gabriela brushed her cheek with the side of her fist. "I'm not going anywhere."

"You should know one thing," Rose went on. "Daniel and I used to be close. Our grandmother raised us after our parents were killed. He tell you that?"

"Yes," Gabriela replied. What the hell did Rose think, that she had met Daniel a week ago? What their relationship lacked in length of time it made up for in depth from all they'd been through together.

"When Daniel went east and I stayed west, we had a falling out," Rose explained. "He kept saying he wanted to reinvent himself." Gabriela heard the judgment in the way Rose said those last two words. "I accused him of abandoning where he'd come from. We still talked once in a while, then Vicki got sick. It consumed him. I reached out, but he had no time for me. I guess I wrote him off. I didn't even know Vicki had died until six months later, when he finally sent me an email. That was our last communication."

"And now this," Gabriela said.

"Yeah. I only hear from him when the shit hits the fan." Rose paused. "I'll do what I can, but I'm not sure my brother will be thrilled to see me."

"I can tell you that *I'll* be glad to have you here," Gabriela said, her voice swelling with emotion. "When the shit hits the fan is exactly when we need each other. You're Daniel's only family. And I'll be there for you too."

The line fell silent.

"I'll book a flight and call you with the details," Rose said after a moment. "In the meantime, I'm going to call the hospital and demand that they let you see Daniel."

After Gabriela thanked her over and over, Rose mumbled a good-bye and the call ended.

Gabriela listened to her voicemails and returned the calls in order. First, she informed Delmina that she would be there the next day. Next she thanked Charmaine for all she had done the night before and assured her that she was feeling better, and then spoke quickly with the library trustee. She left the call she truly dreaded making until last. After a brief hold, Gabriela heard the line click through a series of transfers, then Trooper Doreen Ellwood was on the line.

The state police investigator asked her a series of routine questions, and Gabriela answered them thoroughly: why she had gone to the construction site, what time she had arrived there, and what she had discovered when she arrived.

"You probably saved his life," Trooper Ellwood said. "If Daniel had taken in any more smoke, he might be dead now."

For that at least, Gabriela could be grateful. "Daniel didn't set that fire."

"Who said he did?" the state trooper retorted.

Not wanting to disclose her conversation with Trooper Doug Morrison, Gabriela fumbled for a reply. "Well, ah, the newspaper says arson. So somebody set it. And that wasn't Daniel."

"Why would you think he might?"

Gabriela rang her tongue over her dry, cracked lips. "I don't think that. And you shouldn't either. Because he didn't. Daniel loved that old house. He put countless hours into it. Far beyond anything he was paid for."

"Was he paid?" Trooper Ellwood asked.

"As far as I know. You should ask Everett Brooks. I don't have anything to do with Daniel's business."

"Okay, this has been helpful."

"Wait," Gabriela interjected. "That house goes back to 1770. It was built by a Revolutionary War hero. That history means something to Daniel. He was devoted to restoring it."

"Uh-huh," Ellwood replied. "But in my business, I've found that money means more. And I don't think Daniel got paid. Setting a fire might have been a nice way to make a statement."

"That's not what happened," Gabriela said.

"I'll be back in touch." The state trooper disconnected the call.

Her lungs couldn't take much exertion, but Gabriela pushed her body into motion—down the block, around the corner, through the neighborhood. She wouldn't go far, but she had to get out of the house to clear her thoughts and figure out what to do next. It was only a matter of time, she knew, before the police charged Daniel with arson. She needed to get him a lawyer, someone from out of town. A bigger town.

Mary Jo answered with a cheery hello. "I was just going to call you."

"Oh?" Gabriela wondered if Mary Jo had read the news about the Thorsen Manor fire and connected it with her and Daniel. But if her friend was aware of what had happened, she told herself, she wouldn't sound so upbeat.

"I have a little good news to share," Mary Jo said and launched into what she called a victory over her stubborn husband by convincing Clem to start looking for a house in Binghamton. "I told him I can't stay in this condo five more minutes. It has all the charm of an airport terminal."

"That's great," Gabriela said, though she couldn't make her voice sound convincing. She started walking again, her pace slow.

"What's wrong?" Mary Jo said. "You sound awful, and here I am blabbering about house hunting."

Gabriela approached an intersection of two side streets, about five blocks from her house, and stopped. "Listen, I have something really bad to tell you." She proceeded to explain everything that had transpired in the past eighteen hours.

"Oh, Lord, this is horrible," Mary Jo said. "What can I do?"

"We need a lawyer for Daniel. Somebody experienced."

"Let me call Clem. The pre-law department at Binghamton is pretty good. Somebody there will be able to make a recommendation. I will get back to you as soon as I can. Then we're coming up to help."

A car passed by slowly. Gabriela looked at the driver but didn't recognize the person who stared back at her. Just someone driving down the street. "You've got so much going on."

"Damn it! Don't tell me what I can and can't do. Daniel is in trouble and he's in ICU. If you don't need support now, when the hell will you?"

Her friend's flash of anger shattered her defenses, and Gabriela began to tremble. "If Daniel is charged with arson, his business dies—even if he's not convicted."

"I'm calling Clem now and then I'll get back to you with some information," Mary Jo promised. "As soon as I get some stuff squared away here, I'm coming."

"What about your house hunting?"

"It can wait!" Mary Jo's voice rose shrilly. "And you can be damn sure Clem will be with me."

Gabriela walked another two blocks, telling Mary Jo about the hospital's refusal to give her any information and her conversation with Rose Red Deer. Loosening her pent-up emotions, she gave voice to her fear and anger. Tears brimmed and rolled down her cheeks, and Gabriela didn't bother to hide them. But when she approached a house with a family in the front yard, she turned quickly and headed toward a small neighborhood park. A lone bench on the periphery offered a minimum of privacy and a place to catch her breath.

"I'm so scared of what's going to happen next," Gabriela admitted.

Mary Jo made a soft sound. "I know, and you have reason to be worried. I wish I could say differently, but you might as well face the truth. Daniel is an outsider. People around there see him as someone different."

Mary Jo was right, Gabriela admitted, and that further eroded her hope for reasonable doubt in any investigation or a trial—if it came to that. He would be tried and convicted, in the court of public opinion at least, and perhaps in the legal system as well.

At the end of the afternoon, on a day that seemed two weeks long, a hospital case manager called Gabriela. She introduced herself as Vera and explained that she had spoken with Rose Red Deer. "I have her permission to update you on Daniel's condition."

"Just a second, please." Gabriela opened the back door and left the house, not wanting her mother and Ben to overhear anything. She needed to speak freely, to ask questions without self-censorship, and to demand answers when necessary. "Okay, I'm with you," she said, and listened to an update on Daniel's condition—smoke inhalation, second- and third-degree burns, the first round of skin grafts.

Taking in that information, Gabriela noticed shadows casting a pall across the backyard as the sun lowered toward a horizon of billowing clouds. Rain was predicted, and Gabriela could feel the heaviness of the air. "When can I see him?" she asked Vera.

"He's pretty sedated right now. But probably tomorrow. For a little while."

As Gabriela listened, she walked to the fence behind her garage and surveyed her neighbor's backyard. A sandbox filled with brightly colored toys, a small bicycle with training wheels—the trappings of a much simpler life.

"What time can I see him?" Gabriela insisted.

"Let's speak in the morning," the case manager said.

At the fence line, a dandelion bloomed bright yellow on a long stem. Gabriela reached down to pull up the weed, but it broke off at the root. "I need to know now."

"I understand," the case manager said. "Let's plan on meeting at the visitors' waiting area at eleven. If that changes, I'll let you know."

After their call ended, Gabriela lingered in the backyard among the flowers she had planted—purple pansies, pink and white impatiens, coral-colored geraniums. When she'd put them in the ground just a few days ago, her biggest worry had been Daniel working too hard. Now she faced a nightmare.

Retrieving the hose coiled on a holder on the side of the house, Gabriela unwound it to its full length and sent a spray over the newly planted flowers. She gave them a gentle soak even though rain surely would begin to fall.

Chapter Twenty

Nurses and doctors in scrubs and white jackets, volunteers in street clothes with long lanyards around their necks, and a maintenance crew sporting tool belts paraded down the hallway. Sitting in the visitors' waiting area at the hospital on Tuesday morning, Gabriela watched them all come and go.

A woman wearing a bright blue dress and a kind smile approached. From first glance, Gabriela surmised this was Vera, the case manager, and stood to greet her.

"How's Daniel?" Gabriela asked.

"Better," Vera said. "You'll see him soon. But first, there are a few things I want to discuss with you."

As they walked down the main corridor of the hospital, Vera asked about how long her drive had taken that morning, whether traffic had been light or heavy, and whether she was from the area. Gabriela answered in a friendly tone while fighting against the rush of questions she wanted to ask about Daniel.

When they stopped at the hospital coffee shop, Gabriela wondered why. "We're not meeting here, are we?"

"Heavens, no. But if you want coffee, get it here. The stuff in our office is abysmal."

Gabriela allowed herself to relax a little at Vera's good-natured approach. She ordered a latte and Vera did the same. With their to-go cups in hand, the two women continued on to Vera's office. Unlike the muted tones of the waiting rooms, here photographs and a framed poster splashed bright colors on pale walls. A stuffed frog sat on the corner of the desk, its back emerald green and its stomach sunshine yellow.

"I spoke with Daniel a little while ago," Vera said. "He's still sedated. But when I asked him for permission to let you see him, he nodded."

A nod—that was all he could manage? Gabriela knotted her clenched hands. "He can't speak?"

"Not easily. He's on some pretty heavy pain medications. They needed to do a bronchoscopy—a scope into the lungs. That, plus the grafts. He's in considerable pain."

"But he's going to be okay," Gabriela said.

"As of this morning, the doctors said he's in stable condition. That's a big improvement from critical," Vera said. "He'll probably be moved out of ICU and into a regular room in a day or two."

"How long will he be here?" she asked.

Vera shook her head. "Not sure at this point. They need to monitor the graft sites for infection, so it could be up to ten days."

Gabriela's mind whirled with competing thoughts—his health, the police investigation, his business. Until this moment, she hadn't given a thought to DRD Roofing. Perhaps she should reach out to Ernie, the foreman she'd met several times. How could she make sure the guys got paid? Would there even be any business after the current jobs were completed?

Pulling herself out of the mental morass, she saw Vera looking at her with a gentle expression. "One day at a time," said the case manager. "Now, before you see Daniel, you need to set your expectations for a brief visit. He'll know you're there but may not say much to you."

"I just want to see him. It's been two days."

"I understand." Vera got up from her desk. "Let's go then."

Light from the quiet hallway seeped into the doorway of a darkened room in the ICU. Soft, periodic beeps punctuated the quiet hum of machines. Gabriela paused at the threshold, knowing that once she saw Daniel like this, she could never erase it from her memory. Pushing her right foot forward, she stepped inside.

Eyes closed, lips slightly parted, Daniel breathed on his own. Wires sprouted out of the loose hospital gown he wore. An IV dripped into his body, and a catheter tube drained away from it. He seemed so fragile, Gabriela feared touching him. Extending her hand, she rested it on the cap of his shoulder and felt bone through muscle. His body radiated warmth, and his chest rose and fell. These ordinary signs of life suddenly seemed miraculous, and her eyes flooded and spilled.

"Daniel," she said, her voice low but firm. "It's Gabriela."

Steady breathing continued. He showed no sign of recognition. She touched his face, his hair. "I'm here, and I'm not going anywhere. I spoke with Rose. She's coming in a couple of days."

She caressed his arm. "You don't have to worry about anything. We're going to get through this. All you have to do is get better."

Cradling his fingertips in her palm, she told him how Mary Jo and Clem wanted to help, how Agnese said a rosary for him every morning and evening. "Everybody is there for you," she assured him. "Especially me."

Vera appeared at the doorway. Gabriela bent down and kissed Daniel's forehead and then his lips, which felt dry and papery.

In the hallway, Vera introduced her to a nurse who gave Gabriela a brief update and the plan for the next few days—weaning Daniel off the pain medications, transferring him out of ICU, getting him up and around.

"Here's the number," the nurse said, handing Gabriela a piece of paper. "If you want to check on his condition, just give us a call."

Gabriela studied the note as if it held more than just a phone number. "Have the police been here?" she asked.

The nurse and the case manager exchanged a glance. Vera spoke first. "Yes, I'm told that they have. Daniel is mostly unresponsive of course."

As Daniel became more alert, the police would be back, Gabriela knew, asking more questions, making accusations. She needed to get an attorney involved before that happened.

Leaving the ICU, they returned to Vera's office, where they discussed a plan for Daniel's eventual discharge.

"Daniel will stay with me. I have a guest room and a bathroom on the first floor, so he won't have to climb stairs," she said. "I can work from home part of the time. I have people who can help too." She pulled her mouth into a lopsided grin. "My Italian mother would love to fuss over him."

Vera nodded. "This all sounds good. We'll see what the doctor says as Daniel gets closer to discharge—whether he has to go to rehabilitation for therapy or if that can be done outpatient. A physical therapist might even be able to come to your home. We'll see what Daniel's insurance covers."

Although she wanted to stay, Gabriela knew it was time to leave. She needed to go to the library, then would work from home that evening. "I will be here every day," she told Vera. "As soon as Daniel is more alert, call me." Hearing how her anxiety sharpened her tone,

Gabriela dipped her chin and paused. "Please," she added. "I would be so grateful."

Standing by the circulation desk that afternoon, Gabriela dropped her purse and tote bag on the floor as she surveyed the room. Wiring disgorged from the library ceiling, and hardware scattered across tables shrouded in plastic. "It looks like a war zone in here."

"Darkest before the dawn," Francine said as she scanned a bar code on the back of a returned book.

Gabriela pivoted. "Where's the contractor? Are they leaving it like this?"

"Everything's fine." Delmina's voice drifted down from the second floor as she descended the stairs. "They needed some kind of bracket for the fixtures. They're coming back tomorrow morning."

"It's a hazard. Junk all over the place." Gabriela fisted her hands in her hair. "Somebody's kid falls in here, and we'll be sued."

"Okay, chief." Pearl's voice gave her a start. "Lemme show you what we've done."

Pearl led her over to a table by the front door, which Gabriela hadn't even noticed when she'd entered the library. Covering the table were books from the children's collection. Three or four small volumes for young readers were bound with rubber bands and labeled "Take-home bundles." Chapter books for more advanced readers were grouped singly or in pairs. "Grab and go—just like at the take-out restaurants," Pearl said.

Picking up one of the bundles, Gabriela examined three softcovers then set it back down with the others. "This is a great idea."

"Folks can call ahead for books too." Pearl nodded toward the stacks out of place and pushed together. "Of course finding them is sometimes entertaining, to say the least."

Gabriela shook her head. "I'm sorry. I shouldn't have left you with all this."

Pearl jabbed the air with her finger, almost to Gabriela's nose. "Hey, I'm the first to complain around here, so you know what I'm saying is the truth. Everybody is pitching in. Emilie is worth her weight in gold. When she's not working with Mike, she's helping us."

In her peripheral vision, Gabriela noticed Emilie hovering, as if unsure whether to intrude on their conversation. She waved her over. "Tell me what you're up to."

Emilie explained the reconfiguration of the bookshelves as the contractor moved the scaffolding and ladders around the room. "But we haven't mixed anything up too badly," she said. "No encyclopedias in Fiction and stuff like that."

"Thank you for doing all this work," Gabriela said. "I'm sorry I haven't been around these last few days."

Emilie sobered. "How is Daniel? I've been afraid to ask."

"Getting better," she said, but offered no further details.

"Do you think?" Emilie held her bottom lip between her teeth. "No, it's stupid."

She suspected Emilie had an idea for the library. "Why don't you just tell me what's on your mind?"

"Do you think the Traitor's Map could be cursed or something?"

The question took her aback. "I don't really put stock in such things," Gabriela said. But she had to admit that an inordinate number of tragic events had occurred since the day they first saw the map at the museum: Ricky's murder, then Clawson's, the farmhouse fire, Daniel's hospitalization—and his arrest that could come any day now.

"I've spent most of my career around old and sometimes rare artifacts," Gabriela continued. "A lot of them have a tragic backstory.

I can remember coming across a letter sent from a mother to her daughter, begging her not to make a sea voyage. The letter did not reach the young woman and so she left." Gabriela paused for effect. "On the *Titanic*."

Emilie winced. "That's so sad."

"It's the people—their actions and intentions. That's what makes things happen. Ricky went looking for a boat because of the map, and somehow that led to his death. But the map itself didn't cause it."

Emilie lifted one shoulder in a half shrug. "Yeah, I knew that. Crazy thought."

"No, not crazy. You're trying to make sense out of a friend's senseless death."

"Thanks," Emilie said. "I'm glad you're here today."

Gabriela watched the young woman turn and make her way back into the hodgepodge of shelves and books stacked on every available flat surface in the main room of the library.

Pearl came around the corner. "Tried not to listen, but I have to say, I like what you said to her."

Gabriela kept her eyes on Emilie, who filled her arms with books to carry across the room. "It's hard to know what to say at a time like this."

"Well, how about you try to say this next. You can repeat after me: 'See you tomorrow, folks. I'm going home now.'"

"Pearl, I've been gone too many days already," Gabriela said.

"She has twenty-three days of vacation." Delmina stood off to the side. "Didn't even take all her days last year."

Gabriela protested the unfairness of leaving them with the construction and keeping the library open.

"Oh, right, because you're going to be home watching soap operas and giving yourself a facial." Pearl grimaced. "Daniel is in ICU, and you look like you're about to fall over."

Pearl took one arm and Delmina the other. Francine swept in from the circulation desk, holding Gabriela's purse and tote bag.

Together, the three women steered Gabriela out of the library and walked her to the car.

"I'll be working from home. Just send me my messages," Gabriela said.

Delmina raised one eyebrow. "Anything I can't handle I'll send to you. But there isn't much I can't take care of."

Sitting at her desk at home, Gabriela performed email triage, as she thought of it—answering the most urgent, acknowledging the updates, and deleting what did not require a reply.

At four thirty Ben came home from school on his bicycle, sweaty and grass-stained from playing at the park. He tracked mud in the back door, across the kitchen, and through the living room—a trail Gabriela decided to ignore as soon as she saw the worried look on his face.

"You see Daniel today?" he asked.

Gabriela closed the browser on her computer. "Yes, I did. He sleeps a lot, but he's doing better. He's going to stay in the hospital a little while longer, and then he'll be here for a few weeks as he gets stronger."

Ben leaned against her, and Gabriela drew him into a one-armed hug. "Is he going to be different?" the boy asked.

Reading her son's face, Gabriela tried to discern his question. Was Ben concerned about how Daniel would look, how he would act—or both?

"We know he got hurt in the fire, but he's healing," she told Ben. "He might have a little trouble walking because of that. But he's still Daniel."

Launching himself toward her, Ben tightened his arms into an embrace. Shoulders shaking, he cried.

Chapter Twenty-One

A caller ID with a 505 area code appeared on Gabriela's phone early on Wednesday morning. New Mexico, Gabriela registered, and answered quickly.

"Hello?" Gabriela said into the static that bristled on the line. "Rose?"

"Can you hear me?" Rose replied. "I'm driving to the airport. Be in around six this evening. You see Daniel yet?"

Gabriela winced at the realization that she hadn't called Rose as she'd promised to do. "Yes, yesterday. I was going to call you this morning. Last night was very emotional for me."

"So how is he?"

She repeated what the case manager and the nurses had told her—heavy sedation now, then weaning Daniel off the pain medications. As soon as that happened, he'd be out of ICU and receiving physical therapy.

"Gotta get him the hell out of there as soon as we can. Daniel hates hospitals; I'm no fan either," Rose said.

"He'll be staying here, at my house. Unless he goes to rehab first," Gabriela explained. "I'm afraid they're going to charge him with arson."

"Count on it!" Rose barked into the phone. "Have the cops spoken to him yet?"

"They stopped by, but Daniel was in no shape for questioning," Gabriela said. "Once he's more alert, though, they'll be back."

Rose swore and muttered something inaudible. "He needs a lawyer who will be there when the police question him. If Daniel's not fully alert, he could accidentally say something he'll regret later."

Gabriela related her efforts to hire a lawyer from outside Ohnita County. "I've asked good friends at Binghamton University for their recommendation."

Road noise echoed on the line for several seconds. "Okay. Keep me informed. I'll call you when I get in."

"If it's six, I might be at the hospital already," Gabriela said.

The call ended without Rose saying goodbye.

By midmorning Gabriela had received a text from Mary Jo with the name and phone number of an attorney in Utica who had been recommended by one of Clem's colleagues at the university. Gabriela left a detailed message with the law office, asking to hear back as soon as possible. Now she had to wait, Gabriela told herself.

With hours to go before she made the trek back to Upstate Medical to see Daniel in the early evening, Gabriela settled in to work from home. First she wrote an email to the staff, thanking them for their concern and alerting them that she would be mostly working remotely for the next several days but would be reachable by phone, text, or email. To prove that point, she promised updates on several projects and proposals by the end of the day.

Keeping that commitment busied her until lunchtime. While eating a sandwich at her kitchen counter, Gabriela grabbed her cell phone on the second ring.

"This is Gordon Laxalt," the man on the phone told her in a clear, firm voice. "I'm an attorney with Emory, Arnold and Laxalt. I received your message from earlier today."

She thanked him for calling and gave him an update on the fire at Thorsen Manor, the police investigation as best she understood it, and Daniel's current condition. The attorney listened then asked a few questions, including whether Daniel had given any statements to the police.

"I highly doubt it. He couldn't speak at all when I found him, and he's been in ICU. But as soon as Daniel is alert, the police will be there."

"You are exactly correct in that assumption," he told her.

"I can assure you, Mr. Laxalt, Daniel did not set that fire. He's a well-respected contractor, and he loved working on that old farmhouse. Yes, payment has been a problem, but there is a new investor in the property."

"Of course you would think that," he replied. "And it's good to know where you stand on things. If this goes to trial, you will no doubt have to testify as the one who discovered Daniel and reported the fire."

Gabriela hadn't considered that possibility. "I'm hoping this doesn't go to trial."

"You need to be prepared for that eventuality. Unless the investigation takes the police in an entirely different direction, they will most likely seek charges against Daniel. If they do, he will either accept a plea bargain or there will be a trial."

The attorney's certainty banished her hopes that the police would realize Daniel could not possibly have set the fire. Gabriela didn't care about what the investigators saw as motive or opportunity, Daniel would never destroy that property, she knew. No matter how angry he might have been or how much he wanted to get back at Everett, he would never have done it.

"Trials are expensive," Laxalt continued. "Since you've been recommended by a close contact of mine, I'm willing to do what I can to help. But I require a retainer of five thousand dollars up front."

Gabriela groaned. Neither she nor Daniel had that kind of money. She could probably get a home equity line of credit, but it would take a few days. "Could I pay you a little now and more over time? It will take me a few days to scrape together the funds."

"Let me know when you can get the five thousand. Perhaps another family member can help. Whatever he does, Daniel should not speak to the police without counsel present, even if it's a public defender for now."

A swallow left a stone in her throat. "We'll do what we can. I'll be back in touch."

Five thousand dollars. How quickly would the attorney go through that retainer? She googled how much a defense trial costs and saw estimates in the tens of thousands—and much higher for cases that dragged on. She would find the money—there was no other choice.

Early that afternoon, Gabriela took a short walk around her neighborhood for exercise and then went upstairs to shower and change into a bright print dress. She took time with her appearance, not only for Daniel but also to make a positive first impression on Rose.

At four o'clock she picked up her mother, and both women waited at Gabriela's house for Ben to come home from school and playing at the park. Agnese set to work in the kitchen, and Gabriela let her, knowing her mother needed to stay busy. As soon as Ben rode his bicycle down the driveway, Gabriela fixed him a snack of apple slices with peanut butter.

Glancing at the clock, Gabriela chided herself that by waiting, she would run into rush-hour traffic in Syracuse, but it couldn't be helped. She wanted to see Ben before leaving for the hospital. Sitting down at the kitchen table while he ate his snack, she asked him about school and received perfunctory grunts and one-word answers that told her everything was fine.

"You're going now?" he asked.

"Yes. Daniel's sister is coming from New Mexico. She'll meet me at the hospital."

"Is she nice?" Ben asked.

"I think so. We only talked on the telephone. But she's coming all this way to help Daniel, so that's nice." She gave Ben a reassuring smile.

"Okay," Agnese announced from the sink. "You go to the hospital. Ben's gonna do homework. I say my rosary. Everybody's got a job to do."

Soon after getting on the interstate toward Syracuse, a call from Mary Jo came in through her car's Bluetooth connection and Gabriela answered. She updated her friend on Rose Red Deer's pending arrival and her conversation with the attorney. Her mind returned to the fear that had plucked at her nerves all day—the attorney's certainty that there would be a trial.

"He wouldn't even consider that the police might change their mind or find another suspect," she told Mary Jo.

"He's preparing you for the worst, which is good," Mary Jo said. "But that doesn't mean we change our minds about the outcome. Daniel is innocent. The fire must have been accidental."

"But the accelerant," Gabriela moaned.

"What—paint thinner? Some kind of solvent? There are probably a dozen things on a construction site that can catch fire," Mary Jo argued. "And it's all circumstantial."

Traffic on the highway congested and slowed. Other drivers changed lanes and jockeyed for position. "I better keep my mind on the road," Gabriela told Mary Jo. "I'll text you from the hospital."

"You tell Daniel we love him, and we're coming to see him soon." Mary Jo's voice broke with emotion. "I had a nephew accused of a crime he didn't commit. We got him a damn good attorney, and he was acquitted. We'll do the same for Daniel."

Her friend's conviction worked like a shot of adrenaline, girding her for the fight. They would do what it took to hire Gordon Laxalt.

⚬———◇———⚬

The open sides of the parking garage let in a light breeze that smelled of city grime and exhaust, triggering a memory of when Gabriela had taken Agnese to the same hospital for cancer consultations and then pneumonia treatment. She never expected to be in this place for Daniel.

Her phone pinged with a text from Mary Jo, saying she and Clem would give her a thousand dollars toward the attorney's fee. They'd send her the funds electronically the next day. Fingers shaking a little with a wave of emotion, Gabriela misspelled her reply, fixed the typos, and added a string of hearts.

After checking in at the visitors' desk and getting a badge, Gabriela rode the elevator to the ICU. Two nurses in dark blue uniforms stood at the station near Daniel's room.

"He's much more alert now," said one of the nurses. "He's got a little discomfort at the grafting sites, but no infection. We told him you were coming, and he's excited to see you."

Gabriela took a centering breath and tapped on the door. "Anybody home?"

Daniel's eyes fluttered open. "Hey," he said.

That was all she needed to propel her to his bedside. She longed to wrap her arms around him, but worried about causing him any pain. Instead, she took his hand without the IV in it. When she leaned down to kiss him, his mouth felt warm and not quite so dry this time. Her eyes searched his face. "How are you?"

"Better," he said. "It doesn't hurt to breathe. My leg is sore. They grafted skin off my butt and upper thigh to fix my calf. No more shorts for me." The corners of his mouth rounded slowly upward.

"Scars are sexy. Didn't anybody tell you that?" She kissed him again. "You got another visitor coming, by the way. Rose will be here this evening."

Daniel looked confused for a second. "My sister?"

"Hospital called her. You had her down as a contact when you had appendicitis. She and I have talked a couple of times."

"Rose is coming," he repeated.

Gabriela nodded. "Pretty soon. I had to turn my phone off, but I suspect we'll see her before seven."

Daniel shifted in the bed and gritted his teeth with a wince of pain. "I'm surprised."

Gabriela laid her hand on his shoulder, massaging the muscle lightly. "I'm not. She said you two had a falling out but that she always gets a call when the shit hits the fan."

A light laugh turned into a cough. Gabriela held a plastic cup with a straw for Daniel to sip some ice water. "That's Rose," he said finally.

When the nurse came to change Daniel's IV bag, Gabriela left the room. Visits were meant to be short in ICU, so she went downstairs to wait for Rose. In the lobby, she turned her phone back on and scrolled through messages and texts—two more with encouragement from Mary Jo and one from Rose, saying her plane had landed a half hour late.

Gabriela sat facing the front entrance, looking up every time the automatic doors swept open. At ten after seven, a tall woman with short dark hair, wearing jeans and a black T-shirt with a spiral design on the front, whisked through the door.

Gabriela stood. "Rose?"

Dark eyes gave her a once-over, sizing her up. Then Rose extended a firm handshake. A silver cuff bracelet set with turquoise and what looked like tiger's eye reflected the overhead light. "How is he?" Rose asked.

"Better. Much more responsive. He says he doesn't have as much pain. The nurse was in with him, so I came downstairs for a little while."

"I flew across the country. I'm sure as hell seeing my brother whether the nurse is in the room or not," Rose huffed.

Gabriela led the way to the elevator. "The nurses know you're coming."

The elevator opened, and two other people also got on. Rose angled her head down and whispered. "You talk to the attorney?"

"He'll represent him. I need to come up with the retainer."

The elevator stopped and the others got off.

"How much?" Rose asked, as they continued to the next floor.

"Five thousand for the retainer. A trial will cost a lot more. Friends are giving me a thousand. I'm going to see about a home equity line of credit."

Rose blew out her cheeks. "I can help some. What a mess this is."

The doors opened and they stepped out into the hallway. "I'm so glad you're here," Gabriela said. "Daniel was surprised, but really happy."

"You told him?" Rose stopped in the hallway.

"Yes, of course. I wanted to give him the good news that he'd see you tonight." Gabriela couldn't imagine Rose being offended that she'd given Daniel time to prepare.

"There goes my plan to jump in the door and yell surprise." Rose sighed loudly then laughed. "I'm joking."

Gabriela broke into a wide grin. "We're going to get along, you and me."

"Don't count on it. I don't get along with anybody."

"Now I like you even more."

Standing at the nurse's desk, Gabriela urged Rose to go in and see Daniel by herself. After so many years apart, the siblings deserved privacy for their reunion. She heard Rose's greeting, "Hello, brother," then a hoarse sound that she thought was Daniel's laugh. Their voices lowered, and Gabriela made out only every third word.

"Why don't you go back in?" the nurse said to her. "Just don't let him get tired."

"Can we stay another half hour?" Gabriela asked.

"Twenty minutes," the nurse said. "It's getting late."

Rose had pulled a chair close to Daniel's bed. Seeing how she held his hand, Gabriela felt yet another rush of tears as she stood on the other side of the room, watching both of them. Daniel shifted and patted the edge of his bed for Gabriela, and she sat down.

"Fast version—how'd you two meet?" Rose asked.

"Big storm. Chunk of tree hits my house. He's the roofer. A bunch of crazy stuff happens that will take too long to explain." Gabriela said it all in one breath.

"You know, crazy stuff," Daniel interjected. "Like someone trying to murder her at the library."

Rose's eyes widened. "Yeah—you're kidding."

Gabriela pointed to a scar on her neck. "Nope, unfortunately. After all that, we started dating."

"Librarian, huh?" Rose tossed a chin in her direction. "You're more exciting than I thought."

Daniel shook his head against the pillow. "You have no idea. The police basically have Gabriela on speed dial."

"For my sleuthing, not because I'm a—" She stopped herself before saying *suspect*. "Pain in the neck."

Rose nodded and smiled a little. "Yeah."

It seemed to be Rose's favorite word, Gabriela noticed.

"Police come to see you yet?" Rose asked.

"They called. Coming tomorrow," Daniel replied.

Gabriela crossed her arms as if suddenly chilled. "Don't tell them anything without an attorney present. I spoke to Gordon Laxalt—he's an attorney from a firm in Utica. Clem helped me find him. He'll represent you as soon as I get the retainer together."

"No," Daniel said. "I didn't do it. They're not going to charge me."

Rose stood up. "Are you flippin' kidding me? You don't remember anything from when we grew up. The police just looked at Dad and suspected something."

Daniel let out a long exhale. "He was a labor organizer. Strikes. Protests. Getting arrested was part of his job."

"You ever think that the bus accident was rigged?" Rose spat out.

"Not that again. We were little kids; I barely remember it."

Rose flung one long leg over the other. "Well, I don't remember either, but I read a lot."

A tap on the door brought the nurse in. "I'm sorry, but Daniel really needs his rest."

"Two minutes," Rose called back without looking in the nurse's direction.

Gabriela leaned down and kissed Daniel. She pressed her forehead against his. "I love you. Just focus on getting better."

Rose got up slowly. "Okay, see you tomorrow."

Daniel reached for his sister's hand again. "I'm so glad you're here."

"Well, you did go to all this trouble to get my attention." Rose bent down and kissed his cheek. "We're going to fight like hell. Don't forget that."

Leaving the room, Gabriela looked back, but Daniel had shut his eyes.

Gabriela and Rose walked silently down the hall, onto the elevator, and into the lobby.

"Do you want to get something to eat?" Gabriela finally asked.

Rose shook her head. "No, I'm good. I grabbed something at the airport. I'll be back here in the morning."

"Okay. I work during the day, so I'll come up in the evening," Gabriela told her. "But I would like to see you. Maybe have dinner tomorrow?"

"Hardly a social time," Rose replied, and it stung.

"That's not what I meant," Gabriela said tersely.

"Sorry, I don't mean to be such a bitch." Rose exhaled a loud sigh. "I just keep thinking Daniel is going to be all nice with the cops, and they're going to screw him over."

Gabriela raised a finger. "But they *do* know him."

"Look, you don't get this," Rose shot back. "The laws that protect you blame us."

Heat flooded Gabriela's face. Rose was right; she had no idea other than what she read—how the Thanksgiving stories she'd learned as a child of happy Pilgrims and friendly Indians had cloaked uglier truths of lands stolen from sovereign peoples and diseases used as weapons. Daniel was part Native American, but he never talked much about what that identity meant to him. Afraid of saying the wrong thing, she hadn't asked him either. To be his life partner, she would have to change their dialogue.

"Everything you say is true. I know that," Gabriela told Rose. "But the state police around here do know him." She briefly explained how they had discovered two bodies while hiking the previous autumn and became involved in an investigation of a double murder.

Rose grunted a little. "Don't count on that helping Daniel now." She shook the keys to her rental car. "You're wearing our grandmother's ring."

Gabriela stiffened. "Daniel gave it to me."

The way Rose stared at her hand Gabriela wondered if Rose was going to ask for the ring.

"My hotel is not far from here. There's gotta be a bar there. We're having a drink and then you're telling me all this—starting with why someone tries to murder a librarian."

Chapter Twenty-Two

Dusk had turned the sky a grayish blue, and Gabriela squinted as she entered the too-bright hotel lobby. Beside her, Rose pointed in the direction of a ground-floor restaurant. The interior plunged them into near darkness, interrupted by the glow from two flat-screen televisions along the far wall.

Gabriela led the way to the furthest high-top table in the rear, wanting a sound buffer from the patrons talking loudly at the bar. With her long legs, Rose slid easily into her place, while Gabriela had to grip the table as she climbed onto the stool.

When the waiter appeared, Rose ordered a margarita. Gabriela asked for a Diet Coke.

"Tell me about this knife business," Rose said without preamble.

Gabriela related the story of interrupting the attempted theft of a medieval cross donated anonymously to the Ohnita Harbor Public Library. The thief had been the library board president at the time, and he had given her two choices: Jump off the library tower in what would look like a suicide or get her throat slit.

"I decided to take my chances on the tower, hoping I could get away from him. I did—obviously," Gabriela said, but she avoided any further details.

Rose narrowed her eyes. "You're tougher than you look."

"Thanks—I guess." Gabriela paused when the waitress brought their drinks and a shallow bowl of popcorn. "I know Daniel can refuse to answer any questions from the police without his lawyer present. But will that make him look guilty?"

Rose nibbled a little of the popcorn. "Daniel wants to clear his name. But he's got to remember how this game works. He's got a record."

Gabriela felt as if a bomb had gone off inside her head. "A police record?"

Rose waved her hand in dismissal. "Thirty years ago. He ended up on probation. But it could have gone the other way for him."

Crossing her arms on the table, Gabriela leaned forward. "What happened?"

"Assault." Rose looked at her over the salted rim of her margarita glass. "And, yes, I know how bad that sounds. But there's a story."

As Rose recounted an episode from three decades ago, Gabriela pictured Daniel and Rose, two years apart, orphaned at a young age and living with their paternal grandmother in the Southwest. By the time Daniel became a teenager, the sadness of that early loss had become bitterness, then anger.

"Big chip on his shoulder, just waiting for the next person to knock it off," Rose said. "Then he ran across someone who said the wrong thing, and Daniel beat him up. Gave the guy a concussion."

Gabriela found it hard to imagine Daniel being physically violent with someone and told Rose that. She received a rueful smile in return.

"Let's just say he was provoked," Rose said. "Someone made racial slurs against our family—and me in particular." She shook her head as if hearing the echo of those hateful words. "Fortunately, there was a witness, a high school teacher, who told the police what happened. That's how Daniel got off with only probation. That and the fact that he'd been accepted to college. He was lucky, and he knew it."

Gabriela ran her fingers along her sweating glass, turning beads of moisture into a river like tears. "He never told me."

Rose took a sip of her margarita. "I would have been surprised if he had. Daniel put his past behind him, including me."

Feeling the hurt in those words, Gabriela reached for Rose's hand. Rose didn't move, and Gabriela withdrew.

"I know what it feels like to be left behind," Gabriela said. "My father died, and my husband divorced me and moved to the West Coast to be with someone else. My world crumbled after that." She related leaving her dream job in New York City and her apartment in Brooklyn and moving back to Ohnita Harbor in what felt like retreat and defeat. "Now I'm at peace with it, but some days it's still hard."

Rose studied her across the table. "I imagine it's hard most days."

A couple entered the premises, laughing loudly. Gabriela raised her eyes, more distracted than curious. In the dim light the woman's shoulder-length blonde hair looked almost white. The man beside her wore a leather jacket over jeans. As they greeted another couple seated at the bar, Gabriela wondered how it would feel to be so carefree, as if life were one big party.

She backed away from the edge of that pit of self-pity and returned her gaze to Rose. "I have meaningful work here. Our library goes back more than a century and a half. Free access to all and promotion of literacy. Those goals are as important today as they were in the nineteenth century."

She told Rose about her outreach programs in the rural areas of the county, particularly communities where libraries had to shut down because of lack of funding. "Libraries are for everyone. I can't think of one other institution that can say that. Not churches, not even schools."

Rose's grin softened the angles of her face. Reaching across the table, she gripped Gabriela's hand and squeezed her fingers hard. "Yeah, I get you now," she said. "You're an advocate and an ally. You and me, we're going to do just fine."

Gabriela sat up in bed on Friday morning, head throbbing from exhaustion. She and Rose had talked until after eleven. The long drive home, stoked by two Diet Cokes, had made sleep almost impossible. She didn't know how she would manage to get through this day.

Same way you get through all the other days, she told herself. Kicking off the covers, Gabriela planted her feet on the floor, put on her bathrobe, and went downstairs.

Agnese, who had spent the night, sat at the kitchen table, the coffeepot gurgling behind her on the counter. Taking a seat beside her mother, Gabriela related her conversation with Rose, emphasizing what a strong and loyal sister she seemed to be.

"Remember? I tell Daniel it's no good for family to be apart." Agnese seemed pleased with herself.

Her mother's comment triggered a recollection of how Agnese and Cecelia had to leave Italy, even though that meant never seeing their mother again. The sisters remained close, but they were cut off from the rest of their family. Surely it wasn't only distance that had caused that rift. She would have to ask her mother one of these days. But not now.

Gabriela left the kitchen to get Ben out the door to school and herself to work.

Arriving at the library at midmorning, Gabriela could see much improvement. Light fixtures had been installed in the front of the main room, giving patrons more access to the shelves near the circulation desk. The grab-and-go library table remained popular, especially among parents picking up books for young children.

Delmina gave her an update on the latest calls and inquiries. Hearing that Charmaine had been in the library the day before, Gabriela wondered what had prompted that visit.

"To see the progress," Delmina said, "and to find out how you are doing. She asked me what I'd heard about Daniel, and I said he was still in the hospital. I think she'd like to hear from you."

Gabriela wanted to reach out to Charmaine—she was the library board president, after all. But Charmaine's relationship with Clayton and Daniel being investigated for setting fire to Everett's property complicated matters.

"Call her," Delmina said. "Avoiding that conversation is a mistake, if you don't mind me saying so."

Gabriela saw the wisdom in her words. This time, she would happily let Delmina place the call for her.

Charmaine sounded like her usual self, and her first question—"How are you?"—sounded sincere. She asked about Daniel's recovery.

"Much better," Gabriela said. "Still in ICU, but no longer in any danger."

"Please let him know that Clayton and I are thinking about him."

Gabriela weighed the right response, then she thought of Rose and waded right into deep water. "I have to address what we're not talking about here. Daniel did not set fire to Thorsen Manor. That fire damn nearly killed him. I don't know what you've heard, but please know this: Daniel is innocent. I intend to stand by him and fight any accusations against him." Her heart thundered so loudly Gabriela heard the escalating pulse in her ears.

Charmaine paused. "I hope only the best for Daniel—and that the truth comes out."

When she ended the call, Gabriela had to wonder what Charmaine believed that truth to be.

Ohnita Harbor Savings Bank sat in the center of downtown. A stone edifice from the early twentieth century, it boasted a huge marble lobby and velvet ropes that guided customers through an unnecessary labyrinth, given that only two people waited in line for the single teller on duty. Gabriela stood in the middle of the cavernous room, looking around for the banker she was scheduled to meet.

A young man approached in khakis and a white shirt worn with no tie. Gabriela assessed him to be a good ten years younger than she.

Seated at a right angle to the banker at his desk, Gabriela looked at the computer screen he turned toward her. It displayed information about a home equity line of credit: how much she could borrow and how much it would cost her. Interest rates had climbed considerably since she had gotten her mortgage a few years before. When the banker asked how much she intended to borrow, Gabriela wanted to keep the amount minimal but knew how quickly legal expenses could escalate. "Ten thousand," she told the banker, feeling the enormity of that number and the very real possibility that before this nightmare had ended, she would need even more.

Gabriela left the bank with the assurance that she would likely be approved for the credit line within a few days. She called Gordon Laxalt's direct number and left a message for him. The attorney called back fifteen minutes later, saying he would be pleased to represent Daniel as soon as the retainer was paid.

"Tell Daniel not to say anything until he has his lawyer present," Laxalt said. "Call me back when you have the funds from your bank."

Gabriela sent a text to Rose. *Attorney will take case when I get him retainer. Probably next week. Tell Daniel NOT to say anything to police.*

Rose responded with *OK.*

A minute later, Gabriela's phone chimed with a text. *Any way lawyer can move faster? Police coming today.*

She made three calls in rapid succession—first to Ben's school, requesting that they tell him to go to his grandmother's house after dismissal, and the second to her mother, informing her of this change of plans. The third was to Delmina, saying she was heading to Syracuse and wouldn't be available until later that day.

Before she left, Gabriela made one more phone call.

Billy Bulcher's cell phone number was in her contact information. She studied the 914 of the area code for Westchester County and the digits that followed. Gabriela knew Billy might not take her call; even if he did answer, he probably would refuse to listen to her plea about Daniel's innocence. But he'd been so kind to her, so fatherly. Surely he'd give her a moment of his time.

Billy answered on the second ring.

"Mr. Bulcher, it's Gabriela Domenici."

"Billy, please. How are you, dear?"

The softness of his tone brought tears to her eyes.

"Listen, I know I shouldn't be making this call, but I couldn't just stand by and let this spin out of control. You saw Daniel's work. You know his passion for Thorsen Manor. He would never damage the farmhouse. He loves that place."

"This is beyond tragic," Billy said. "And I can only imagine how much you're hurting right now."

"Daniel is badly injured. I'm trying to get him a good attorney. I have to get a home equity loan. I'm doing this because I know he's innocent, and you have to know it too. You and Everett both."

Billy sighed loudly. "Nothing would make me happier than to know this is one big, ugly mistake. Some raccoon chewed on a wire and set off a spark or something. I know Everett feels the same way. The police are investigating, but I think it will all work out."

"Oh, God, I hope so. I've been so scared." Tears flooded her eyes and choked her voice. "Please don't think Daniel did this. Because he wouldn't. He couldn't."

"The best thing you can do right now is take care of Daniel. And when you speak to him, please give him our best. We're sending our prayers."

"Thank you," Gabriela said, her voice hardly more than a whisper.

If Billy and Everett stood by Daniel, the police would have to look in a different direction.

The low heels of her shoes beat a staccato rhythm against the tile floor as Gabriela headed to the ICU nurses' station. Two nurses clustered together; their heads angled toward each other. "How is Daniel?" she asked.

The nurses shot a glance at each other before one explained that the state police were in there now. "His sister too."

Without saying another word, Gabriela entered the room. Two state troopers in uniform stood at the foot of the bed, while Rose sat in the chair beside Daniel, her hand on his arm. Rose glanced up at her, expression fixed and tense.

"My name is Gabriela Domenici," she said from the doorway. "I am Daniel's fiancée. I was the one who found Daniel at the scene."

Both state police officers darted their eyes toward her, but their bodies remained squarely in front of the hospital bed. "I spoke with Daniel's attorney, Gordon Laxalt, this morning," she added. "He does not want Daniel questioned without representation."

"When can Mr. Laxalt get here?" asked the female state trooper. Gabriela could see the nametag "Ellwood" and remembered her phone conversation with Trooper Doreen Ellwood.

"He's not able to make it today," Gabriela said. Not a lie, but hardly the full truth.

"These two are doing all the talking." Rose pointed from one state trooper to the other. "Daniel has nothing to say other than the obvious. He remains in ICU with severe burns and smoke inhalation. Whoever set that fire tried to kill him."

Trooper Ellwood set a card on the tray table beside the hospital bed. "Here's my card. When Mr. Laxalt can be here, we'll be back. You know your rights as a suspect."

"Yeah, you read them loud and clear. So appropriate in a hospital, which is supposed to be a safe place for *victims*," Rose shot back.

"If for any reason Mr. Laxalt cannot represent you, an attorney will be appointed for you by the court," Trooper Ellwood continued.

The state troopers filed past her on their way out of the room. Gabriela watched them leave. No matter what they said, it seemed the state police had already made up their minds. They had tried and convicted Daniel in the court of their own assumptions.

When Gabriela turned back, she expected Rose to start spewing vitriol. Instead, Rose's mouth gaped a little as she put her head down on the edge of the bed and began weeping.

Reaching over, Daniel stroked the back of his sister's hair. Gabriela walked around the bed and stood on the other side, not interrupting their moment.

"I gotta get out of here for a little while," Rose said, wiping her eyes. She left with a kiss on Daniel's cheek and a tight hug for Gabriela.

The nurse came in, informing Gabriela that she couldn't stay long. "He's had quite a bit of company."

"Is that what you call it? Two state troopers accusing him of nonsense," Gabriela said.

The nurse's widened eyes made Gabriela regret her harsh comment aimed at the wrong person. "I'm sorry. As you can imagine, this is all upsetting," she said, and the nurse nodded.

"Give us a few minutes, please," Daniel said.

Taking her hand, Daniel tugged a little and Gabriela sat down on the edge of the bed. When she kissed him, his top lip felt damp. Tears rolled out of his eyes and down the lines of his face. "I'm scared," he said. "Honey, I don't know what's going to happen."

Honey—a word Daniel rarely used. That more than anything told her how vulnerable he felt.

Wrapping her arms around him, Gabriela burrowed her hands into the pillows behind his head to complete the hug without shifting his body and causing him any pain, but the embrace went only halfway. It made her feel disconnected, as if he'd already been taken from her.

"The cops are right. I had a huge argument with Everett. Right in front of everyone," Daniel said. "Everett's last check bounced. My guys were there. They heard everything. Everett kept saying he'd fix it. I told the guys to leave. And I stayed."

Gabriela waited to hear what happened next—maybe a car pulling in, someone approaching the house.

"I can't remember much after that." He rolled his head from side to side. "There was an explosion, then I was in the ambulance."

"You didn't set that fire," Gabriela whispered.

"We were using a torch to seal seams in the roof. Maybe that caused it," Daniel's voice drifted off.

Gabriela straightened her spine. "You didn't cause that fire," she repeated. "Something or someone else did. Everett knows that. If the police ask him, he'll vouch for you."

A tap on the door turned her attention. A doctor stood in the doorway and, behind him, the nurse. The doctor walked in and introduced himself to Gabriela.

Today was the day, the doctor said, to get Daniel on his feet. The physical therapist would be there soon. "Once that happens, we'll transfer you out of ICU."

"Okay," Daniel said. "That's good."

Gabriela kissed him again. "Just focus on getting better. I love you."

"Love you, too," he said, and another tear rolled down his face.

Sitting in her car in the hospital parking garage, Gabriela called the attorney's office and asked if she could put the retainer fee on her credit card. After a long hold and a transfer, she spoke to someone in accounts payable who told her the arrangement had been authorized. Hands shaking, she pulled the card from her wallet and read the numbers over the phone. Then she called Gordon Laxalt's office a second time and gave his assistant the contact information for Trooper Doreen Ellwood. She hung up with the assurance that Laxalt would call the police before the end of the day.

Her dashboard clock read 2:26. She called Rose Red Deer, reached her voicemail, and left a message with the update. Her phone rang before she left the hospital parking garage, and she pulled over to take it.

"You think this attorney is any good?" Rose asked.

Gabriela could only say that he'd been recommended by someone who knew someone who knew her friend. The firm's website looked professional, and Laxalt's bio listed that he had gotten his law degree from Syracuse University. "I think so. More to the point, he's the one we have right now. I gave him my credit card number a little while ago."

"Hope you can pay that off fast," Rose said.

"When my home equity loan comes through," Gabriela added. Using a loan to pay off a debt, she thought ruefully, hardly a great plan.

"Daniel's lucky to have you," Rose said. "Listen, I know I was hard on you that first time at the hospital. I should have apologized last night."

"It's okay. You're right. I don't know what it's like to be him. And he never talks about it."

"Nope. Never does. At least he didn't change his name."

Gabriela couldn't imagine Daniel ever doing that. Names fascinated him, she told Rose. "One of the first things he ever asked me was about my full name—Gabriela Annunciata Domenici."

"That's a mouthful," Rose said. "So listen, I'm leaving in two days. I can't stay longer."

"I wish you could. I'd love to spend more time with you—and I know Daniel would too."

Rose swore under her breath. "Not exactly the family reunion I had in mind. I always knew we'd break the impasse. One of us would reach out to the other. But I wanted him to do it. Now I've wasted all this time, and my brother might go to jail."

"Don't say that!" Gabriela gasped. "He isn't going to jail. This attorney will help. Daniel doesn't even remember what happened. And there's no real evidence against him."

Rose huffed a rueful laugh. "I used to work for a legal aid society. I saw it a million times. The fight just becomes too much, and innocent people agree to plead to a lesser charge to make it go away. The police get a conviction, but it's not justice."

"Not Daniel. Not him." Gabriela shook her head vigorously as if trying to convince herself.

"I hope you're right. Why don't I meet you for breakfast tomorrow? Say nine thirty? Then we'll go to the hospital together."

"That sounds great," Gabriela agreed.

Putting her car in gear, Gabriela continued out of the parking garage and followed the signs for the highway that would take her northward back to Ohnita Harbor. With every mile she put behind her, though, Gabriela felt the tug back to Daniel. Physical therapy, she reminded herself, and a transfer to a regular hospital room. All signs of progress for his body. But right now, she needed to find a way to help protect his freedom.

Chapter Twenty-Three

An hour later, Gabriela pulled into her driveway. As she neared the garage, she saw Agnese on her hands and knees in the grass and Gabriela's heart lurched. Fearing the worst, she threw the car into park, pushed the car door open, and ran to her mother.

Agnese pulled up a dandelion with a long taproot and held it like a prize. "You cut, they come back. You pull, it breaks off. You gotta dig it out."

Gabriela crouched down beside her mother, dizzy with relief. "I'm surprised to see you here. Ben was supposed to go to your house after school."

"He called me to say he goes to the park," Agnese said. "I say okay and walk over here. Your gardens are a mess."

Gabriela noticed the bag of organic fertilizer she'd bought two weeks ago but hadn't had time to apply. The top was open, and a trowel rested beside it. "Thank you, Mama."

Agnese looked up with moist eyes. "I do this and say my prayers. For Daniel."

Gabriela helped Agnese to her feet and guided her to a small table on the back patio. Sitting there, Gabriela recalled when she'd bought the table and chairs on sale last fall, splurging for the umbrella and stand as well. Back then, she'd imagined backyard cookouts and quiet evenings with a glass of wine under the stars. That all seemed so distant now.

"You see the sister?" Agnese asked.

Gabriela nodded. "Rose. She's great. Tough, but she has a fierce heart."

"It's her name," Agnese agreed. "People think a rose is sweet and soft. They forget the thorns."

Gabriela had to smile at that one as she went inside the house to get iced tea and returned with two tall glasses topped with lemon slices. "I always wondered what it would have been like to have a brother or sister," she began.

"After you, no more babies," Agnese said. "We try, but..."

Gabriela took her mother's hand. "I loved having you and Dad all to myself. But the bond between siblings fascinates me. I see it with you and Aunt Cecelia."

Agnese took another sip. "Cecelia and me, we have history. We remember Italy."

"I love your stories—the olive groves, the church bells ringing over the hills." Gabriela smiled. She'd seen it all herself, years ago, when she'd visited Tuscany and her mother's hometown of Poggibonsi.

"Not all stories are good stories," Agnese continued.

"Tell me, Mama," Gabriela coaxed. "I know you were poor, and there were few jobs. But I think maybe something else made you and Aunt Cecelia leave."

Agnese tapped her fingertips on the tabletop. "Okay," she said. "I never told you. Maybe it's time."

Gabriela held her mother's gaze in encouragement, then Agnese dropped her eyes and began. Their father had died when she and

Cecelia were young girls, and their widowed mother constantly worried about money. "That's when she decided to marry off Cecelia. She was eighteen. Me, I was sixteen," Agnese said.

Gabriela stiffened. This story did not match what she knew. Aunt Cecelia had met Uncle Nick in the United States. A few years earlier, they celebrated their fiftieth anniversary.

"There was a man in town. Older—fifty-two. He had money. His wife died. My mother, she wanted Cecelia to marry him. Not a good man."

A man, Gabriela noted—his name withheld like a curse.

"Cecelia, she cry and cry. 'Mama, don't make me do this. I am afraid. I don't want to marry him.' She tried to go to the convent—that's how much she didn't want to do this. But the sisters wouldn't take her without Mama's permission. I think they were afraid of this man too. So Cecelia, she had to marry him."

Gabriela put her head in her hands. "Oh, that's horrible."

"He kept her in the house like a prisoner. His old mother sat in the kitchen like this." Agnese pantomimed crossed arms and a scowling face. "She watched and told him everything. So I went to see Cecelia in secret—at the church. I hid in the confessional, and we made a plan."

Agnese's voice shook a little as she described one night when the man was out of town, how Cecelia made a big show of saying good night to her mother-in-law and went upstairs with a candle and a few matches hidden in her pocket. Watching from the shadows across the street, Agnese saw the small light in the window and then the curtains burst into flame. She heard Cecelia's shouts and smelled smoke.

Cecelia went out that window, across the roof tiles, and down a trellis on the other side. Agnese and Cecelia joined hands and ran away as fast as they could, with only a small valise and the few lira that Cecelia had managed to steal from the kitchen money the day before.

"We walked all night through the fields. We picked grapes and olives—that's all we had to eat," Agnese said, her eyes focused on a distant point across the backyard.

Agnese recounted how they had walked as far as Siena and caught the bus to Florence. When no one would rent a room to two unaccompanied women, they stayed at a brothel. The two sisters slept together on a single mattress with a table up against the door.

"Cecelia, her nerves were bad. She was sick all the time. So I worked washing dishes in a restaurant. I brought home food and paid for our room. But we couldn't stay. Too close to Poggibonsi," Agnese said. "I told the madam everything. And that lady—she was so good to us. She gave us money for the train to Rome."

The story became sparser in details: Agnese and Cecelia getting jobs in Rome, finding a room to rent, saving money for the voyage, and finally leaving for the United States. "We didn't know nobody. We spoke a tiny bit of English. On the boat, we met a family. The husband had a brother in Syracuse. So we go there too."

A fat bumblebee droned over the table and landed at the edge of a puddle of condensation from their glasses.

"Did you ever contact your mother?" Gabriela asked.

"No. Many years later, I wrote to a friend. She tells me our mother died. That man, he looked and looked for Cecelia." Agnese made a fist, then opened it. "But we were too far for him to catch."

"You're amazing, Mama. What you did for your sister, and so young." She had always considered her mother a fighter, but this story took that perception to another level. "I assume Uncle Nick knows."

"*Si.* Your father too. But Cecelia never told her children."

Gabriela thought of her two cousins—one in New Jersey, the other in California—who came home every year to visit their parents. "Don't worry. I won't say anything to them. But thank you for telling me."

Agnese got up from the table and walked back toward the garden. Gabriela followed but did not hover, knowing her mother might need some space. They knelt side by side, gloves on and trowels in hand. Silently, they worked fertilizer into the ground, nourishing what they wanted to grow and rooting out what they wanted to obliterate.

A short while later, Ben came home, sweaty and muddy, and went upstairs to his room. Gabriela called the hospital, got an update on Daniel's transfer out of ICU, and spoke to the nurse when the phone in his hospital room went unanswered. He'd been given a light painkiller after his first attempt to walk, the nurse told her; now he was sleeping.

Agnese sat at the kitchen table scraping and chopping radishes and cucumbers. Gabriela started to boil water for pasta but then turned off the burner. "I have to go," she announced.

Running the peeler down the length of a carrot, Agnese nodded. "Okay, where? I stay with Ben."

Gabriela laid her hand on her mother's arm. "I can't just stay here, waiting. I have to prove Daniel's innocence. I'm going to Thorsen Manor. Maybe being there will help me think of something."

"That's why I told you the story. Somebody started that fire that burned Daniel. When you know why they did that, then you know everything."

Dressed in jeans and sneakers, Gabriela grabbed a windbreaker to wear over her T-shirt in case the air cooled. Getting in the car, she checked the gas gauge and filled up at a station on the way out of town. The sun had only started to slide toward the horizon when she reached the first sign for Thorsen Manor. At the access road she expected police tape or a barricade, but nothing blocked her way. Driving slowly, she passed surveyor stakes with neon strips fluttering like tiny flags but no other signs of development.

Toward the end of the road, Gabriela slammed on the brakes. Seeing the charred hulk of the old farmhouse squeezed the breath out of her. She fought for a deep inhale, but her lungs would not take it in. Eyes closed, she willed calmness into her body and, with it, a steady stream of air. She drew in one deep breath, then another.

When she opened her eyes, Gabriela saw the top story of the house had been destroyed—all of Daniel's restoration work. The lower story still stood, but the front door was gone. Yellow hazard tape ringed the remains.

Gabriela turned off the engine and put the key in her jacket pocket, leaving her purse locked inside the car. Walking slowly toward the house, she searched for the spot where she'd found Daniel. With each step, it all came back to her. Her heart rate spiked as she recalled the panic that night, and her eyes burned as if she were still engulfed by smoke. The intensity of the memories nearly sent her back to her car and away from a place she never wanted to see again. Then Gabriela reminded herself why she'd come. Somewhere in her memories of that night could be something—anything—that could exonerate Daniel.

Forcing herself ahead, she approached the front steps of the house crisscrossed with police tape. The wind picked up, carrying the acrid smell of burnt wood. Turning to the left, she shut her eyes to mimic the sensation of stumbling away from the choking smoke. A few steps away from the house, she remembered her feet had connected with something solid—Daniel's body lying on the hard earth.

Crouching down, she touched a tuft of grass, still green amid everything that had been scorched. Curling her fingers into the coarse blades, she recalled how she'd grabbed Daniel and rolled him over, pushing his body across the dirt until he'd roused enough to crawl away. Something nagged at her, begging her to pay attention. Getting to her feet, Gabriela stared at the ground as if an imprint of Daniel's body had been traced there. He'd been lying face down—she'd tripped over one of his legs. It didn't take a forensic expert to guess he'd been running away from the house. The police theorized he'd set the blaze, tried to get away, but wasn't fast enough.

He'd been alone at the house—even Daniel admitted that. And then she'd found him. Within that lapse of time was the truth of what had happened here. Gabriela paced a tight circle, hoping something would jump out at her. Nothing did.

Giving the house a wide berth, Gabriela headed toward the trampled and matted backyard, littered with charred debris. In the rear of the property, the three gravestones still stood, marking the resting places of Penelope Thorsen, her infant, and someone else—a family member most likely, perhaps another child. Gabriela entertained a fleeting thought that these three had witnessed what had happened here to Daniel, but the dead weren't giving up any of their secrets.

Sitting on the grass beside Penelope's grave, Gabriela felt an odd comfort to rest for a moment beside a woman who had died nearly two hundred years ago. Penelope had known pain and sorrow—the death of loved ones, her husband severely wounded during the Revolutionary War. How had she survived those losses and hardships?

The same way she had overcome her own, Gabriela admitted. In the past five years or so, she'd gone through divorce, her father's death, and her mother's two bouts of cancer. Her life had been threatened twice. And now this. Just as she and Daniel planned a life together, he could be taken from her. She had no choice but to go on, the next day and the one after that—no matter what happened from here.

The police had no other suspects, she knew, and Daniel had both motive and opportunity. Feeling disloyal, she tried to keep those thoughts from igniting into condemnation, but her spinning brain fanned the flames of her own fears and suspicions. Daniel had worried constantly about his crew being paid—everything hung in the balance of getting paid for the Thorsen project.

She could easily imagine him kicking over a bucket of tar or paint or a can of turpentine. Just like Cecelia's tiny candle had destroyed the man's house in Italy, one spark here could have wreaked havoc on Everett Brooks's plans. In that moment, sitting in the tiny cemetery, Gabriela could see it so clearly. Daniel had been truly desperate. Whether intentionally or accidentally, who else could have caused this fire?

No. She knew his heart and his character. Daniel loved this place and its history, and he never would have intentionally destroyed it. No circumstantial evidence could convince her otherwise.

Leaving the graves, Gabriela decided to walk the path to the lake just one more time to bring back the pleasant memories of that Sunday afternoon when Daniel had taken her, Ben, and Agnese to see this property. They had been so happy, so optimistic. Something about this place had triggered that joy, and it wasn't hard to figure out. Daniel had been proud of his work and the opportunity to do something more than tear off and replace roofs. He had created something here and had wanted them to see it.

As she made her way down the path, Gabriela took in how the ample spring rains and lengthening days had thickened the brush on both sides. Overhead, trees budded with canopies of new leaves. A patch of wild violets spread their delicate, pale lavender faces across the ground, and three-petaled white trilliums stood between two wild apple trees. Natural beauty enveloped and soothed, coaxing her onward.

In a flight of fancy, Gabriela pictured herself walking in Penelope's footsteps. She imagined the lady of the house in a long calico dress with a basket over her arm, picking berries or wildflowers. The vision beckoned her to follow, and Gabriela continued to the next big tree, then around one more bend. She kept moving until she finally reached the edge of the rocky beach.

It was already after six o'clock, and the sun would set a little after eight. She had to turn back soon but decided to take a short stroll along this peaceful stretch of shoreline. Up ahead, the beach curved outward into a point that jutted into the waves, forming a small, secluded cove. Curious, Gabriela approached, telling herself that this had to be her final turnaround.

A small boat with an outboard motor floated in the shallows. Gabriela scanned her surroundings for whoever it might belong to but saw no one. Recalling the skiff Ben had found in the marsh at Peninsula Point, she decided to take a closer look. Picking her way across the rocks, Gabriela recalled what Thelma Tulowski had told her—the partial registration number in the photo Gabriela had taken that day matched one of the small boats stolen out of Cape Vincent.

There had to be hundreds of skiffs like this in and around the area, but Gabriela couldn't shake the idea that this was the same one Ben had found. Peninsula Point was only a mile or so away. Scrolling through her phone, Gabriela found the photo that showed the first four digits of the registration number: 7842.

It was the same boat—the second stolen boat.

Quickly she took a picture and texted it to Thelma, reporting the boat's location. She waited for a reply, then texted that she was leaving and would be home in less than an hour.

Another thought occurred to her. Maybe Clawson, who fished this shoreline nearly every day, had come across this same boat and whoever piloted it. Whatever he'd seen had been enough to get him shot—just like Ricky.

Gabriela stumbled backwards a step, then turned. She needed to get out of there and tried to run but the rounded rocks tripped her repeatedly. For better footing she walked quickly along the water's edge where rocks mixed with a little sand. Up ahead she saw the path back to Thorsen Manor and accelerated toward it, finally entering the woods. Pressed into the soft ground were the footprints she'd made earlier, and she followed them in the other direction. Her fast pace worked up a sweat, and Gabriela stopped to unzip the light jacket she wore.

She heard something and froze—a man's voice, carried by the wind off the water. Straining to hear, she tried to make out the words, then discerned another man's voice as well.

Two men talking was hardly out of the ordinary, Gabriela told herself. They could be anyone—fishermen wondering whether the perch were biting, people with a camp nearby, someone walking down the beach with a friend. But that boat turning up here made her want to know who those men were and what they were saying. To do that, she had to get closer.

Leaving the path, Gabriela headed into the woods to keep from being seen. She pushed away branches, skirted thick clumps of brush, and climbed over trunks of felled trees. As she neared the shoreline, the sound of waves amplified and the voices disappeared.

She nearly gave up until a man spoke so loudly, she flung herself against a tree trunk. The wind stirred the branches with a whoosh that brushed away every other sound. Then, in a brief pause as if the air itself drew in a breath, she heard, "...got rid of that damn Indian."

The downstate accent, the clipped words, the hardness of the vowels. It was Billy Bulcher's voice—she'd bet on it.

Revulsion sent bile into the back of her throat. All his interest in the farmhouse, his fascination with the old fireplace and its history—it had been some kind of ruse. She'd been taken in by him, the way he'd fussed over her the day she discovered Clawson's body, so fatherly and kind. He hadn't stepped in to save Thorsen Manor but to destroy it.

Her mind reeling, she clamped onto his words, knowing they could only refer to one person. This proved Daniel's innocence—the victim of a fire, not the arsonist who set it. She waited to hear more, but the wind picked up again and the words flew in another direction.

The first text she sent was to Thelma Tulowski. She copied what she'd written and, after scrolling through her contacts for Trooper Doug Morrison's cell, sent him the identical text. *This is Gabriela. I am at the shore behind Thorsen Manor. Do not call me. Text me. I need to report something.*

As she waited for a reply, Gabriela heard the men's voices and wanted to put as much distance between herself and whoever approached. She moved as fast as she dared, the soggy ground absorbing her footsteps.

A voice broke through the quiet of the woods, close enough to make her quicken her pace. "Insurance will give us a nice enough payout. That farmhouse was nothing but a money pit."

That sounded like Everett Brooks, though Gabriela couldn't be sure. But it made sense that Billy and Everett would be here together, investor and developer, father-in-law and son-in-law. And she had no doubt that they were talking about the fire at the farmhouse—and getting rid of Daniel and a costly restoration project.

Gabriela plunged into the trees on the other side of the path. Squatting down beside a huge hemlock, its trunk gnarled and knotted, she examined her phone screen. A cascade of text messages awaited her from Thelma Tulowski and Doug Morrison, both wanting to know where she was and what was happening. She sent a group text to both: *Heard 2 men talking at beach. Something about the fire and getting rid of Daniel.*

Twigs snapped, and Gabriela dove face down onto the ground. Pine needles prickled her cheeks. A large beetle walked across her bare hand, but she didn't flinch. She wanted to raise her head enough to glimpse the two men as they passed but couldn't risk them seeing her.

Her phone vibrated with a text from Doug. *Get out of there.*

As she thumbed a reply, she heard another set of footsteps. Was there a third person? Or had one of the other men doubled back?

Burying her face against her arms, she took in the musky smell of moss and old leaves. A footstep scraped a rock, and Gabriela held her breath. Whoever passed did so without saying a word.

Another text came in, this time from Thelma. *Leave. Get to safety.*

Gabriela answered. *Men going toward Thorsen Manor. My car there. They'll know I'm here.* She sent a second text. *Going to Peninsula Point.*

Heading west through the woods, Gabriela stayed parallel to the water to keep from going too far inland. Thick undergrowth scratched and clawed at her. A bramble of wild blackberry bushes tore at her flesh, right through her clothing. She barely felt their sting.

Her phone buzzed with an incoming call, and Gabriela answered in a whisper.

"It's me—Doug. You safe?"

"Yes." Gabriela kept moving, holding the phone in one hand and pushing back bushes with the other.

"I called Doreen Ellwood," Doug said. "Where are you?"

She tripped and a branch snapped. Stock-still, she waited but heard nothing.

"Gabriela?" he repeated.

"I'm going to Peninsula Point."

"Stay where you are. Wait for someone to come for you."

"No. I don't want them to find me."

"Who?"

"Billy Bulcher. And somebody else—probably Everett Brooks. I have to go." Gabriela disconnected the call so she could focus fully on heading in the right direction.

Thick woods and impenetrable brush forced her to veer to the left, away from the shore. When she could, Gabriela angled to the right toward the water. Her footsteps made sucking noises in the mud. Forced out of a swampy area, she reached the shoreline.

Scanning the water's edge and seeing no one, she began running. She recalled the boat launch at Peninsula Point, the arched bridge leading to a small island ringed by marshes, and the trail that led to the road. The images encouraged her, pushing her onward, knowing that's where she would find safety.

Then she ran out of land.

A wide creek swollen by rain separated where she stood and the marshy island at the tip of Peninsula Point. A text from Doug asked again for her location. Gabriela texted back: *At marsh. North side Peninsula Point.*

Walking upstream Gabriela reached a bend where she judged the stream to be just six feet across. Plunging in, she held her phone over her head. With each step the water deepened, covering her knees, then her hips. The current pushed her, and she fought to keep upright in her sodden clothes. Cold cramped her muscles, turning each movement into agony. Her upraised arm ached, and the phone buzzed in her hand, but she didn't dare look at the screen for fear of dropping the device.

Finally, she waded out of the water and climbed the embankment, tripping and sliding several times. At the top she sat on the wet ground and shivered. Curled into a ball, Gabriela tried to absorb warmth from a sky streaked with sunset colors. Peaceful beauty surrounded her, and she watched two ducks flap their wings rapidly and settle onto the water.

For the moment she felt safe, but the men she'd heard at the shoreline were so close. If they came looking for her, it would be obvious where she'd gone. All they had to do was follow her footprints.

A boat engine rumbled nearby then stopped. Peering through the tall grass Gabriela saw a small skiff bobbing in the current and a man in dark clothing onboard. She couldn't make out who it was and wondered if it might be someone from the state police or maybe even the Coast Guard. Then the boat turned sideways, and she recognized it as the one she'd seen in the cove. She couldn't see who was at the wheel but guessed it had to be Everett Brooks. Billy Bulcher in his Italian loafers wouldn't go anywhere near a swamp.

Crouching low, Gabriela recalled the layout of Peninsula Point and focused all her mental energy on the location of the small arched bridge. She ran toward what she thought was the right spot but found only a historic marker with the title "A Turning Point in the War." It was the story Daniel had related to her—of the two Continental Army soldiers who had overheard the British commanders in the marsh plotting their invasion.

Because sound carried over the water. Gabriela repeated that fact to herself like a warning.

She heard marsh grass rustling and snapping and surmised that whoever had piloted the boat was pushing it into a hiding place. That person would be preoccupied for a moment and, she hoped, unable to hear her.

Looping around the edge of the island, she spied the wooden footbridge up ahead. Pausing a moment, she weighed whether to cross it now and head straight to the road or wait and let whoever had come by boat to leave first. But what if he stayed on the island until someone else came? Could she risk staying hidden and silent in such a small place with danger so close by?

Her phone buzzed again, the faint vibration jolting her out of indecision. She read Trooper Morrison's text, *WHERE ARE U*, and thumbed a brief reply. *Peninsula Point. By the footbridge. Someone here in boat.*

Gabriela dashed for the bridge, her footsteps thudding dully against the wooden planks. She slipped on a mossy patch and fought for balance but went down on one knee. The strike against the boards stung, and Gabriela limped off the bridge. Ignoring a sore kneecap she started to run, allowing adrenaline to push her forward.

The path narrowed with an overgrowth of brush on both sides, a tunneling effect that cast everything into shadowy darkness. Gabriela plunged in, feeling the coolness against her skin dampened by sweat and creek water. She could hide here undetected.

Something grabbed her arm, knocking her off balance, and she hit hard. Wondering if she'd tripped or failed to see a branch in the gloom, Gabriela looked around. A man emerged from the thicket.

She scrambled backward like a crab on the sand. Everett Brooks took an easy step toward her.

Her brain muddled from fatigue and fear, Gabriela tried to make sense of how Everett had managed to hide the boat in the marsh and get this far down the path without passing her. The realization crept over her like a long, slow chill. Everett hadn't been on the boat. He'd been here, waiting for someone else.

Gabriela tried to yell, but her constricted throat only let out a hiss. "I heard what you said on the beach. You and Billy."

"You heard nothing." Everett took another step toward her. "It's all in that vivid imagination of yours. You'd say or do anything to help your boyfriend. But Daniel is an arsonist."

Gabriela got to her feet and found her voice. "He didn't do it, and you know it! Billy said that you got rid of Daniel—or as he put it *that damn Indian*." She hated repeating those vile words. "You're expecting a nice big insurance payout for the farmhouse—the *money pit*."

She watched his face for a reaction, but Everett only smiled. "You're delusional. Wandering around out here, making up stories. But here's one thing you should know. I never burned that farmhouse. Arson by the owner? Insurance company would be all over us. No, someone did me the favor. That was Daniel."

Everett was a sociopath and a liar, Gabriela told herself; she couldn't believe him. But when she looked at his face, she saw confidence in his eyes.

"I've called the state police," she told him.

"And told them what?"

Gabriela thrust her phone screen in his face. "I've been texting them. They're coming for you, so nothing better happen to me."

Everett grabbed her arm. "Plenty is going to happen—trust me."

She screamed, praying her voice would carry and alert anyone nearby. Everett loosened his grip on her arm and slapped her.

Her head jerked back, and she tasted blood in her mouth. Righting herself, Gabriela saw the gun in Everett's hand. Her eyes darted in all directions for a way out, but the woods seemed to press in on all sides.

"Let her go," said a man's voice.

Gabriela swung around. For a moment, the man's bulky build and camouflage jacket made her think of Clawson. Then she remembered he was dead. Recognition widened Gabriela's eyes.

Chapter Twenty-Four

Walt Seymour ambled down the path, his weapon fixed on Everett. Watching him approach, Gabriela pressed into the bushes beside the path, praying the branches would open up and swallow her.

"It's okay," Walt told her with a courtly nod. "I don't mean you no harm. My only business is with him."

Everett aimed his weapon straight back at him, and Gabriela sucked in her breath.

"Nah, you ain't gonna shoot me," Walt said. "You do, and I shoot you. Then Gabriela here runs down the path to the police and tells all about what you said and did."

In the distance a siren blared. The sound made Gabriela exhale with relief. This would all end soon—Everett in custody and Walt a hero for saving her.

"They're here," Gabriela said to Walt, but he shook his head.

"I ain't leaving this to them," Walt told her. He took one more step toward Everett. "You killed my boy," he said and squeezed the trigger.

Everett crumbled to the ground.

Gabriela screamed as his body convulsed once, then stilled. The dark forms of trees, black against the indigo of the evening sky, seemed to swirl, and she staggered. Walt reached out his hand, and Gabriela shrieked as she jumped backward.

"Please don't kill me," she begged. "I don't have anything to do with whatever is going on here."

"I told you, it's okay," Walt said. "I shot that bastard before he could hurt you." He nudged Everett's body with the toe of his shoe. "He's gone—and straight to hell."

Panting deep breaths through her open mouth, Gabriela fought to clear her mind. "You said he killed your son. What did Ricky have to do with this?"

"Ricky was a good boy," Walt said. "Never got in no trouble. Real smart—whole lot smarter than me. But Ricky found out about the boat and wanted to borrow it."

Before she could formulate her next question, voices pierced the quiet around them. A woman shouted Gabriela's name.

"I'm here," she called back. "I'm okay."

Trooper Doreen Ellwood came at them at full speed. Doug Morrison was a step behind.

Gabriela moved forward, putting herself between Walt and the state police. "Everett Brooks is dead. He threatened me with a gun, and Walt Seymour shot him."

Walt set his weapon down on the ground and kicked it toward the state police. "I don't care what happens to me. I just wanted justice for my boy."

Ellwood barked into her radio. "Armed male shot dead. Shooter apprehended. Witness on the scene."

Doug secured Walt's gun and ordered him to sit on the ground, hands on his head. He recited his rights, then cuffed him.

Gabriela approached, ignoring Doug's demand that she stay back. "Walt has something to say. He knows who killed his son."

"A guy named Clawson pulled the trigger. But he was working for Everett Brooks," Walt said. "I killed both of them."

"We're taking you to the station," Trooper Ellwood said. "You heard your rights. If you want an attorney present—"

"I told you what I done," Walt interrupted. "I don't need no lawyer."

"Wait!" Gabriela insisted. "Don't you want to know why they killed Ricky?"

"You are interfering with an arrest," Doug snapped.

"They're running guns!" Walt yelled. "They buy them cheap down South then bring them up here to smuggle into Canada. They had two boats for a while, making a run every week or so. Small loads brought over to the Canadian side on fishing boats, as easy as you please. Clawson got me in on it. We'd done a job together."

The way he said *job*, Gabriela thought of work in the traditional sense. Chronically unemployed, Walt clearly functioned in a different economy.

"Ricky never knew nothing about the guns. He thought I was helping Clawson with fishing charters." A sob broke Walt's voice. "When the police told me Ricky had been looking to borrow a boat, I figured out what musta happened. Ricky went to talk to Clawson. They used to keep one of the boats about five miles from Ohnita Harbor. Musta found them loading guns, so they shot him." Walt shook his head.

Gabriela imagined Clawson forcing the young man onto the boat, shooting him offshore where the shots wouldn't be heard, then pushing his body overboard near Ohnita Harbor.

"Why didn't you go to the police with what you knew?" Doug asked.

Walt made a face. "Like they'd believe me. Everybody kept saying Ricky had to be involved in drugs. They had their minds made up. Nobody did a damn thing, so I did."

His story rambled, but Gabriela captured the pertinent details of Walt's plan—how he'd reached out to Clawson with the pretense of another boat he could get his hands on, replacing the one lost in the storm. When Clawson refused to meet at first, Walt had come up to Peninsula Point and found him getting ready to go out fishing. "He didn't want anything to do with me. Bastard even shot at me."

"It was a Sunday," Gabriela interjected. "I heard you arguing, then two shots."

Walt looked at her with weary eyes. "Maybe. I can hardly remember one day from the next."

He continued his story, how he kept calling Clawson, telling him he needed money and offering to help with another gun run. "I played like we were still friends. Bought a six-pack and drank it with him," Walt said. "That's when he said he'd meet me to see the boat."

Walt shifted on the ground as if tired of talking. "I met Clawson at a bar near here. He was feisty at first, then he got lit and settled down. When we left, I had him follow me down this road—ain't even got a name—where I knew nobody would be around. I pulled off in this field and flagged Clawson down. Told him he'd have to drive the rest of the way in his truck. Guess he figured it was a setup and tried to get away. I shot him, and he drove right into a swamp."

Killing Clawson had been enough at first, Walt said. Then Everett contacted him, saying he'd gotten his name from Clawson a week or so before. They needed someone to take another load to Canada. "That was my chance to get even with who was behind all of this."

Walt described getting the boat out of the marsh at Peninsula Point, bringing it to the cove behind Thorsen Manor, and hiding in the woods—waiting for Everett.

Walt turned toward Gabriela. "Then you came along—walking around and taking pictures. Didn't want to get you in the middle of it. You left just before Everett and the other guy showed up."

"Billy Bulcher," Gabriela told the state police again. "I recognized his voice."

Then something else occurred to her. "I didn't see their car at Thorsen Manor, and I don't think they walked the path to the lake."

Walt shook his head. "Can't take a hike with two crates of guns. There's another access road. Comes out near the cove. Everett bitched about having to drive his nice shiny SUV down it."

Trooper Ellwood crossed her arms. "You saw the guns? You know where they are now?"

"Yeah, I can show you," Walt said, then continued. "Everett kept texting me—*Where are you?* They went looking for me, I guess—no idea I was following them."

He glanced at Gabriela again. "Figured you'd go back to your car, so I said I'd meet them at Peninsula Point. Told Everett I'd bring the boat there, then we'd get the guns. I didn't know you'd be here."

Doug leaned down. "I want to be clear about this. Everett and Billy were the ones Gabriela overheard talking about the fire at the farmhouse. Is that correct?"

Walt nodded. "Guess they thought some guy burned down their old house. But he didn't. I did."

"You?" Gabriela gasped.

"I wanted to take away something from them," Walt said. "But I didn't know anybody was coming back to the house that night."

Walt described dousing the upstairs with kerosene, turning the acetylene torch on with a low flame so that when the fumes ignited, the place would explode. "I'm awful sorry that guy got hurt."

"He's my fiancé, Daniel Red Deer." Saying his name brought a wave of tears. The charges against him would be dropped now that the police knew who set the fire.

Trooper Ellwood reached down for Walt's arm to help him to his feet. "We've heard enough. The rest will come out later."

"I'll tell you everything," Walt said.

Gabriela began trembling, and someone handed her a blanket. When she looked to see who it was, she saw a paramedic. She hadn't even heard them arrive on the scene. Another was tending to Everett's body.

"Thank you," she called out to Walt. "You saved my life."

Walt turned his head toward her as Trooper Ellwood urged him forward. "Ricky liked you. I did it for him."

Pulling the blanket tighter around her body, Gabriela started walking down the Peninsula Point trail toward the road. Doug Morrison caught up with her in a few steps. "Think you can make it?"

"Let's see. I ran through the woods, waded through the creek, faced down Everett with a gun, watched him get shot, and heard Walt's confession. I think I can walk down a little path."

After a few steps, Gabriela felt the weakness in her legs but pushed herself onward. Sapped of adrenaline, she had only determination to take her the rest of the way.

The woods closed in around them, and Gabriela heard the chirps of tree frogs singing in the night. Peepers, her father used to call them. The gentle memory calmed her brain and stirred questions as she processed what had happened in the past few hours.

"I'm not complaining, but what took you so long to get here?" she asked.

"I wasn't on duty, and Doreen was up in Watertown at an arrest." Doug paused. "Keep this between you me? Doreen didn't think you were in any danger. I'm not even sure she believed you heard anybody on the beach."

Gabriela's growl of frustration turned into a sigh. "Yeah. I can see that."

"I'm sorry," Doug said. "It wasn't my case."

"I know. Thank you for all you did."

Gabriela fell silent, her words spent. Later, she would need to tell so many people what had happened—Daniel, Rose, her mother. For now, she walked silently, her eyes filling with tears of fatigue and relief.

⁓

Dressed in white slacks and a blue top, Gabriela showed up at the hospital the next morning. She had left the state police station after one o'clock in the morning and had only three hours of sleep. Now she carried a large coffee for reinforcement. What she had to say to Daniel could not be delivered by phone.

"How about some good news?" she asked after entering his hospital room.

Daniel gave her a smile and returned her kiss. "That I could use."

"Well, let's start by saying you won't be needing that attorney I hired." Gabriela sat on the edge of the bed and took his hand. "A whole lot happened yesterday that's going to take a while to explain. But the bottom line is, you aren't facing any charges of arson. The police know who burned down the farmhouse."

Daniel sagged back against the pillows. "Oh, my God. I've been wracking my brain, trying to figure out if I'd done it accidentally. They almost had me convinced."

Gabriela told him everything, a long story she tried to condense. When she was finished, she gripped Daniel's hand. "For what it's worth, Walt is so sorry that you got hurt." Tears dripped off her chin and landed against the blanket covering Daniel's chest. "He wanted to get back at Everett for what happened to Ricky."

She repeated what Walt had confessed to the police, about the kerosene and the acetylene torch on low to ignite the fumes. "Except you came back," Gabriela said. "Apparently after your fight with Everett and everyone left, you went out for a little while."

"Yeah," Daniel said, nodding. "I think I went to get something to eat. My memory is still a little scrambled."

Emotional trauma, a mild concussion from hitting his head when the exploding fire sent his body reeling—Gabriela could think of a dozen reasons why he couldn't fully remember that night. Maybe he never would, or maybe, as with her own past traumas, the memories would resurface and replay in vivid detail. She'd be there for him, no matter what he had to face.

"You weren't running out of the farmhouse, like the police said all along. You were going back in," Gabriela said, piecing the scenario together. "When you opened the door, the rush of air was all it took."

She reached for him, and as they held each other, Daniel shook with sobs. Gabriela's tears wet the neckline of his hospital gown. Then, resting her head against his shoulder, she told Daniel what she'd learned from the state police—about Billy Bulcher's ties to organized crime on Long Island and involvement in criminal activity that had long been suspected. Until now no one had been able to make any charges stick. When Everett went deeper into debt at Thorsen Manor and rising interest rates shut him out of legitimate financing, Billy stepped in.

"The police think Thorsen Manor was all part of Billy's larger money laundering," Gabriela said. "Gun smuggling was just a small but lucrative part of it."

"Thorsen Manor being on the lake must have made it even more attractive to Billy," Daniel said. "They could load the guns right from the beach."

"They used two stolen boats, hidden along the shoreline," she said. "That big storm we had washed one up. The other was hidden at Peninsula Point." She smiled at Daniel. "You always said it was a hideaway for smugglers and spies."

Gabriela continued with the last part she'd learned from the police about the rise in gun smuggling into Canada. "Private ownership of guns is very restricted. A handgun smuggled out of the States goes for ten times as much in a place like Toronto or Montreal. Something like 90 percent of all the guns used in violent crimes in Ontario started out in the U.S. Billy had quite a network set up."

"So, where's he now?" Daniel asked.

"In custody. They picked him up about one o'clock this morning along the New York State Thruway outside Albany. He was driving Everett's SUV. When he heard the shot Walt fired, he took off and stranded his son-in-law. Nice guy, huh?" Gabriela grunted her disgust at ever having compared Billy with her father.

Others waited to see Daniel, but she needed a few more moments alone with him. She sent a text, asking for fifteen more minutes.

"There's something else," she said. "Rose told me what happened to you when you were younger. The assault charge."

"Ancient history," Daniel replied, and Gabriela saw a muscle twitch in his thin face.

"Yes, it's in the past. But it's relevant to our future," she said. "I need to know more about how you grew up so I can be the best life partner for you. Not to judge—but to understand." She felt the warmth of his palm against her cool fingers. "No secrets."

Daniel kept his hand in hers but didn't respond right away. Gabriela waited, wanting to give him all the time he needed.

"I was a really angry young man and in so much pain," Daniel began. "Our parents dead, our grandmother struggling financially to raise us. And a lot of prejudice. There was one kid—used to call me Geronimo, like it was an insult. Geronimo was a great leader— until the government imprisoned him then carted him around to county fairs."

Daniel closed his eyes and shook his head. "That kid used to taunt me—'Hey, Geronimo. You take any scalps lately?' But what really got me was when he went after Rose. He used to call her 'squaw.'"

"Oh—" The guttural sound escaped like Gabriela had been punched.

"Made sure he never said that again." Daniel turned toward the window, and Gabriela followed his gaze toward golden sunshine seeping through gaps in the blinds. "If I'd gotten convicted of arson, I was going to leave you. That prior felony assault charge would have come out. I couldn't have you and Ben waiting for me to get out of prison."

"But we would have appealed," Gabriela began.

Daniel shook his head. "No, I love you both too much for that. I'd made up my mind. In fact, I was going to tell you today."

Pressing her forehead against his shoulder, Gabriela's words muffled against skin and fabric. "Good thing I had better news."

———

A knock sounded on the hospital room door. Ben divebombed toward the bed as Gabriela tried to steer him away from Daniel's legs, which were still healing. Daniel caught the boy in a bear hug, telling Ben over and over how much he loved him.

Agnese leaned down and kissed Daniel on both cheeks. "You gonna be my son now."

"Thanks, Mama," he said. "*Va bene.*"

"See? You half Italian already." Agnese looked around the room and spotted his half-eaten breakfast of gelatinous oatmeal and watery orange juice. "*Bah!* How you get better eating this? You come home, I make you peppers and eggs. Vincent, he loved this. Make you strong."

"I could go for peppers and eggs," a voice said from the doorway.

Clem stepped into the room with Mary Jo, bearing flowers and a balloon shaped like a teddy bear with a smiling face. Ben insisted they tie it to the foot of Daniel's bed.

Clem gave it a swat, and the balloon bobbed in the air. "You can blame Mary Jo for this one."

"It's so obnoxious, I love it." Daniel laughed.

Mary Jo kissed him on the cheek. "That was the point."

Rose entered last, having heard the story when Gabriela called her from the state police station at midnight. "You sure know how to draw a crowd, brother," she said.

Gabriela saw the fond look that passed between them and beamed.

"That I do, little sister," Daniel said. "And you're going to find yourself wrapped up right in the middle of it."

Agnese made her way around the end of the bed and reached up to put a hand on Rose's arm. "When you come back, you don't stay at a hotel. That's no good for family. You stay at my house. Very close to them."

"Thank you," Rose said. "I'm not sure when I'm coming back."

"What do you mean?" Agnese threw her hands in the air. "For the wedding."

Chapter Twenty-Five

On a Saturday in mid-June, Gabriela knelt by her garden beds in the backyard, putting in the last of the annuals—asters, zinnias, and petunias—that would bloom until the frost. Daniel walked across the patio, leaving behind the cane he only used when his leg tired. The grafts had healed without infection, allowing him to go back to work, though it would be a while before he climbed any ladders. DRD Roofing had continued working on jobs without him, thanks to his loyal crew.

Ben appeared at the back door and announced that someone had come to see them. Gabriela brushed the grass and dirt from her knees and walked down the driveway. Charmaine and Clayton stood by the front door with two large potted plants.

"Gifts for the garden," Charmaine said, and Gabriela beckoned them to follow her to the backyard.

They sat at the patio table, and Gabriela went inside for iced tea and lemonade. Charmaine offered to help, and Gabriela handed her the glasses filled with ice, then carried two pitchers to the table.

When she returned, she caught the last of what Clayton said to Daniel—something about wanting to meet with him at Thorsen Manor.

"No thanks, I'm done with that place," Daniel said.

Clayton reached over. "There will be new owners soon—Charmaine and me. The state seized all of Billy Bulcher's property in its racketeering investigation against him. But when Thorsen Manor is released for sale, we've reached an agreement to buy it."

Daniel tipped his head back and rolled his eyes skyward. "I can't rebuild that old farmhouse. It's too far gone."

"Agreed," Clayton said. "But we do need to design and build a monument there. And we want you to be the one to do it. Please come out to the property so we can discuss it."

The next day Gabriela drove with Daniel in the front seat beside her and Ben in the back. She glanced over at Daniel, who seemed lost in thought. Whatever he decided to do, she would support him.

Another car was parked by the charred remains of the farmhouse. "Oh, God," Daniel moaned, gripping Gabriela's hand at the sight of the destruction.

"You okay? We can leave if it's too much," she said.

"We'll stay," he replied, huffing out a breath. "If nothing else, it's some closure for me."

Ben raced off toward the path, and Gabriela called after him to be careful. The site had been cleaned up, but police tape still wrapped the exterior of the old farmhouse.

Clayton and Charmaine waited for them by the first of the building lots that had been surveyed and marked. "We want to go ahead with the plan for Thorsen Manor," Clayton explained. "Nice homes for families. But no marina. No golf course."

"And we are going to make a park, accessible to the public, that will include a monument, the Thorsen family cemetery, and the path to the lake," Charmaine said.

Daniel turned toward what remained of the farmhouse. "There's nothing salvageable here."

"No," Clayton agreed. "But that old fireplace is still standing."

Gabriela saw something in Daniel's eyes as he studied the ruin and knew some idea had taken root. "What are you thinking?" she asked him.

"We can tear down everything and just leave the fireplace," Daniel suggested. "That could be your monument. It was the heart of that home."

Using a stick, he scratched out a simple design in the dirt—an A-frame, enclosed on three sides, with a rebuilt chimney protruding from the roof. "Leave the front open. Put in a few picnic tables on a cement floor. You'll have a nice community space that honors the original building."

"With one more touch," Gabriela added. "The stone with the family crest mounted on the chimney."

"Say you'll do it," Charmaine said, a note of pleading in her voice. "You invested so much here. And not just time and effort."

When Daniel looked at Gabriela, she told him it was his decision.

"Okay," he said. "I'd like to finish what we started here."

"Good. Now I suggest we head to my house." Charmaine hooked her arm through Clayton's. "Give me an hour or so. I've got to get something from the museum. Then we've got some reading to do."

<hr>

After dropping Ben off at friend's house, Gabriela and Daniel went over to Charmaine's, where she met them at the front door and led them into the dining room. There, on a long table that could hold ten comfortably, sat the metal box that had been hidden in the wall of the old farmhouse. After storing the artifacts in her office, Gabriela had brought them to the Ohnita Harbor Maritime Museum for safekeeping. Her promise to Everett not to show them to anyone had ended with his death.

The map that had been discovered in the wall had been examined and compared with the Traitor's Map. The similarities between the two proved the same cartographer had drawn both maps. That mapmaker was Henry Thorsen.

Charmaine opened the box and revealed the stack of letters inside. The paper was so old and brittle, Gabriela cautioned them not to touch any of them. Those letters would need to be handled by a conservator. Charmaine agreed and said the museum would store them under climate-controlled conditions until they could find a more permanent solution.

That left the diary, preserved for more than two centuries thanks to its leather cover that had insulated its pages from dampness and variations in temperature. That the water seeping through the walls and blistering the plaster had not gotten inside the metal box would never cease to amaze Gabriela.

Wearing protective gloves, Gabriela picked up the diary and admired Penelope's name tooled into the leather cover. She opened it to the first page and saw the graceful handwriting and brimmed with excitement at the prospect of reading the story of this woman and her family.

In a slow and steady voice, Gabriela brought life to Penelope, a young woman of sixteen who had married a man she barely knew— Jacob Elijah Thorsen. From the account, Gabriela could imagine how Jacob's military career left little time for home or to notice the loneliness of a young wife. And so his brother, Henry, became her friend, confidante, and then, as Penelope described him, *the dearness of my heart.*

Most of the entries were sparse, just a few lines to chronicle a particular event, such as a visit to the homestead or her husband's homecomings. Gaps of weeks and skipped months led Gabriela to surmise that Penelope only wrote when she had something to say. Long stretches telegraphed loneliness or the tedium of days that felt achingly the same.

One entire page was devoted to the birth of her first child, a son. After a few short entries dated months apart, Penelope wrote of feeling a quickening inside. The next entry announced the birth of another child, a daughter.

The dated pages skipped forward in time to the American Revolution. With Jacob gone off to fight, Penelope stayed at the farm with her son and daughter and the housekeeper. She did not see Jacob for months on end and seldom received word from him.

Her voice hoarse, Gabriela took a sip of water, then handed the gloves and the diary to Charmaine to continue reading.

Charmaine picked up with the account of Henry's arrest and Jacob's vow to punish his brother for the betrayal. When Jacob returned to the fort the night before the execution, Penelope accompanied him, saying she wanted to see justice done.

Blessed laudanum made my husband sleep. I left him to his slumbers and made my way to the stockade. I told the guard my husband wanted me to pray with his brother. A bottle of rum convinced him more than my words alone.

Penelope recounted Henry's confession to her, that he had made a detailed map showing every stream, cove, marsh, and path along the lakeshore to aid the British and exposing where the Continental Army hid its supplies. But Henry could not bring himself to hand over that map to the British. Just hours before his appointed rendezvous, he drew another map, purposefully obscuring it with enough errors to render the drawing worthless.

Hearing this, I brought out the keys I had taken from Jacob and set Henry free. Where he is now, I know not. I do not expect to see him on this side of the veil of death again.

"Unbelievable," Clayton said.

"Strong women in your family," Charmaine said, her voice as low as a purr. She handed the diary back to Gabriela. "Your turn."

Gabriela skimmed entries that contained only bits of home life—planting crops, a new cow for the household. Months skipped, and Penelope picked up again in a tighter hand, the letters losing their graceful curves. The date on the page was October 1781.

My husband lies in bed, near death of mortal wounds from battle. They say the leg is gone, but Jacob refuses to let them take it. Poultices and powders do nothing to help him.

Then, on the next page, appeared one line: *Henry is home.*

Gabriela paused at that, raising her eyes to the others around the table.

Penelope's next entry from four days later described how she dismissed the physician, insisting she would tend to her husband herself. All visitors were turned away at the door. The housekeeper was sent back to her own home, taking Penelope's two children to shield them from their father's death.

In sparse accounts, Penelope described *Jacob's feverous rages,* and *a putrefying which makes the air noxious. Pallor paints death's mask on Jacob. Henry speaks to him tonight.*

A page was skipped, and when Gabriela turned to the next, she read, "*This morning Jacob is dead. We will bury him beside the baby.*"

"The third grave!" Gabriela exclaimed. "That's Jacob."

"Then who's in the Old Post Cemetery?" Clayton asked. "Jacob Thorsen served in the War of 1812. There has to be some mistake."

As Gabriela scanned ahead, a paragraph jumped out at her, and she read it aloud: "*Only a few years separated the brothers and hard life has marked both. They always appeared so much alike, even to me. And so we have decided that Henry is Jacob now. He is my husband and father to my children.*"

The following entries described life in seclusion over many months. To become Jacob, Henry adopted his dead brother's identity and mannerisms. *He walks with a purposeful limp to seal the believability of the story. Even the children do not question who he is.*

The next entry was eight months later, announcing the birth of a child. *Our son, Alden, comes into the world.*

"That's our ancestor," Clayton blurted out. "We descended from Henry, not Jacob!"

"No wonder you always loved his map," Charmaine said. "You felt the connection."

Gabriela skimmed a couple of pages about farm life, the children growing up. Then the entries stopped.

Turning to the last pages, Gabriela found a final notation dated 1812. *My husband, though older and gray, goes to battle. He tells me this is his duty to honor his father and his brother. He goes to war in Jacob's name to fulfill a debt he must repay.*

Pro Patre, Gabriela thought, recalling the family motto.

Penelope reported how the soldiers under the command of Colonel Thorsen marveled at his leadership and bravery, despite his advanced age. In the Battle of Ohnita Harbor in May 1814, Colonel Thorsen thwarted a British attack. Hailed as a hero, he retired at last and returned to the farm with his beloved wife. He died in 1818 and was given military honors at the fort.

The diary ended on the next page: *The Good Lord willing I will see them both in eternity, my two husbands—brothers.*

Gabriela closed the book, her hand resting on the cover. Daniel set his arm along the back of her chair, and she leaned into his touch.

Clayton brushed tears from his eyes, as Charmaine spoke softly. "Henry is buried in Jacob's grave. And Jacob is at the farmhouse cemetery. They became one person. What do we do about that?"

Gabriela smiled. "We make a petition, and have these brothers reunited."

On a bright August morning, a small crowd gathered at the Old Post Cemetery. Standing beside Daniel and Ben, Gabriela scanned them all: Wallace Kersey and the staff from Fort Ohnita, two representatives from the New York State Department of Parks, Recreation and Historic Preservation, Officer Thelma Tulowski in her dress uniform, and a chaplain from the local Coast Guard unit. Nearest the monument stood Charmaine and Clayton. The last to arrive were Emilie Hernandez and her parents.

After two months of petitions, and with the support of Fort Ohnita, approval had been expedited to exhume the body of an adult male in the third grave at Thorsen Manor. DNA testing and comparisons with a sample given by Clayton Brooks led to permission to rebury what were believed to be the remains of Colonel Jacob Thorsen at the Old Post Cemetery.

At the start of the service to commemorate this burial, Clayton spoke of a long-awaited reunion between two brothers, Jacob and Henry. "Despite their differences, they can rest together in peace," Clayton said. "That's the best we can hope for any of us."

As he wiped his eyes, Gabriela felt her own tears as she wondered if Clayton thought of Everett in that moment, the brother with whom he'd never had a chance to reconcile.

The chaplain read from a prayerbook, asking for peace and blessings on all those buried in this sacred place and those who bore witness to their lives and sacrifice.

Gabriela reached over and took Emilie's hand. "For Ricky Seymour, whose passion for history and love of authentication helped bring us to this moment."

"We love you, Ricky," Emilie whispered, her voice as soft as the summer breeze that rippled the grass.

Chapter Twenty-Six

Late summer sun on Labor Day weekend cut across the water and tinted the sky with the first tones of orange and pink, a resplendent backdrop. From the bluffs on the grounds at Fort Ohnita, the lake appeared to be a shimmering mirror, reflecting an untroubled and cloudless sky. Mary Jo Hinson, in a long blue dress with a multicolor silk scarf draped around her neck, stood with her back to the water. Beside her, Clem beamed in his role as best man. Daniel approached from the right, dressed in pearl-gray pants, a white shirt, and a navy blazer. A thin black cord held his gray hair in a ponytail at the nape of his neck.

On two rows of folding chairs sat family and close friends. Agnese took her grandson's arm as she walked along the grass and settled into the first chair on the left. Ben grinned at Daniel, then his eyes quickly returned to Gabriela, who waited at the rear and watched it all. She wore a sheath of light pink lace that skimmed her body and ended at midcalf. A ring of flowers crowned her dark hair—long, curly, and unfettered.

"You ready?" Thelma Tulowski asked.

"Oh, yes," Gabriela replied. "I think I've been waiting for this all my life."

Wearing wide-leg pants and tunic top in soft green, Thelma approached the group. A guitarist strummed the first chord, and Thelma began to sing a folk song about love and growing old together—her voice low and throaty. The untraditional wedding march could not have been more perfect.

Rose Red Deer in a long dress with swirls of red, rust, and yellow—the colors of the Southwest—led the way down the makeshift aisle between the folding chairs. She wore a simple band of flowers over her short dark hair. Earrings of beads and feathers dangled from both lobes.

Taking her son's arm, Gabriela carried a bouquet of white roses and green ivy as she walked in low-heeled shoes across the grass toward Daniel. At the front row of chairs, she kissed Ben and leaned down to embrace her mother. "Love you, Mama," Gabriela told her.

"Love is too small a word for all I feel today," Agnese said.

Then Gabriela stepped forward to join Daniel. Clasping hands, and with Mary Jo as the officiant, they made promises of lifelong love and fidelity.

Clem read from *The Song of Solomon*: "The voice of my beloved. Behold he comes, leaping upon the mountains, bounding over the hills. My beloved is like a gazelle, or a young stag."

A deer, Gabriela registered and wondered if this Bible passage had inspired Henry to design a family crest, perhaps to honor his love for Penelope.

Clem's voice rose, full and melodious, as he turned the last words of the verses into a song that rose and fell with beautiful inflection to the final stanza of the reading: "My beloved is mine, and I am his."

With the kiss to seal their commitment, Gabriela felt a rush of tears at first, then laughed with uncontained joy. "Yes," she said aloud. "Oh, yes."

Ben let out a whoop and raced over, wedging himself between Gabriela and Daniel. They walked three abreast, a chain forged in love. When they reached the last row of chairs, Ben pulled them up short. "So," he said, "when are we getting that dog?"

Epilogue

Thorsen Manor
October 1781

Death hung thickly in the air, and even the candles struggled to keep the darkness at bay. Henry listened to the unnatural quiet of the house. By Penelope's order, no one was allowed to enter—not the man who tended the livestock nor the boy who worked in the field. Even the doctor had been sent away.

Only he, the prodigal brother returned just days before, was allowed to stay.

News of Jacob's mortal wounds had reached Henry by chance in a tavern at the edge of the Adirondack Mountains, where for four years he had hunted and trapped and lived under an assumed name. In that moment, he'd known he had to come back, to make peace if Jacob would give it or to receive the final curse of a dying man. Now, waiting to be summoned, Henry had little hope for the former and prepared himself for the latter.

He stood at the fireplace with its great yawning mouth, large enough to swallow a man standing upright. Something bubbled in an iron kettle hanging from a hook over the fire, but Henry had no appetite. Not with the anticipation of seeing the brother who had once condemned him to execution and would probably do so again.

A door opened and Penelope slipped out, bringing with her the stench of putrefying flesh. Henry swallowed a gag and breathed through parted lips. How could she stand it, day after day, hour after hour? But it would not be for very much longer.

Penelope approached—her face thin, eyes shadowed by lack of sleep and abundance of worry. Henry fought the urge to gather her into an embrace, one he might have done as a brother under any other circumstances. But, here, he would not play the cad.

"Go to him," she said.

Nodding, Henry took his leave of her, feeling more anxiety in this moment than he had in the stockade four years prior, when he had waited through what should have been his last night on Earth. When he opened the door, light fell upon the bed, illuminating the cadaverous man who had once matched him in height and build and strength. Now, Jacob appeared withered and dried, like a turnip left in the root cellar come spring. Then this form took shape again, a man raging in fever and agony that laudanum could not tame.

Henry stepped closer, willing himself to show his face without a handkerchief to block the stench.

Jacob's eyes rolled back in his head as a moan escaped his lips. Then, with a shuddering inhalation, Jacob turned those eyes toward him. "Henry," he croaked.

Tensing, Henry prepared again for the damnation that would come from his dying brother's lips, a condemnation that would last until Judgment Day.

"Take...Penelope," Jacob said.

Henry leaned in. "Where, Jacob? Where should I take her?

"Take her," Jacob said, his breath spent.

Later that night, Henry confided to Penelope what Jacob had said and asked where she would like to be taken.

"Jacob means for you to take me as your wife," Penelope said.

Henry denied it. "No, he would not want that. I still have a price on my head."

"Not if you become Jacob," she said. "It would be a tribute to him. He will live on in you, and you will redeem yourself in his good name."

Crossing the room to clear his thoughts, Henry reached a looking glass on the far wall. He studied his own face and remembered Jacob as he had been years before. They had the same eyes, same nose, same hair.

"Yes," he said simply.

For the rest of his life, Henry vowed he would live as his brother. Together, he and Jacob would become a far better man than either of them had been on their own.

Pro Patre.

Author's Note

Oswego, New York, my hometown and inspiration, is steeped in history. Overlooking Oswego Harbor is a star-shaped fort of gray stone, built in the early 1840s. It is the fourth Fort Ontario, built on the site of three earlier fortresses that date back to the 1700s. Fort Ontario was a US Army post through World War II and, from 1944 to 1946, housed Jewish refugees given safety and shelter from the Holocaust. History buffs take note: Oswego and Fort Ontario with its Old Post Cemetery are worth the visit.

I have taken much liberty with the history of what I call Fort Ohnita. The same applies to the fictional Peninsula Point, which is based on Spy Island near Mexico Point, New York, where a man named Silas Town overheard British General St. Leger making battle plans. Silas warned the Continental Army, which led to the British loss at the Battle of Saratoga, a turning point in the Revolutionary War. (My deepest thanks to Cousin Melanie Stanfill and her husband, Alan, for the tour and explanation on a rainy October day.) A visit to Spy Island is a delightful immersion into history and the natural beauty of the area.

Colonel Jacob Thorsen and his brother, Henry, did not exist. However, it's not too hard to imagine families split by rivalries and politics—then or now.

Finally, the Traitor's Map is a product of my imagination mixed with a memory that may or may not be real. I recall (at least I think I do) being told as an elementary student about a spy map given to the British that contained inaccuracies meant to throw them off. But research never turned up any evidence of such a map. So my thanks to whoever might have told me a story that I tucked away long ago, only to be brought to life in this novel.

Wanting to recreate the Traitor's Map, I had the good fortune to be introduced to Dave Imus of Imus Geographics (visit his amazing website at ImusGeographics.com). When I described the premise of this novel and the fictional provenance of the Traitor's Map, Dave enthusiastically took on this project and created the illustration that appears in this book. Dave brought the Traitor's Map to life for me and, I hope, for you.

About the Author

Patricia Crisafulli is an award winning, New York Times best-selling author. Her debut novel, *The Secrets of Ohnita Harbor*, was published in 2022 by Woodhall Press, followed by *The Secrets of Still Waters Chasm* in 2023. She earned a Master of Fine Arts (MFA) degree from Northwestern University where she received the Distinguished Thesis Award in Creative Writing. Widely published and featured on many blogs and podcasts, Patricia is also the founder of www.FaithHopeandFiction.com, a popular e-literary magazine.

Patricia is a past recipient of the grand prize for fiction from Tall-Grass Writers Guild/Outrider Press and was published in its anthology, *Loon Magic and Other Night Sounds.* She was also nominated for a Pushcart Prize. A collection of her short stories and essays, *Inspired Every Day,* was published by Hallmark.

Acknowledgments

My sister, Jeannie Zastawny, to whom this book is dedicated, is an ardent lover of history, especially of the American Revolution. Thank you, Jeannie, for your enthusiasm and love of this story. And to her husband, Ben, my faithful first reader. Ben, I'll never write anything without you weighing in with your valued opinion.

To my husband, Joe Tulacz, my partner, supporter, and love of my life. You keep my feet on the ground while my thoughts spin in all directions. Thank you, dear Joe, for your unwavering belief in me and for being my sounding board.

To my son, Pat Commins, and daughter-in-law, Grace Vangel. Your adventurousness, creativity, artistry, and overall sense of fun are infectious. Let's go hiking again, soon!

To my cousins—especially Melanie Stanfill, Colette Robinson, and Peter Regan—I treasure you. To Aunt Margie and Aunt Mary Helen, you are the epitome of aging gracefully and courageously. To my niece, Stephanie Crisafulli, who loves to go walking with me to Fort Ontario whenever I visit my hometown.

Special thanks to dear friend Cindy Jensen, who skillfully read these pages and proclaimed this story to be her favorite. Much gratitude to fellow writer Laura Roe Stevens and avid reader Velda Matsdorf for reviewing my page proofs with me.

To friends, longtime and new, who accompany me on this journey: Janie Gabbett, JoAnn Locy, Margo Selby, Judy Jones Davila, Cecily Morrison, Beverly Ahlbeck, Susan Dolan, Marsha Meyer, Susan Gilpin, Mary Favia, Ella Indra and Len Seligman, Malia Lazu, Alexandra Zizmor, and so many more. To Loren Fleckenstein, student of Latin, who helped me with *Pro Patre*.

To my agent, Delia Berrigan Fakis, and to Sharlene Martin, both of Martin Literary Management—I will always be grateful.

To my publisher, Woodhall Press, for bringing my books to life, especially David LeGere and Miranda Heyman, and Margaret Moore for helping to spread the word through social media. My gratitude to Paulette Baker for her thorough editing and helpful suggestions and to LJ Mucci for the gorgeous cover and design.

To Dana Isaacson for his incomparable wisdom and editorial guidance as I wrote multiple drafts. You are the best!

To Avita Broukhim, publicist extraordinaire, who built my online presence, expanded my guest blogging, landed two television interviews, and helped me expand the conversation about my writing and my mystery series. Thank you for your energy and tireless drive.

And to everyone who has ever read, commented on, reviewed, or asked me about my books—thank you, thank you, thank you.